He takes a step forward, his big chest rising and falling. "I know I'm pushing it, Snaps. But I'm dying over here."

I'm dying, too. No denying it. This attraction is very bad for my mental and physical health. He probably won't even show up tomorrow night. His romantic comedy costar will distract him with an invitation to eat grapes on a sun-drenched rooftop somewhere and I . . . I could never get another chance to kiss this outrageously beautiful man. This trip to New York isn't only a career opportunity, it's a chance to shake off my comfort zone.

Do it, Katie. Don't regret it. Don't be a coward.

What's the worst that could happen?

"Just one, then," I whisper.

His green eyes go molten as he takes two big strides and swoops in. I hear my backpack hit the ground and then nothing, nothing, but Jack's mouth has any part of my focus.

What's the worst that could happen?

By Tessa Bailey

The Academy Series
DISORDERLY CONDUCT • INDECENT EXPOSURE

Romancing the Clarksons
TOO HOT TO HANDLE • TOO WILD TO TAME
TOO HARD TO FORGET • TOO BEAUTIFUL TO BREAK

Made in Jersey Series
CRASHED OUT • ROUGH RHYTHM
THROWN DOWN • WORKED UP • WOUND TIGHT

Broke and Beautiful Series
CHASE ME • NEED ME • MAKE ME

Crossing the Line Series
RISKING IT ALL • UP IN SMOKE
BOILING POINT • RAW REDEMPTION

Line of Duty Series
PROTECTING WHAT'S HIS
PROTECTING WHAT'S THEIRS (novella)
HIS RISK TO TAKE • OFFICER OFF LIMITS
ASKING FOR TROUBLE • STAKING HIS CLAIM

Serve Series
OWNED BY FATE • EXPOSED BY FATE
DRIVEN BY FATE

Standalone Books
UNFIXABLE
BAITING THE MAID OF HONOR • OFF BASE

TESSA BAILEY

Indecent EXPOSURE

THE ACADEMY

AVONBOOKS

An Imprint of HarperCollins*Publishers*

Excerpt from *Disturbing His Peace* copyright © 2018 by Tessa Bailey.

First Avon Books mass market printing: February 2018

Print Edition ISBN: 978-0-06-246710-2
Digital Edition ISBN: 978-0-06-246711-9

Cover design by Nadine Badalaty
Cover photographs: © Michael Frost Photography (man); © rabbit75_ist / Getty Images (background); © Shutterstock (kisses)

FIRST EDITION

HB 09.01.2023

For Uncle Alex

ACKNOWLEDGMENTS

Thank you to the following people who helped shape this book! Patrick and Mackenzie, my support system and forever loves. Nicole Fischer, my fabulous editor at Avon, for letting me throw out my original outline for this book after meeting Jack and understanding him more. Fiona Clarke, my consultant on Dublin-isms and ruiner of fun when I wanted to use the word shagging. Okay, it's an English term, I get it. *Chill.* Eagle of Aquila Editing for top notch beta reading. And Karen and Georgia of the My Favorite Murder podcast for helping inspire Katie's character. SSDGM.

Indecent
EXPOSURE

CHAPTER 1

—————— *Jack* ——————

Growing up in the brothel where my mother worked had a couple of drawbacks. Here is the main one: I know way more about women than any man should.

For instance, sometimes when they say they're fine? They're actually fine and you should stop asking and shut the fuck up. I learned my lesson the hard way, as one does when sharing a bathroom with a rotating door of females, not to mention a best friend with the almighty X chromosome. Those lessons have served me well, though, haven't they? Knowing when to retreat carefully, push forwards, or backpedal like a motherfucker during a conversation with a girl means I never go home alone.

Alone is a funny word, though, isn't it?

Sometimes I'm the most alone when surrounded by women. And that situation happens a lot more often for ol' Jack than it does for most guys. Is that a brag? Damn right. When women see me coming, their hormones whisper my name. I'm a demon in the sack. And most important, I treat girls with respect. Why shouldn't they want to go home with me at the end of the night? A couple of hours in my bed means laughs, some patented sweet talk, a few orgasms and cab fare. They could definitely do worse.

It's not their fault that I'm barely there when it's happening. That I'm watching myself touch them from above like a creepy, naked angel and wondering how long the mild queasiness will last. But like I said, that's not the girl's fault, is it? Women get blamed for enough without me adding to their plate. I'm there to give them a safe, shameless, satisfying ride and send them off with a smile.

Jack Garrett. Superhero. Protecting New York City's women from two-pump chumps one night at a time.

Look. I've witnessed the way men can disregard women as garbage once they've had their fun, so this calling of mine is not such a joke. Am I arrogant to think my dick is making a difference in the world of women? Yes. Am I apologizing? Hell no. Did I mention the orgasms and cab fare?

I've just come from a visit with my mother, who

now works as a pet groomer's receptionist—thank Christ—and as always, I marvel over how my old neighborhood of Hell's Kitchen has changed. They're calling it Clinton now but I don't have time for that nonsense. It's the Kitchen to me and it always will be. Doesn't matter how many gastropubs and yoga studios pop up, I can still see the grit beneath the glitter. I pass the doorway where I finally got a hand up Melissa Sizemore's shirt when I was thirteen, only to find out she'd been wearing a Wonderbra the whole time we'd been dating—and that's when I spot the redhead.

There is a lot of new blood in the Kitchen. Midtwenties Millennials, like myself, trying to make it in the city, while crammed into an apartment with three roommates. Right now I'm calling the East Side neighborhood of Kips Bay my home while I train to be a cop under the annoyingly watchful eyes of my NYPD instructors, but someday I'll come back to the Kitchen.

And if this sexy redhead is an indication of what awaits me, it'll be sooner rather than later.

What the hell is she up to, though? She's on her tiptoes, peering through the window of a dive bar I know too well. In her hand is a shiny pink camera. She's snapping away with a look of total awe on her face. A face I can see only in profile, but that's enough to peg her as . . . cute. Cute as a button, even. Huge eyes, full cheeks, the kind of red, puffy lips that stop traffic. At least when I'm at the wheel.

When it comes to women, I don't have a type. Tall, short, curvy, freckled, pierced, black, white, etcetera. All applications are accepted and approved. This redhead, though . . . I can't quite put a name on what pulls me towards her on the sidewalk. Is it her smile? The wobbly tiptoe dance she's doing to make up for her lack of height? I've established she's adorable, but she's probably not looking for a hookup. Yet. Although, I never pursue women outside of bars, where I spend a lot of my time. If you ask my best friend, Danika, way too much time. But the alcohol makes it a shit ton easier to say yes. Yes to the girl, yes to what my body wants right now, but will regret later.

I push the troubling thought aside and focus on the redhead.

Coming to a stop beside her at the window, I get a nice whiff of mint and wonder if it's courtesy of lotion or direct from the herb. "Need a boost?"

She drops back onto flat feet and flicks me a glance. "I'm grand, thanks."

Irish girl. Her accent loops around in the air, but doesn't distract me from her huge blue eyes. Nothing could. They're the color of pale denim, outlined by a crowd of black lashes.

Hot. *Damn.*

Those twin beacons scan my face in slow motion, like a couple of bar code readers . . . and go right back to spying in the window. Huh. Disinterest from a girl is definitely new, but then again, this is why meeting women on a night out works so well. There's no mystery. For all I know, this girl is waiting for her husband to exit the dive where I had my first beer. No ring on her finger, but maybe they're traveling from Ireland and she left it home to be safe.

My mouth screws up in disgust when I realize I'm performing detective work involuntarily. Freaking academy is actually working.

"What are we looking at?" I ask, trying again.

"You're looking at me. I'm looking at this historical landmark."

"O'Keefe's?" I wave at the familiar bartender through the window. "Are you sure you didn't confuse this for the Empire State Building? Easy mistake. Happens to everyone."

One end of her incredible lips gives an upwards tug. "I know what I'm at. Could you get lost now?"

"You're asking me to leave when I just made you smile?"

"I imagine it's not difficult for you to make a girl smile. What else you got?"

My chest vibrates with a laugh. "What else do you want?"

Thoughts skitter across her face like a blown dandelion. "I won't know until I see it."

I prop my shoulder against the building and wink at her. "Look no further."

She peers up at me and I swear to God, she's not even seeing what I've got on the surface.

She's digging deeper, deeper . . . looking for *more*. When is the last time that happened? Never. Not that I can remember. She's not playing a game with me. She seems to be *truthing* me. Being totally honest.

Who *does* that?

"I'll decide when I'm done looking." With a jolt, she goes back to looking through the window. "But I think that's enough for now."

I'm not even offended. I'm more fascinated than anything else. It's not that I've never been turned down before—it has probably happened at least once—and I should really walk away now. No means no. Zero excuses. I'm just finding it pretty difficult to walk away and never hear the tilting notes in her voice again. To forfeit a chance to look into those unmatchable eyes at least one more time. And damn, she was searching for something below my surface and I'm kind of bothered that she hasn't found it yet. Hell, I'm not even sure what's there. But the fact that she tried at all makes me want to stick around. "I'll make you a deal. Just tell me why you're out here like a Peeping Tom and I'll go. Just satisfy my curiosity, would ya, honey?"

The twin patches of pink on the girl's cheeks tell me she's not totally unaware that I'm attractive. The cajoling did it. Women like it when I beg, whether or not it's only for show. This time doesn't feel like it's for show.

When she drops back onto her heels, humor is

dancing in her expression. "Once I tell you, getting rid of you will be easy enough, I suppose."

Now that I finally have her undivided attention, I just want to hold on to it. Even though she wants to get rid of me. Maybe the lighting on the street is bad and my face is hidden by shadows. Or the sun is blinding her. That has to be it. "Let me be the judge of that."

Lips pursed, she tugs a book out of her back pocket. It's titled *The Ultimate Guide to Famous New York City Mob Hits*. She gestures towards the window with the book spine. "In there is where Whitey Kavanaugh was whacked during the mob wars of eighty-seven." Her eyebrows give a mischievous waggle. "You're kind of interrupting my murder tour here, good-looking."

Katie

In Dublin, we have a word for this kind of man: *a ride*.

I'm fighting the temptation to peek over his shoulder and see if he walked off a movie set. Honest to God, he's a dream. A taller version of James Dean, charisma gliding off him in lazy, rolling plumes of smoke. His smile is its own story altogether, the way it crinkles the corners of his eyes and creates dents in his cheeks.

I wouldn't call them dimples, because they're more like twin, side-by-side dips on both ends. Like his mouth is in quotation marks.

All manner of things are happening here. The dead center cleft in his chin. His stubbled cheeks and jaw. Dark, sweeping eyebrows over green eyes. His hair is in a crew cut, but I can see it's black and if it were long, would probably flip just perfectly over his forehead, framing his gorgeous face. Tall. He had to be tall and fit, as well? Really? It seems an awful gluttony of five-star qualities on a single person. God should have spread them around His other creations a bit.

I could have used a few inches of height myself. My neck is already beginning to protest being craned so long to look into the face of such flawlessness.

Good thing he'll be moving on soon. No one sticks around for a girl who has a long-standing fascination with organized crime. At least, I don't think so. I've never voiced this interest of mine out loud to a man. I barely speak to men at all, although I have plans to change that while I'm visiting New York. As soon as this completely unrealistic, possibly CGI creature stops trying to knock me into a coma with his physical charms, I'll be off to the races.

"Good-looking, huh?" Of course, he focuses on the name I called him. "And yet you're so impatient for me to leave."

"Oh, em . . ." When his smile sags a touch, I realize I've been outright rude. But I'm too embarrassed to explain why. That I thought he was just having a laugh at my expense on his way into the pub . . . and couldn't possibly be interested in me. I mean, I'm only after getting off the plane at JFK, no shower or hairstyle to speak of. My jeans and tank top are rumpled from traveling and will probably have to be burned. What could possibly have drawn this man in my direction? "I apologize. I just assumed you had somewhere else to be and I was . . . giving you leave. To go there."

He tilts his head, interested. "Where do you think I'm headed?"

"Hmm." I lean back and size him up. When I reach his eyes, one thing is obvious. He already thinks he knows my answer. "Piano fingers."

Shock transforms his expression and the digits in question twitch at his side. "What about them?"

"Maybe you're a piano teacher? On the way to a lesson?" Why is he so quiet all of a sudden? "Am I that far off?"

"No, but . . ." He shifts. "You look at me and think I could be a piano teacher?"

"What do you *want* me to see?" His lack of response jumbles my nerves. "Wherever you're headed, I was just trying to be polite and give you an easy send-off. I didn't mean to sound eager or anything."

He gives a quick shake of his head. "You don't need a reason for wanting me gone." He seems intent on impressing this important point upon me. "It's your decision and I should have listened the first time."

I'm suspicious by nature. "Are you being this agreeable now because I'm murder sightseeing and you're trying to get away from me?"

"No, actually I think murder sightseeing is pretty fucking cool."

"Is that why you're still here?"

"Yeah. And the fact that you're beautiful." He arches an eyebrow when all I can do is sputter. "If you've changed your mind about ditching me, I'll bring you inside to get a decent picture. Do you know which chair Whitey was sitting in when—"

"Third from the end."

"Had a feeling you would know." With a half-smile, he offers me his arm, which is wrapped in the soft cotton of a black hoodie. "Come on. I'll kick whoever is in it out."

"I don't go into bars. That's why I'm out here probably looking like a bloody lunatic." The reasoning behind my no bar rule is personal—too personal to tell a stranger—so my gaze automatically evades him. Otherwise he might see the hurt and I don't share that with anyone. It's mine. But I feel him watching closely as I tuck my camera back into its case and replace it in the pocket of my backpack. "Thank you for the offer . . ."

"Jack." His throat sounds crowded when he answers me, along with his eyes. "And you're . . ."

"Katie." I sling my backpack on over my shoulders, trying to remember if I thanked him for calling me beautiful. Or if I should even call attention to the fact he did, because he might repeat the word and I'm not sure I can handle hearing it twice in one day. Not without giggling and making a complete arse out of myself.

The last four years of my life have been spent training for the Olympics nonstop. Grueling hours of practice that meant zero time for the opposite sex. Now, at the first sign of freedom, I'm thrown right into the arena with James Dean's great-grandson. When I decided to sandwich in a torrid love affair during my business trip to New York, I had someone more approachable in mind. Like a nerdy desk clerk. Or a portly crossing guard. "Listen, I'm not judging or anything. About the bar. Really. You can go on in—"

"There you go, trying to ditch me again." His thousand-watt smile turns back on and steals the breath straight out of my lungs. "Are there any other famous mob hit locations in the neighborhood or is this your last stop?"

"There's one more," I hear myself say. Shite. How am I supposed to relax when he's smiling at me like that? If he concentrated the full power of that smile on a stick of butter, it would be a gooey puddle in seconds. Needing a distraction from his face, I consult my mob hit guide. "McCaffrey Park. Is that close?"

"Right down the street." He ticks his head in that direction. "Ready?"

No, I'm not ready. For one thing, he's a stranger in an unfamiliar city and might be planning to harvest my organs. Two, he's fresh and stunning, while I'm in ratty runners and wearing a purple backpack like an oversized toddler. And three . . . I just have a feeling mysterious Jack is going to be bad news for me. Call it a sixth sense or common sense or what have you, but this ride with the bad boy smile has trouble oozing out of his pores.

This should be a no brainer. When a stranger shows an unlikely interest in me, it's probably for the best to avoid walking with him to a dark park where mob hits have taken place. Just as a rule. I've been expected to act beyond reproach my entire *life*, though. I barely survived a strict Catholic upbringing before being thrust under the Olympic microscope. Every day of my life has been scheduled and executed without fail.

This man is not on my agenda.

Then again, I did promise myself adventure during this two-week trip. Swore to myself I would fulfill a vow to someone I love, by living without constraint. After being under my father's thumb so long, I'm so light. So without responsibilities, I didn't even take the time to clean up after my flight, throwing on my runners and bursting out of the hotel. Could Jack be part of my adventure?

No, it's impossible. Surely he's filming a romantic comedy down the street and he's method acting right now. Then again, those piano fingers . . . the way he acted so surprised that I would point them out has me reluctantly intrigued.

His green eyes cloud with disappointment the longer I take to answer him, though. His smile winds down in degrees until his mouth is nothing more than a grim line. I'm about to turn him down for the walk to the park, when he says, "No hard feelings, Katie. Huh?" He winks, but it's a sad one. "Even if it is going to take me a damn long while to forget those eyes."

My heart is in my mouth when he goes. His hands shovel into his pockets and he walks backwards a few paces, keeping me in his sights, before turning and strolling down the block. It's insane, the anxious bubbles that begin to pop in my belly. My hands tighten into fists at my sides and the backpack starts to feel heavy. "Wait," I shout. Then I cringe. Because everyone on the sidewalk, including Jack, turns to look at me. "Ah . . . sure go on. Just the walk, then?"

Even from a distance, Jack's mouth spreading into a slow smile is breathtaking.

As I walk towards him, my feet on the warm concrete seem to be chanting one word.

Trouble, trouble, trouble.

CHAPTER 2

Jack

I'm taking this girl home.

Katie trots towards me on the sidewalk, making her small tits jiggle underneath her tank top. The wind sends that red hair flying off behind her and I can already feel it wrapped around my fingers. Feel it rubbing down my stomach and catching on my thigh hair. Most times, I would be well on my way to reaching that portion of the evening with a girl. Instead, I'm walking her to the park. There's a first time for everything, I guess.

Not like I'd had much choice if I wanted to keep hanging out with her, since she doesn't go to bars. *Doesn't go to bars.* Where I tend to close my nights. Every night, lately. Meaning she's not a drinker. A good girl. It was right there in her denim eyes that she has a good damn reason for not wasting hours in watering holes. So God knows that should have been my cue to bail the second she dropped that information, but I still stood there. Waiting for her to choose me. Why?

I have no idea if I'm good for this kind of activity anymore. Park walks. Small talk. In high school, I focused more energy on dates. Hanging out with girls when the focus wasn't on getting each other into the sack. Around sixteen, sex became a given and I loved it. I listened to the johns talking. I paid attention to my mother's friends discussing their customers and I learned how to murder in bed. It kind of gave me a sense of . . . value. And there didn't seem like anything wrong with that when everyone around me was living with that same sense.

I'm good at . . . fucking. No, I'm a great fuck. Do I have other skills? Sure, I can entertain any crowd with a tried and true set of card tricks and the occasional arm wrestling competition. But beyond that, I'm not sure what I think I can bring to the table with Katie.

Katie hasn't offered too many details about herself, but here is what I've gleaned. She's organized. Those little dog-eared pages in her mob hits book and the way she sealed her camera neatly in its case tell me so. She's got a sense of humor, but doesn't use it to flirt. At least not with me. Murder is her jam. Her eyes make my stomach hurt.

And she's got a great rack.

What do I have going for me? Obviously she doesn't give a shiny rat's ass about my devastating good looks. I might be able to impress her by mentioning I'm training to be a police officer, but something tells me she would cut through my bullshit and see the academy is just a necessary evil for me. That it's not something I'm proud of, unlike my fellow recruits. Getting my badge is just a way to pay the rent and help my mother out with grocery money. If I hadn't lost a bet to Danika and gotten stuck enrolling, I would have found another way to make ends meet. I always have.

It frustrates the hell out of Danika and our other roommate, Charlie—whose father and brother are big dogs in the department—that I don't take training seriously. That I show up with a vodka buzz half the time and waltz through the drills like a sleepwalker on Ambien. Maybe I just don't see the point. A room full of shithead twenty-somethings are preparing to call themselves New York's Finest and I can't relate to being confident in anything beyond bedroom and parlor tricks. I'm there. I'm training. But I never actually feel *present*. It seems like an elaborate dream to me, the halogen lights and drills and sweatpants. I'm not meant for it. I'm not sure I'm meant for anything at all but a good time.

Katie catches up with me on the sidewalk, her thumbs looped under her backpack straps. I've got a good eight inches on her and since I'm the furthest thing from a saint, I let my attention drop to the edge of her tank top. My body responds to the sight of her breasts swelling against the white cups of her bra and I swallow a groan, aching for the feel of them in my palms.

I'm seriously attracted to this girl. More attracted than I've been to anyone in my memory. I'm also anxious to stop pretending I'm the kind of guy who chaperones an innocent out-of-towner to the park and find a flat surface where I remind myself what I'm good for, just for a while.

"So . . . do you live around here?"

Katie looks up at me a split second after I take my eyes off her cleavage. Close call. "Not anymore. I grew up here, but I live on the East Side."

"Oh, I think that's where I'm staying." She's like a curious meerkat, ducking and shooting up onto her toes to look into the shops we pass. Her camera is back out and she's taking pictures of damn near everything in sight. "I just flew in this afternoon and I haven't really gotten my bearings yet, but the hotel is somewhere around the UN. Is that east?"

"Yeah." I edge closer to Katie as two men pass by us on the sidewalk. Would she have done this walk to the park alone if I hadn't come along with her? I'm not sure I like that idea at all. No, I definitely don't like it. "Are you here in New York by yourself, Snaps?"

She pulls to a stop and blinks up at me. "Snaps?"

"On account of you taking literally one picture per second."

Her whole face brightens with a smile. And then she keeps walking.

Feeling . . . bemused? I jog to keep up. "Look, I'm not saying women aren't capable of taking care of themselves, but it's almost nighttime and you don't know this town. Some precautions might be in order."

"I appreciate your concern."

"But you're ignoring it."

"Yes." We're a block away from the park now and I can see it's empty, except for one old man in a ball cap feeding the pigeons. I'm trying to decide on another tactic to keep this cute-as-a-button redhead from getting mugged while she's in New York, when she cuts off my uncharacter-istically noble line of thought. "Tell me a story about this park. If you grew up here, you must have one."

Is she really so confident in my ability to enter-tain her with my memories and thoughts? The idea both pleases me and makes me nervous. "Sure." I scratch at my sideburns, a series of images and sounds flickering in my head. "All right. Some of the locals used to have chess tour-naments in the park." I squint an eye and point off into the distance, rubbing our shoulders to-gether in the process. "At those tables near the basketball court. Only six or so regulars would be allowed to play and the same dude won every time. Isaiah. They had like a . . . trophy of sorts the winner would take custody of, but it was really just some knife carvings on a plaque."

We reach the corner across from the park and I slide an arm across Katie's shoulders. Maybe I do it because I don't usually go this long without touching the girl I'm interested in. Or maybe I've designated myself as the one looking after her tonight and the responsibility is making my palms sweat. I don't know. But I do it and she stiffens, but doesn't pull away.

"Anyway . . ." I let the oxygen in my lungs seep out slowly. "Same guy won the chess tournament again, only the loser didn't feel like being gracious for the hundredth damn time. So he tossed the plaque into the back of a passing garbage truck."

"No," she breathes. "Terrible sportsmanship, that."

"Terrible." God, the fluid, husky way she talks is addictive. As soon as I'm finished with this story, I'm done talking so I can listen to all her, all the time. "So off goes the winner, chasing after the garbage truck and his beloved plaque. He manages to stop the truck after four blocks, but the compactor has already mangled it."

She shoots me some narrow-eyed suspicion. "Is this going to make me cry?"

"If it does, be forewarned that a woman's tears have no effect on me. Sob a brand-new river straight through the city. I'm completely immune."

"Is that true?"

"Hell no, it's not true. I'd curl into a fetal position and beg for mercy."

Her laugh tickles straight through my bones. "Better make it a happy ending, then."

I let out a slow whistle. "Isaiah walked back to the park with the mangled plaque and the runner-up helped him put it back together?"

"Oh no, you don't, liar." She gasps and pokes me in the ribs. "You changed the ending. I want the real one or I will launch a formal protest."

"With who? The storytellers' union?"

"Yes." She giggles through the word and I realize two things. I'm doing all right here. Not a single drink in me. No expectation of sex. Yet. And I'm doing fine. I'm not sure how long I can keep it up, though. We've been walking for only five minutes and already my heart is starting to hammer, my tongue feeling thick. I want a drink. I want Katie spreading her legs for me in bed. I want the high of feeling useful I only get from giving pleasure.

"Uh . . ." I tug on the string of my hoodie, forcing myself to chill the fuck out. But seriously. What am I doing here? Walking with this girl who giggles and wears a backpack. Trying to pull off the long game. Why? What is it about her that's got my chest so tight? "Okay, here's the real ending. Don't say I didn't try to soften the blow."

We walk into the park and she eases away from me, turning in a circle to take in the scenery and, I swear to Christ, for a second I really believe she's a mirage and I'm imagining the whole thing. "Fair enough. I'm prepared for the worst."

"Isaiah fell down a manhole on his way back to the park."

The old man feeding the pigeons on the bench behind me hums. Mmm-hmm. Probably because he was sitting in the same spot a decade ago and witnessed the whole thing.

Katie is staring at me as though the fate of mankind is in my hands. "Did Isaiah survive the fall?"

"He did." I ease the backpack off of Katie's shoulders because it looks heavy and I decide I should be holding it for her. She doesn't even seem aware I'm removing it, she's so intent on the story's ending. "He would have landed on a subway gear switch, but the plaque blocked it from sticking him in the ribs."

Her nod is slow. "So the moral of the story is, it's okay to be a shite loser."

"No, the moral of the story is this city has hidden dangers and you shouldn't be exploring it all by yourself."

I take the camera from her hand and snap a picture of her adorable outrage. Which makes her bristle even more. "How dare you try to teach me a lesson when I'm on holiday."

Time for more cajoling. I tilt my head to one side, slipping into a contrite smile. "Forgive me, Snaps? I only have your best interest at heart."

"How did you fit my best interest in there with all the lies knocking about?"

"Persistence."

Our fingers brush as she takes her camera back. "I'll be keeping my head around the likes of you, Jack."

"We'll see about that."

I don't like the touch of worry I see trickle into her expression as she leads the way farther into the park, but I follow anyway, wanting her more with every step.

CHAPTER 3

— *Katie* —

I f I'm not mistaken, Jack is the Big Bad Wolf and I'm Little Red Riding Hood.

Or at least that's how I'm feeling as he saunters along behind me in the rapidly falling evening. It's strange. One second I feel safe as houses with him. The next, I wonder if he's deciding how best to prepare me for his supper.

I'm picturing myself trussed up like a turkey when the wind begins to kick up, sending goose-bumps prickling up my arms. There's a cardigan in my backpack but Jack is carrying the feckin' thing and I'd have to stand there and dig it out while he holds it open in his big hands. And then I'd essentially be required to don clothing in front of him, which is basically, seriously way too close to intercourse to even consider. Slide on my cardigan under his watchful green eyes? We might as well be stretched out in my hotel bed doing the bloody business.

Where did that thought come from?

I must be jet-lagged. That's why I'm picturing Jack above me, half of his amazing face lit by the lamp on my hotel side table. No. No no no. I can no more tell this man I'm a virgin who's been locked in a firing range for four years than I can recite the ancient Greek alphabet. And I would have to tell him. Anything else wouldn't be proper behavior. While I might be on a rebellious streak, I can't set aside every ounce of politeness and Catholic guilt that has been hammered into me for years.

He could help me check an item off my Katie Conquers New York list.

As soon as I consider the notion, I discard it. Jack would chew up the likes of me and spit me out. I glance over my shoulder and find him watching me, as if chewing and spitting is exactly what he has in mind. Maybe some flambéing and glazing while he's at it.

But then. Then he frowns at my shivering, unzips my backpack and pulls out my cardigan, holding it out for me to take. "If that's not enough, you can have my sweatshirt."

"Oh." Lord does it sound lovely, the chance to be swallowed up by his rich scent, but I can't. That would pretty much be like *double* intercourse. And I'm back to being confused over whether Jack is the Big Bad Wolf . . . or a sheep in wolf's clothing. "Ah, th-this'll do. Thanks," I say, taking the cardigan.

Watching me closely, he nods, before zipping the pack once more and casually tossing it over one wide shoulder. "So where did this hit go down? Talk to me, Snaps."

"Right." I whip the mob hit book from my back pocket, lick my index finger and flip to the correct page. "This one was more quick than brutal. It happened in broad daylight during the mid-eighties and the victim was . . ." After studying the black-and-white crime scene photo a moment, I turn and point back towards the benches. "He was found over there, single GSW to the left temple. Witnesses claim the perpetrator walked with a severe limp. Therefore, the rumor was that local baddie Frank Donahue was the shooter, but no one in the neighborhood would confirm which of the shooter's legs was bad, putting the kibosh on that theory. And then the witnesses changed their stories altogether, probably afraid of retaliation or being called a snitch. So technically it went unsolved."

Jack appears to be holding his laughter. "Technically?"

"Well . . ." I drop my voice to a whisper. "It wouldn't be difficult to fake a limp if you wanted to frame someone obvious. Someone the police would already suspect. I'm just putting it out there, mind you."

"Jesus. This is exactly why you need me with you on this little holiday in the city."

Him be my guide? When had that subject been broached? "I don't follow."

"Going around, stirring up old homicide investigations. Throwing out new, dangerous theories." He bites his bottom lip, dragging his green eyes from my feet to the tip of my head. "You need me along for the ride. I can't have you ending up in the updated version of that book."

A laugh bubbles out of me before I can stop it. "And you would be willing to throw yourself into harm's way for a mere stranger?"

Silence glimmers between us. "Yeah, I think I might." His boots fall heavy on the asphalt as he comes closer. Close enough that I have to tip my head back. "And you won't be a stranger too much longer, will you?"

Languid, purple—I'm guessing on the color— heat billows in my tummy, reaching down to my knees and loosening them. Feckin' hell. It's settled. He's the Big Bad Wolf and while, yes, I am quite clearly attracted to Jack—who wouldn't be?—this burning he kicks off inside me is far too bright. Too intense.

I've had none of the experiences most twenty-five-year-old women are meant to have at this point in their lives. There was no time after the tragedy. After my father tunneled all his focus into the Olympic trials. Maybe Jack sensed that I would be an easy conquest? Something in my gut tells me he wouldn't do that, but damn, I don't have the experience to be sure.

It doesn't help that I'm suspicious by nature and I'm fascinated with true crime.

Doesn't help whatsoever.

"Em. I don't think a bodyguard is necessary." Pretending to be engrossed once more in my book, I back away from the magnetic presence of Jack. "Don't you know people fear the wrath of the redhead? My hair protects me wherever I go."

"Or it makes you more recognizable," he mutters. "Is this all you plan to do while visiting? Tour old crime scenes?"

"Oh no, it's only one item on the list."

The second the words are out of my mouth, I know I shouldn't have let them loose. No one knows about the list, save myself. It's tucked into the back pages of the book in my hands, flat as a pancake and unseen by human eyes. It might as well be my diary, it's so personal. But I know when Jack's eyebrows lift and his devilish mouth curves, I'm not getting away without an explanation. Not without some effort. "List?"

"Shopping list. I love a good sale. Did you know that about me?"

"Try again."

"Grocery list. I have wheat allergy so I have to stock my hotel room with food. It's very inconvenient, but I've gotten used to it."

"That was pretty good, but I'm still not convinced." He crosses his arms. "What list?"

I clomp over to a bench and drop down onto it, noticing that the pigeon-feeding man has gone home for the day, leaving Jack and me alone in the empty, now dark, park. Even though I've decided he's a wolf, I'm still not nervous for some reason. Thinking maybe I should be and my sheltered upbringing has made me less perceptive of danger, I do a quick scan behind the park's perimeter bars, confirming there is a decent amount of foot traffic, plus one hot dog vendor I could call out to if I was in trouble.

When I return my attention to Jack, there's a furrow between his brows, as if he knows my thoughts. "Hey. We can go somewhere more out in the open if you want, Snaps."

The memory of him walking away, prepared to leave me outside the bar sails past. He might be seductive, but he's not aggressive. "I'm grand. You want to sit?"

He falls onto the bench beside me like a prince draping himself over a throne, one arm stretched along the back, his fingers just shy of brushing my neck. The heat of them alone makes me shiver, along with Jack's steady eyes. "Tell me."

"It's silly—" I stop myself. "No, actually, it's not silly. I have a list of things I want to do during the two weeks I'm in New York. They're not big, world-shattering accomplishments. It's more for a bit of fun. I haven't had fun in a long time." I sense his fingertips creeping close to my nape and hurry to speak out of pure nerves. "That's not to say you should feel sorry for me, Jack. I'm fine."

"Okay. If you say you're fine, I believe you."

"Just like that?"

His middle finger slides right down the center of my neck. "Just like that."

I feel the rich texture of his voice and that featherlight touch between my legs, but I force myself not to press my knees together, lest I give myself away. "How about we make a deal?" Jesus, I sound like I need a new set of lungs. "I'll reveal one list item."

"How is that a good deal for me?"

"I'll let you come along."

He's strumming my neck now like a guitar, slow, slow brushes designed to drive me mad. And it's working. His huge, warm, male presence on the bench is sucking me in, making me want to turn and crawl straight into him. "So if I agree to the deal, I only get to come along on one adventure?"

"How did you know I was calling it an adventure?"

Those dimples wink at me. "Seems like something you'd say." He appears to be pondering the terms of the deal. "What if I hold out for the entire list? All or nothing."

I straighten my back. I'm not sure if it's a voluntary move or what, but he's now cupping my nape, sliding his thumb through my hair and I can barely breathe. "Didn't you learn anything from your plaque story? When you wish for too much, a manhole comes along and swallows you up."

He expels a harsh breath. "Christ, you're fucking cute, Katie. How long am I supposed to pretend I don't want to kiss the shit out of you on this bench?"

My knees snap together to block the bolt of lightning that blows up both thighs. "Th-this is you pretending? Really? With the whole thumb massage thing?"

"You don't know the half of it, Snaps." His laughter is pained as he stands, pacing away. My neck feels achingly cold without his hand. "Fine. You have a deal. One item on the list and I get to be there. Sold. For now."

"For now?"

Jack inclines his head. "You might decide to tell me more at a later date."

"Is this the part where you tell me you can be very persuasive?"

He crooks a finger at me. "If you're going to put words in my mouth, honey, at least be nice and use your tongue."

I shoot to my feet. "I'm way out of my league here."

"Shit, Katie. Wait." His burrows his fingers through the short ends of his hair. "I'm sorry. I'm the one out of his league. Most girls aren't interested in having a heart-to-heart with me on a park bench, all right? I don't know what you expect from me."

"I hadn't gotten round to expecting anything just yet."

"Don't go. Just . . . don't go." He drops his hands slowly, as if trying to will me back into a sitting position, but my heart is pinging all over the place and I'm . . . I'm thinking of doing a legger. Just juking left to throw him off, then sprinting straight out of the park. I thought I understood how hypnotic and overtly sexual Jack is. But right up until he told me to come over and use my tongue, I was underestimating him. I only met this man a half-hour ago and I want him to throw me down and make a harlot out of me. And for someone who felt guilty over her own private fantasy about the Tonga torchbearer in Rio, it's a lot at once. A lot.

He could tease me for being a virgin. Once we get the general hilarity out of the way, I could disappoint him. I could . . . yeah, I could start to like him. Maybe I already do. But he has to have a million options for companionship at his disposal, and that's far too intimidating for me.

"Thanks for coming with me to the park, Jack . . ." I pick my backpack up off the bench. "But I have to go."

"Fuck. I really blew it, huh? You're just going to go."

I think it's the hollow tone of his voice that propels me to blurt, "I'm going to dance in Cherry Hill Fountain in Central Park. Tomorrow night."

He's very still and somewhere in the distance a horn begins to blare. The universe telling me I've made the right decision sharing my plans? I guess I'll find out. "You can get arrested for that."

"Then I suppose I could do with a lookout." There we go. I've lost the plot. The plot vanishes from sight completely when Jack's upset expression is cracked open by a mile-wide, slightly piratical smile . . . and my pulse flies on butterfly wings up to my throat. "I'll see you then."

"One kiss." He takes a step forwards, his big chest rising and falling. "I know I'm pushing it, Snaps. But I'm dying over here."

I'm dying, too. No denying it. This attraction is very bad for my mental and physical health. He probably won't even show up tomorrow night. His romantic comedy costar will distract him with an invitation to eat grapes on a sun-drenched rooftop somewhere and I . . . I could never get another chance to kiss this outrageously beautiful man. This trip to New York isn't only a career opportunity, it's a chance to shake off my comfort zone.

Do it, Katie. Don't regret it. Don't be a coward.

What's the worst that could happen?

"Just one, then," I whisper.

His green eyes go molten as he takes two big strides and swoops in. I hear my backpack hit the ground and then nothing, nothing, but Jack's mouth has any part of my focus.

What's the worst that could happen?

He could kiss like my taste will set him free. And that's exactly what he does. One giant hand cups the back of my head, the other resting on my cheek. He tilts me so gently, I don't expect the ravenous sweep of his tongue, smooth and wicked. The power of it knocks me back a step. Jack follows, towering over me, groaning into my mouth, taking, absorbing, demanding more. Holding me right where he wants me, his firm lips slanting and slanting. He's the Big Bad Wolf and I'm the meal he's snared in his trap. Only, I'm not sitting there taking it like good prey. After the initial shock of sensations, I willingly drown in them.

My hands twist in the front of his sweatshirt, my back bowing by primitive demand and he counters me perfectly, giving me his hard lap to cushion my softness. His rough exhalation shakes out into my mouth when our lower bodies meld on a single grind, his eyebrows slashing down as though he's in pain.

"One more, Katie. One more, one more, one—"

I yank him back down, cutting him off with my waiting kiss and his hands, they become these sweeping sources of hot want, dragging down my sides, clutching my hips and pulling me up onto my toes, sliding me side to side against his large arousal. There's nothing gentle about the way he's kissing me now, and I imagine this is what he does with his mouth while thrusting into a woman. Just overwhelms her senses until she's a mass of lust and urgency, letting him have her in any manner he deems suitable.

And I was worried about putting on my cardigan in front of him.

Maybe it's ridiculous—maybe I'm ridiculous—but that's the thought that forces me to break away, sucking in deep gulps of chilling night air. Jack's forehead is pressed to mine, twisting side to side like he's shaking his head. Or in denial. I don't know.

Somehow I find the strength to extricate myself from his hold, stooping down to pick up my bag. "Just so we're keeping count," I manage, breathily, "That w-was two kisses. Never say I wasn't generous with you."

His green eyes cut towards me and I read determination there. A lot of it. "I'll see you tomorrow, Snaps. Don't you dare doubt me on that."

I nod, the heat of his body reaching out to grab me as I pass towards the park's exit. The entire way to hail a cab, I feel his eyes burning into my back. And I wonder how the heck I'm going to check off the mad love affair on my list with Jack nosing about, giving me kisses like that.

CHAPTER 4

Jack

There's nothing like a little hair of the dog that bit you, right?

I wait for the locker room to clear out to take my final swig of cheap vodka and orange juice out of my water bottle, before stowing it back on the shelf. My head loosens up and the burning in my throat eases. Right as rain. It's rare that I wake up with a hangover anymore, but you can bet your ass I tied one on after that kiss in the park last night with Katie.

What the hell happened?

She asked me to tell her a story. Through the whole thing, straight through to the end, she'd been interested. Watching me, holding her breath, waiting. I started to wonder what else I could do to hold her interest, outside of bed.

What do you want me to see?

After the way her searching questions and honest vulnerability stripped me down without a single piece of clothing removed, though, I'd been prepared to sign over my kidneys for that kiss. Both of them. Maybe I'd been desperate to come to my senses and kissing her was the only way to achieve that. No way the kiss could live up to the girl, right? With all her teasing smiles and wit and intelligence and that rack. Only, the kiss had turned my blood to rocket fuel. I'd thought, no way, no way we're ending the night any other way but naked, sweaty and filthy. But she'd walked away, leaving me standing there with a beating heart in my throat and a boner that took seven shots of whiskey to kill.

I still haven't recovered. The academy is the place I least want to be on most days, but this morning? I'm counting the minutes until I see her again. Get those steady, yet curious eyes on me and hold them. Hold them longer this time. That damn kiss threw me off my game so bad, I didn't even get a phone number or the name of her hotel last night. If she doesn't show up tonight, I have no idea what I'll do. Facebook is an option, but there have to be five thousand Katies in Ireland. There's only one that's got me itchy, though.

It'll go away. This itch. Soon as we get between the sheets and I bang her into next Thanksgiving, I'll go back to being good old Jack, the one who takes nothing and nobody seriously. The downwards slide after Katie might be even harder than usual, but she'll be worth it.

Although, what if I *don't* feel like shit after I'm with Katie? I've begun to think the crash into regret after sex is something I speed towards on purpose. What happens if it's taken away?

Maybe with Katie I won't feel used and shitty afterwards. Is this the time?

My stomach drops. Do I even *want* to feel good afterwards?

Hands everywhere, my head stuffy with the scent of floral perfume, low laughter, heavy breathing.

The vision hits me out of nowhere and my hand shoots back into the locker, wrapping around the water bottle of vodka and drawing it out. It shakes in my grip as I bring it to my lips.

"Garrett." Danika's voice whips straight through the center of my ugly thoughts. My oldest childhood friend is standing at the entrance to the men's locker room—the girl has no boundaries—and she's giving me that tilty-headed stank face she does so well. "Drills are about to start. Are you waiting for a formal invitation?"

"A simple Evite should do it," I quip into the bottle, taking another drag.

"Cute." She crosses her arms, letting me know she's not in the mood to shovel my bullshit. It used to take a lot more to make her angry with me, but her irritation seems to be coming easier lately. We lived in the same building on 10th

Avenue growing up and were friends for three years before I got up the nerve to tell her why I never invited her over to watch television. But she'd already figured out what my mother did for a living. While I sat there gaping like a fish, she'd socked me in the shoulder and told me she'd aim higher if I ever held out on her again.

Danika is the only person I love, besides my mother. That love is ironclad. It means I'll go to the ropes for her any damn day of the week. When her first boyfriend got angry and clipped her in the chin "on accident," I tied him to a fire hydrant on the West Side Highway and stole his pants. Then two weeks later, I stole his new girlfriend.

I tell anyone who asks that Danika is my sister. They don't believe me, on account of her being Colombian, but I don't care. That's exactly how I feel about her.

And right now, she seems to be feeling murderous towards her brother.

"Put that shit away." She wants to tap her foot. I can tell. "Would it kill you to show up on time once in a while without being dragged?"

I shut my locker door and make for the exit, giving Danika puppy dog eyes as I approach. "Aw, don't be mean to me, D." When she doesn't budge from the doorway, I tap her on the nose. "Maybe I just don't like walking alone."

She crams her lips together on a sigh, then digs

in the pocket of her uniform. A second later, she pops a breath mint into my mouth. "You should know by now that I'm not going to swoon over your helpless bachelor act."

"You think this is an act?"

"I used to." Chewing her lip, she looks like she wants to say more, but the clock on the wall over my shoulder makes her curse. "We don't have time for this. Move your ass." I follow her down the concrete hallway towards the gymnasium, balancing myself on the wall when my feet get tied together. "Lieutenant Burns is introducing a new instructor and he's being all furtive about it."

"Cool, cool. And furtive means . . ."

"Secretive."

"I knew that." I wink when she throws exasperation at me over her shoulder. "When is the L.T. not being furtive?"

Danika stops at the gymnasium door, spine snapped straight. "How would I know? I don't pay attention to what the man is doing."

Like I said, I know way more about women than any man should. "Try not being so defensive next time and I might believe you."

Light blinds me when my "best friend" smacks the gym doors open—totally purposeful—and stomps off towards our regular mat. We aren't even close to starting drills, which has me weighing the pros and cons of dipping back to the locker room for one more swig. But when

I see our roommate and pal, Charlie, lying under the oversized halogens with a sappy smile on his face, I remember. This thing with Katie has me so distracted, I actually forgot I'd participated in a flash mob yesterday afternoon, right before going to visit my mother in the Kitchen. A flash mob designed to win back Charlie's girlfriend, Ever. Along with the fact that he never came home last night, the smile on his face is a clear indication that our public humiliation was effective.

"Charlie boy." I drop down onto the mat, ignoring the way the room tilts. "You're going to sprout a pair of tits if you don't stop mooning like a schoolgirl. You've gone straight past creepy couch-jumping Tom Cruise and smack into uncharted territory."

"Ever is spending the night at our place tonight." Apparently Charlie can't hear a damn word I say over the birds chirping in his head. "I need to wash my sheets."

Danika's nose wrinkles. "When is the last time that happened?"

"No clue."

She groans. "Some Febreze wouldn't go amiss, either." Her elbow meets my ribs. "That goes for you, too, Garrett."

"And yet the complaint department has been totally silent." I think of Katie walking into my room and what her reaction would be. Would she laugh at the Rat Pack bobblehead collection my mother gave me for Christmas or head straight for the bed? Would she ask me to tell her another story? The tightness in my chest makes me force the curiosity away. "Does Ever staying the night mean we should invest in some ear plugs, Charlie, you dirty dog, you?" A full minute of silence passes in which I have completely lost my bro to the power of pussy. "You all right over there, man?"

"Oh, uh . . . yeah. Yes, I would look into ear plugs." His dreamy sigh is straight up unacceptable coming from someone with testicles. "Because we're going to be doin' it."

"Thanks for the clarification," Danika says dryly. "Do you want to give me the birds and the bees talk, too?"

Now here's an opportunity for some fun. Not to mention a way to get back on Danika's good side. I hate it when she's mad at me. "Well, you see, honey. When a man and a woman have established a mutual respect for one another—"

"Stop." She's laughing as she smacks both hands over her ears. "Make it stop."

That laugh means I've earned another day of friendship and my relief makes me double down, digging my fingers into her ribs, same way I used to do when we were kids. And on cue, she loses it, squealing and batting my hands away. If I was sober, I still wouldn't give a shit that everyone is watching, but I especially don't give a flying fuck now.

Not until the lieutenant walks into the gym.

Charlie's brother, Lieutenant Greer Burns, is a world-class prick. At age thirty, he's been decorated by the department so many times that his shit has ceased to stink, at least in his mind. I've never once seen him crack a smile. His face is made of stone. But if he thinks I haven't noticed his interest in Danika, he's not as much of a genius as everyone thinks.

Or else he just assumes I'm stupid.

His jealousy snaps in his face like a live wire when he sees me tickling Danika. I would assure him he has nothing to worry about—I've never had romantic feelings for my best pal, worthy though she is—but he *should* worry. Because over my dead body will Danika get run over by that emotionless dickhead.

Growing up, she looked out for me. The code of friendship demands I return the favor. In terms of favors, I am way behind, too. Before the academy, I was content to work on the docks forever, unloading cargo ships at night on the West Side for decent cash. Enough to get my mother out of the brothel. Danika wasn't content with my half-ass life plans, though. She threatened me with violence if I didn't pass the department-required amount of junior college credits, which I justified to myself by admitting my days were open, might as well give those studious ladies something nice to look at besides a book. Once I'd racked up the credits, Danika tricked me into taking the written civil servant exam with a sucker's bet about the Knicks making the playoffs. To this day, I can't believe she managed to con me into the academy. Or that I ever bet on the Knicks.

Nor will I ever understand why women don't run the world.

"Keep your damn hands to yourself, Garrett," the lieutenant growls.

Danika shoots to her feet, back straight, heels clicking together. A split second later, she's annoyed with herself for doing so, but holds her position with gritted teeth. Me? I throw the son-of-a-bitch a lazy smile and don't even bother standing.

My smile slides right off my face when Katie—my Katie—walks in.

At first, I think someone slipped a hallucinogenic into my water bottle. Something way stronger than vodka. Because why would Katie be here? Holding a clipboard? Maybe I never even got out of bed this morning and I'm having a whiskey-induced dream. If I was imagining Katie being in the gym, though, wouldn't my brain put her in the same jeans and tank top she wore yesterday? Instead, she's wrapped up in these sleek, black spandex pants and a tight as fuck academy T-shirt. Oh, and rest assured, everyone with a dick—with the exception of the Burns brothers—is sitting up and taking notice of Katie. My Katie.

"Listen up, recruits," Greer shouts, still watching Danika and me with annoyance. "This is your new arms instructor, Katie McCoy."

Pretty sure my jaw hits the mat. "Fuck. Me."

CHAPTER 5

— Katie —

S hite. Bollocks. Fuck.
   Is he still there?

I close my eyes and give my head a bit of a shake. When I open them, Jack is still reclined on one of the mats, spearing me with disbelieving green eyes. Or he was reclining a moment ago. He's slowly rising to his feet now, stretching to his full height. If he was standing in front of me, my head would be falling back to keep him in my sight lines about now. Good thing I'm shaking like a newborn lamb across the room, yeah?

Not really. Is this actually happening?

Forget that the odds are completely stacked against this being a real-life occurrence. How am I supposed to use my presentation voice now? If I open my mouth, I'm fairly sure a squeak or a string of giggles is going to come out. Your man Lieutenant Burns is arching an eyebrow at me, waiting for me to speak. Thinking fast, I give him an identical look. He's going to think I'm a diva now, needing a big intro and some pomp before I'll roll over, but I hardly have a choice if I want to get my nerves back under control.

An Olympic stadium chockablock with spectators? I'm golden. A room full of Americans in sweatpants, including one green-eyed ride that makes them all look like lumpy mash? I'm useless.

"Miss McCoy is here from Ireland for the next two weeks, thanks to the International Police Exchange Program," Lieutenant Burns continues smoothly. "If you're unfamiliar, it's a government funded program designed to keep our departments abreast—" Someone in the back row snickered at the word *abreast*. This lot is going to be a challenge. "—of global techniques so that we might improve on our own. There is always room for improvement, especially among this pack of jackasses."

I snort a laugh. My hand flies to up contain it about four milliseconds too late.

Burns is not impressed.

Neither is Jack, who is still trying to burn a hole into my face with green laser vision. Which I find rather annoying when I'm attempting to get my pulse back under control. I frown at him to let him know it. And for some insane reason, that appears to relax him.

I'm beginning to wonder if men are worth everyone's trouble.

My stare down with Jack is interrupted when a gentleman in aviator sunglasses pipes up from the front row. "She a cop or what?"

The lieutenant whips his head around and glowers at the speaker. "She's an Olympic gold medalist in the air rifle competition and more proficient with firearms than anyone in this room, including myself. After the Olympics, she completed her training with the Garda Emergency Response Unit and graduated at the top of her class. Now she's a special weapons instructor." The audible shift of energy in the room has my eyes shooting to the floor. Apart from standing on the podium in Rio, I haven't had my accomplishments waved in the air like this. At least not while I'm standing there to watch it happen. "So how about showing a little respect, recruit?"

"I was just—"

"You can begin by removing those ridiculous sunglasses." That command hangs in the air while the recruit follows orders, tucking the item into his back pocket. "Did your mother put them on you while she combed your hair this morning? He has sensitive eyes. Is that what she tells all her friends while she shops for your pajamas?"

"No, sir."

Well. It's safe to say he won't be interrupting Lieutenant Burns anymore. I almost feel bad for the poor lad. His friends look as though they're getting their insults ready for the moment my introduction ends. Instead of joining with everyone else in witnessing the demise of Sunglasses Boy, I allow my gaze to drift over to Jack. That's when I notice the beautiful girl standing beside him and my legs turn somewhat watery. She's watching Jack with guarded curiosity and following his attention straight over to me, elbowing him in the side and getting no response.

Is that his girlfriend, then? It would be, wouldn't it? Her dark waves of hair are tied back in a perfect ponytail while mine looks like a bloody whale spout.

I don't realize Lieutenant Burns has given me the floor again until he clears his throat. His clipboard taps against his thigh. *Whap whap whap.* And I have no choice but to step forwards, mentally reviewing everything I remember from my required public speaking course in college.

Then promptly forgetting it.

"Good morning." I go on autopilot, reaching for my backpack to get out my camera. Same as I always do when I have something remarkable in front of me—and a hundred sweaty lads totally qualifies. The dozen or so ladies don't look so bad themselves—definitely picture worthy. My pack is back in Burns's office, though, so I grab the next best thing, my phone. "Would you mind terribly if I just took a quick snap for Instagram? I don't even have any followers, really, so I don't know why I bother. Being a slave to social media has become something of a habit, I think, hasn't it? We've no choice. Show us your pictures or it never happened. Okay." I stab a few buttons and hold up my cell, certain I've turned the color of watermelon. "You'll all follow me now, won't you? Please?"

There's a beat of silence. Then I swear every single one of them breaks out into a grin at the exact same time. One bloke makes a bloated monkey face, tugging out his ears on the side. After that, it's a sea of silly poses, men attempting to yank one another's pants down and Burns blowing the whistle, attempting to restore decorum.

"Sorry about that," I call to the lieutenant over the noise. "I ramble when I'm nervous."

He ignores me and continues to blow the whistle. While I snap a few shots, I notice Jack in the frame, pushing his way closer. That same determination I saw in him last night is back and my stomach flips just being in the path of it. I can't have a conversation with him here, can I? No. But I saw the way Jack blew off his instructor's irritation when I walked in, so I'm guessing he doesn't give a flying fig about appearances. I do, though.

This program bought me two weeks in New York. Two weeks of freedom I can't afford on my own just yet, but that I desperately need after years of grueling preparation for the Olympics, followed by Emergency Response Unit training. This adventure isn't only for me, either. It's for someone close to my heart who couldn't be here—and I don't want to let him down.

When I kissed Jack in the park last night, I didn't know he would be under my guidance for the duration of the trip. Now that I do? Any kind of communication between us needs to be on the up-and-up. An indiscretion could lead to me being sent home early or losing my position as an instructor back home. Having gone through Garda training, I know instructors and recruits are placed in close quarters for months and often make mistakes of the Biblical variety. It's just the nature of the beast. But inappropriate contact with a trainee is the fastest way to lose respect from your colleagues. As a woman, I have to work twice as hard for respect—and I have—so this thing with Jack and me . . . it can't go beyond last night.

I'm surprised by the sharp punch of loss in my stomach. Sure, I spent an inordinate amount of time thinking about Jack's kiss while lying in bed last night—and this morning—but I've only known him one day. Surely there's no way I'm already attached.

Whatever I'm thinking must be showing on my face, because Jack's progress slows to a halt and we're left trapped inside unwavering eye contact, as though trying to read one another's mind. I feel Burns watching, though, so I force myself to regain control of the situation.

"As the lieutenant said, I'll be leading a weapons training course for the next two weeks. Six sessions in total." The men quiet down so suddenly, my quick sucks of breath between sentences sounds like nails on a chalkboard to my ears. "In Ireland, the Garda don't carry guns, but Emergency Response does require extensive training, which is where I come in. My role here is to promote safety and sound judgment. I want to leave you with the utmost respect for weapons. In our line of work, they are a last resort. Not the first." I'm quiet for a moment letting that sink in, because I know what's coming next is going to cause a stir and I'll lose their undivided attention. "While I'm here, I've been asked by the lieutenant to identify the recruit who shows the highest proficiency with firearms during training. If you're the lucky winner, my recommendation will go in your file. If you have your sights set on the Emergency Services Unit, you will be fast-tracked when the opportunity to move up arises."

Truthfully, I was surprised myself when Burns dropped that responsibility on my head, but his explanation made sense. He wants to incentivize his recruits into taking safety training seriously. If the buzz of their reaction is any indication, it's a sound plan, and I'm looking forwards to having the group so focused.

Speaking of focused, Jack has not joined in with the rest of the recruits, most of them already bragging they'll come out on top at the end of two weeks. We're the only two people in the gymnasium standing still as statues. Even Burns is joining in the good-natured ribbing, so I feel free to hold Jack's sparking eyes for a few extra seconds. Being pinned under his attention sends bumps rising all down my arms and back, makes my belly muscles contract. How on earth am I going to spend time in this man's company without giving in to temptation?

No clue. But I better find a way fast. Because I can read the message he's sending me and it goes something like this: I don't play by the rules and this new development changes nothing.

Jack

Well if this isn't a wrench in the fucking works.

On the upside, I don't need to go searching Facebook for Katie now. She's fallen right into my lap, hasn't she? Problem is, she's fallen into everyone else's, too, and I don't like it. In fact, the next idiot to wonder out loud if the carpet matches the drapes is getting paint thinner in their shampoo bottle. Any other day, I would have already sent these clowns to the ER for stitches, but starting a fight will get my ass suspended, putting Katie out of my reach.

And I really, really want to keep her within my reach. She gets more incredible by the minute. An Olympic gold medalist? I was hot to get her naked when she was leafing through a mob hits book and peeping through the bar window. Put her in goggles and stick a rifle in her hands? She looks like something out of a World War II cigarette advertisement. A redhead pinup girl showing the boys how it's done.

We're in the firing range for a demonstration from Katie, before we head to our own booths to follow suit. I'm pinging back and forth between two burning urges. One? Join the drooling shitheads around me by staring in awe at the beauty who just landed six quick shots in the center target. Two? Calmly explain I've already had my tongue in her mouth, she's ruined for their pathetic attempts to land her and they can all go home.

There's a not so slight problem with option two, however. Katie might as well have a sign blinking over her head now that says off-limits. As I learned yesterday, she shows every emotion on her face, so it's no mystery she wants to put me on ice now that we're instructor and recruit. And no means no. Zero excuses.

So I just have to make sure she doesn't want to say no.

Easy, right?

Katie finishes her demo to a deafening round of applause from everyone in an academy uniform. Christ. For their next act, they're going to carry her around on a daybed and fan her with giant palm fronds. The fact that I understand why they all fell instantly in love with her doesn't make watching it any easier. She's *my* murder-obsessed, backpack-wearing, picture-taking kiss bandit. Not theirs. I need to get her alone sooner rather than later. Away from the admiration that's making my neck hot. Looking into her eyes and seeing recognition of how explosive our kiss was in the park is the only thing that can make this weird, possessive caveman feeling go away. I think. I've sure as shit never been here before.

Fifteen minutes later, we've been divided into groups. Half of us will remain in the range, while the others head back to the gym for take-down drills. I could wait for my turn in the firing range or . . .

"Bro, I'm going to swap spots," I say to the guy ahead of me, slapping him on the shoulder when he sputters. "I owe you one, thanks."

"Wait, but—"

I'm already snagging headgear, securing it over my ears and shrugging when I can't hear him. *Better luck next time.*

Charlie is in the first group and he's wasted no time aiming for the man-shaped target in the distance, focused and prepared to nail the task in front of him. There's no doubt in my mind Charlie will be the one Katie recommends to Emergency Services. Everyone talking a big game about being the star contender knows it, too. His father is a bureau chief, Lieutenant Burns is his older brother and, bottom line, he wants to be the best. He's wanted it forever.

I've liked Charlie since day one. He's a damn good friend. Sometimes, though, he's hard to be around. He might be the only man I've ever envied in my life. Not because of his looks or anything—I'm the permanent winner of the dude beauty pageant—but Charlie knows his future. Knows where his path leads. And when something is off or he isn't satisfied with a situation, he pokes at it and obsesses over it until it's fixed. Me? I can live with something—inside me or around me—being wrong forever. I have.

Don't get me wrong, when Charlie gets the recommendation I'll be proud as shit. But it will be another reminder I'm only in this job for the paycheck and pension. That I don't have a dream beyond a reasonably comfortable life for myself. Ensuring my mother is never forced back into her old line of work. Bottom line, I wasn't built to be a dreamer. Sometimes, it's hard to live with that when my best friends were.

When Katie sees me walking into the range, her casual expression falters, but she catches herself and continues explaining the proper loading technique to a starry-eyed recruit. It's noisy in the facility, not to mention everyone is wearing headgear, so she's having to speak pretty loud. It's not going to be easy to carry on a decent conversation with her here. Maybe I should have waited for a better opportunity, but it's too late now. And I don't want to wait, anyway.

I'm in my booth when she approaches, sliding into the small space to my right. Lust hits me low in the belly at having her close, even though she's being careful not to touch me. The gunfire camouflages the groan in my throat when she peeks up with those incredible eyes, because finally, there it is. Recognition that she knows me, more than she knows anyone else in the room. An acknowledgment that I've had my tongue in her mouth and she stretched out my hoodie trying to get more of it. Unfortunately, she's gearing up for the big brush-off. Funny how I can tell when I've never been brushed off by a female in my life, but Katie's poker face needs definite work. I'll be keeping that to myself, though, considering I love her open book expressions and apparently I'm going to need every advantage I can get.

Katie squares her shoulders, ready to cut me off at the knees. "Morning, Jack—"

"How heavy are gold medals? I've always been curious."

"Eh—" She tugs on her ponytail with a nervous hand. "Fairly heavy. Sure, I've never weighed it."

My plan was to distract her with conversation until she forgot about breaking our date for tonight, but soon as she opens her mouth, I'm hanging on every husky syllable, damn the plan. "Did you wear it on the plane ride home?"

"God, no, I didn't. Or I wasn't planning on it, anyway." Pink blooms on her cheeks, making her light pattern of freckles stand out. "The flight attendant announced me over the loud speaker, though, so I had no choice but to take it out."

"Was that before or after you hid in the bathroom?"

Pleasure pulls at the ends of her mouth. "Before."

Those lips are doing their best to distract me, but I persevere, watching emotions flicker across her face. Surprise, confusion, determination to stay focused. "Congratulations on the gold medal, Katie. You must have worked really hard for it."

She blinks. "Aren't you going to ask me if I met Michael Phelps?"

"Is that what every one of these shitheads has been asking you?"

"With the exception of one. He was more interested in Al Roker." Her nose wrinkles. "Is he an athlete or what?"

"Close. He's a weatherman."

"Oh." She presses her knuckles to her mouth, suppressing a smile. "It usually takes me more time to find the group weirdo. Thank you for your assistance."

"Any time, Snaps."

We're grinning at each other and I don't even care that I succeeded in distracting her. I'm too busy feeling . . . good. Being around this girl makes me feel good. Not the fake and fleeting kind of good, either, that I get when I talk to girls in bars. The kind I want to hurry and get rid of as soon as it starts. I don't feel as though another drink, and *another* drink will make it easier to be around her. Nah, it'll make concentrating on every word she says harder and I don't want that.

When she looks up at me, totally lacking in guile and seeking—always seeking—something more from me, I wonder if I could be better in her eyes than I am in the eyes of everyone else. Maybe I'm crazy, but the possibility lightens some of the tension in my gut. How long has it been there? As if Katie holds the answers, I move closer like there's an invisible rope tied around my waist, tugging me forwards. Katie's smile dips slowly, replaced by awareness and alarm, so I stop when our toes bump.

"Been thinking all night about this fountain adventure of yours—" Her frown cuts me off. "What's wrong?"

She's staring at my mouth, which should be a good thing, but her expression is nothing short of troubled. Right out of nowhere. "C-can I talk to you outside in the hall?"

Sweet. I thought I was going to have to work a lot harder to get her alone. "Took you long enough to realize how irresistible I am." I wink to let her know I'm joking. Mostly. "Lead the way."

A wrench turns in my gut when Katie doesn't laugh. Instead, she looks dazed as she pivots on a heel and heads for the side exit. Except for a couple of shrewd recruits, everyone is too distracted by their task to pay attention to us leaving. Of course, one of the shrewd ones is Charlie, who raises an eyebrow at me as I walk past. *No idea*, I mouth as I slide out into the deserted corridor. Once the door closes behind us the sound of gunfire fades, leaving only the buzzing, flickering halogen above our heads.

Without dozens of eyes on us, my first instinct is to walk her backwards until she's flattened between me and the far cinder block wall. That thin T-shirt she's wearing needs my hands underneath it, like, right now. My tongue can already taste her moaning into my mouth while I tug down the cups of her bra and thumb those nipples. We'd only have a few minutes to play, though, because the last thing I want is Katie's job suffering because of me. Someone—like the lieutenant—could walk out at any minute. Some primitive part of me fist pumps over the idea of marking my territory, but I order myself to stop being an idiot caveman. That's not me and it never has been. Yet the fist pumping rages on.

I ease into Katie's space, letting my fingertips brush against her hips. God, I want to taste her so bad, but she looks stiff and it's making my stomach churn. "Something wrong?"

"Yes. I-I think so." Her swallow is audible. "Have you been drinking, Jack?"

Clarity slams into me hard. It's like waking up from a dream, but I'm in a different location than where I fell asleep. The veins in my temples pump hard, as if they're full of hot sludge, instead of blood. Dread thins my stomach lining. Apart from the occasional squabble with Danika, I've never had to answer for my drinking. It's part of my days and nights. I don't have to think as much when my mind is numb. Apparently I wasn't thinking *at all* when I entered the firing range buzzed.

I remember Katie's refusal to go inside the bar yesterday and my fuckup blinks like a bright, neon sign. Me being buzzed at ten o'clock in the morning is not good in the eyes of *anyone*, let alone this girl. Forget the fact that I could get in trouble with the academy or that the danger of the situation only occurred as an afterthought to me, Katie is visibly unsettled. I did this to her. I'm unsettling her. If I was ever tempted to apologize for the way I cope with my shitty memories, now is the time, but the stubborn voice inside me excusing my methods is too loud to drown out. I do what I have to do.

"It's no big deal, Snaps, all right?" I attempt a reassuring smile, but she doesn't appear to be biting, kicking panic into my bloodstream. "I just find orange juice boring on its own."

She processes that with a few blinks. "I know you're trying to be funny, right?" God, the step she takes away from me echoes in my chest. That one step might as well put a mile divide between her and me. "But I can't let you handle weapons when you've been drinking. If something were to happen—"

"Listen, I get it." I want to lunge across the space between us, but force myself to stay put. "I can skip this one and make it up later, huh?"

"I wasn't allotted time for makeups." She dodges eye contact while chewing on her bottom lip. "It would have to be after . . . after regular training hours, but I don't think that's a good idea. Especially now."

"What do you mean especially now?" As soon as the words are out of my mouth, I realize I don't want to know. Not yet. Not when I have to hear it through a vodka buzz. She's either going to cut me off because she's my instructor or because I showed up this morning half-drunk. Neither one of those outcomes is desirable. "Never mind. Look, let's just talk about this when we meet at the fountain tonight."

"Jack." Her tone is full of warning. "You have to know everything is different now."

"It's not safe for you to go alone."

"Would you come alone? Or would you . . ." She fidgets. "Bring your girlfriend, or—"

I rear back like I've been coldcocked. "Girlfriend?"

She covers her face. "That was so stupid. I have no tact or clever ways to discern relationship status and that was so, so stupid. And it doesn't matter anyway, because everything is different now, like I said."

Who *is* this girl? I've never come across a single other person like her in my life. She just truthed me again, throwing insecurities up in the air like confetti and as the pieces flutter down, I want to catch them all and stuff them in my pockets. There's no game between us. She doesn't know how to play them, so I'm allowed to not play mine. It's fucking amazing. "Honey, you're the closest thing I have to a girlfriend and you're trying to get rid of me. For the second time. I don't have enough humiliation left over to split between two girls."

When her surprised laugh falters, I realize I've moved closer. Immediately I stop, but the air thrums with awareness. Mine. Hers. She's wary of me, sure, but her gaze continues to dip to my mouth, my chest. Her nipples become noticeable behind the material of her T-shirt. "Aren't you going to ask me if I have a boyfriend?"

"No." My fingers flex, like they're wishing for some imaginary guy to throttle. "You wouldn't have kissed me if you did."

Her smirk is edible. "At least not the second time."

Shit, she's got me so hot. Pressing the advantage of our attraction isn't right when the fact that I've been drinking makes her nervous, though, so I stay put. When we walked into the hallway, I couldn't have been lighter. Now I'm buried under wet concrete and I have to shovel my way out.

Normally, I would just laugh this whole situation off and forget about it. So I don't get to shoot a bunch of big-ass guns? Fine. Less work for me. So I lose my chance with a girl? Whatever. There's literally five million more in this city.

They're not this girl, though. Not Katie. Katie who is balanced on the balls of her feet, seeming undecided between jumping my bones and running away. Katie who looked so guilty over having to kick me out of class, even though it's not her fault, and stumbled her way through asking if I was attached. Katie whose taste I'm still holding on to because I've never experienced anything like her. If I want a chance to experience her again, I have to fix this. Is it crazy to think I can keep it fixed, though? I've never been with a girl longer than one night, maybe two.

"Let's make a deal," I say, struck by inspiration. "You let me come tonight and I promise, I won't make a move on you."

A few notes of laughter trip out of her mouth, her shoulders relaxing. "Is that meant to be noble?"

"If you knew how bad I want my hands on you, noble would be an understatement."

Those nipples of hers tighten even more and I almost collapse a lung keeping my growl from escaping. "You've got me in a weak moment, here, because even though drinking vodka before breakfast is not sound behavior—"

"If you think this stern teacher lecture is getting me any less hot, you're wrong."

"Even though I know that," she wheezes, her

tits trembling. "I'm new to this instructor thing, so maybe I'm a bit of a softy. And I've still got that yucky guilty feeling for making you lose today's course credit."

"You're going to let me make today's credit up, though, right?" My dick is like a steel rod at this point. He wants between Katie's legs and doesn't understand the delay because he's a spoiled jerk. "After hours. Right, Snaps?"

"I haven't decided," she whispers, analyzing my face. "But if we make up the credit, that's all we'll be doing."

"Fair enough. Same with tonight." I tuck my hands underneath my armpits to make my point. "No touching. No kissing. Even though we'll be thinking about it. Wanting it. I'll be there as your lookout, nothing more."

She purses her lips, but there's humor sparkling in her eyes. "You're very arrogant."

"You kissed me last night. Do you think there's a reason?"

"I seem to recall you were the one begging," she says breathily.

My balls squeeze like they're in a vise. "If you like begging, I'll give it to you, honey," I rasp. "I'll wear out the knees on every pair of jeans in my closet . . . begging."

Just like last night on the bench, her thighs cinch together at the insinuation that I would go down on her. And I would. Until she screamed for me to stop. Pretty sure my eyes are communicating that message because her eyes are like silver dollars. Christ, this is the epitome of torture. Knowing you've gotten a girl good and wet, then walking away. And yet, all I can think about is doing it again tonight.

"Do we have a deal?" I ask, as the light above our heads flickers.

Her eyes are drawn to the light, her lips parting on a soft intake of breath. Studying me for a beat, she walks past me, settling a hand on the doorknob. After another pause, she sends me a serious look from beneath a forest of eyelashes. "Don't make me regret this, Jack."

CHAPTER 6
Katie

This is a terrible idea.

Honestly, I thought I had a level head on my shoulders. But not only am I meeting a recruit after hours—I'm preparing to do something sort of a wee bit innocently illegal. So why is there a rush of bubbles floating down the veins of my arms, making my fingertips tingle?

It's just around 11:00 p.m., but the buzz of life in Central Park is still rippling in the air. The occasional jogger trundles past me. People bundled into their jackets walk their groomed dogs, while staring down into the lit-up screens of their phones. I take the occasional picture with my camera, trying to catch the wind slithering through the trees. I can barely swallow around the lump of excitement in my throat. Just to be out. To be anonymous in a giant sea of end-less anonymous. Possibilities for the innocent mischief I was never allowed to indulge in lay in every corner of the park, inside every jagged building sticking up around the perimeter.

When my brother was alive, we used to dream about coming to New York City for a summer holiday. We were going to get jobs in a pub in some trendy neighborhood, a cheap apartment in one of the outer boroughs near the train sta-tion. Everyone would come to our place, because we'd always have something good on the telly and enough crisps to go around. Sean was three years older than me, so he would have gone back to Ireland after our summer trip with only one year left to go until graduation, while I would have just been starting college.

But everything can change in a split second. I learned that the hard way. And maybe it's on the morbid side, but I look back now and remem-ber all these tiny hints the universe dropped in my lap that Sean would be taken away too soon. There's one that stands out more than most. The last time we were together, he'd picked me up from school in his lorry. My passenger side window was fogged because of the chill outside and I remember drawing lazy hearts in the con-densation. His favorite band, The Kinks, drifted from the stereo where he'd hooked his iPhone. The song "This Time Tomorrow" came on and we both sang along—even though neither of us could carry a note—and by that time the following day, he was gone.

I look for signs everywhere now. Tiny hints from your man upstairs that I need to pay better attention to what's in front of me. Much to my dismay, it keeps happening with Jack. Just when I'm ready to employ common sense and write him off—hello, he was drunk at ten in the morning— there's a tiny nudge from the universe. The ancient light flickering over his head today when he offered me tonight's deal. Or the car horn wailing in the park when he asked to come along to the fountain. My own personal Magic 8 Ball that tells me *keep going, there's something here.* Of course, it's entirely possible I'm looking for excuses to keep seeing him because he makes me feel shivery inside and out. I'm just not sure.

But those maybe-nudges from the big guy upstairs reminded me of one thing. Life does move fast. People and opportunities can be snatched away in the space of a heartbeat. Just like Sean. I'm going to do some living for us both while I'm here, the way I've been pining to do in the years since he's been gone. I need to keep my head around Jack, though. There won't be any fanciful notions that he's a permanent part of the adventure. I've got too much at stake professionally to throw it all away on someone who must go through women like Quality Street chocolates on Christmas Day.

There are footsteps to my right and they cut

through every other sound. There he is. Turning the heads of a twosome of female joggers, swaggering a path through the moonlight. He's wearing a bomber jacket and faded jeans, a here-comes-trouble smile playing around the corner of his lips and God, I can't help but sigh. What a beautiful creature. I'm not a badge bunny by any stretch of the imagination, but I can only imagine the droves of women that will faint at the sight of him in uniform someday. When Jack gets close, it takes loads of willpower not to shoot up from my perch on the stone fountain, just so I won't be at a disadvantage sitting down, while he stands. I'm already on the defensive from his charm, giving him an extra two feet of height just seems unwise, but I manage to lean away and remain seated.

"Snaps." He runs a hand over his scalp. "You look more fucking adorable every time I see you. You know that?"

Wings flutter in my chest, but I attempt to hide my reaction by replacing the camera in my backpack. "That's hardly the proper way to speak to your instructor."

One edge of his mouth jumps. "Out here, we're just Jack and Katie, no?"

"Did you forget about our deal this afternoon?"

He sits down beside me on the fountain edge, his face easing within a couple of inches of mine. Close enough that I hold my breath. "Honey, if I was making a move, you'd know it."

"Right." I scoot away, frowning at him when he laughs, low and raspy. "I'm actually glad you're here."

It catches him off guard, his cocky smile slipping. "Really?"

Sexually confident Jack is dangerous. Sexually confident Jack with flashes of self-consciousness? Those glimpses set off doom singing in my ears. "Yeah," I say, refusing to be anything but honest. "It's one thing to picture myself dancing in a fountain and quite another to actually do it. There's way too many people about for this time of night. Doesn't this city ever sleep?"

He laughs warmly at my lame-o joke. "What's the main problem?"

"I'm not sure." Rubbing my lips together, I turn and survey the fountain over one shoulder. "Maybe I expected music?"

"I knew it. This is because of the opening credits from *Friends*."

I cover my face with both hands. "Do you think it's silly? I know the gang didn't actually dance in this fountain. They probably replicated it on a television studio lot somewhere in Los Angeles." He stays silent, but I don't detect any judgment on his face. Only curiosity. "It's just . . . those *Friends* reruns were with me during my training for Rio. All the injuries and bad days and arguments with my coach. Every time I heard that theme song, I knew I could just disappear into a happy place for half an hour."

Jack nods and stares off across the paved court-yard surrounding the fountain. "Thought you'd be more of a *SVU* girl with your mob hits fasci-nation."

"I like that one, too. But Benson and Stabler didn't have a fountain."

His eyes crinkle at the corners, as if he's laugh-ing, but there's something else going on in his expression. Like having a conversation isn't en-tirely within his comfort zone and he's nervous about what to say next. "Training sounds like it was pretty rough."

"Yeah." I sigh. "It was."

He cuts me a sideways look, half of his face covered in shadows. "Tell me about it?"

There have been a lot of interviews in the year since Rio, mostly from news stations and maga-zines back home, so I have my patented answers. Yes, the work is grueling, but at the end of the day, it's worth the pain so I can represent my country. Yes, my brother's death inspired me to work hard in his honor. All true—so very true—but those words only scratch the surface.

"My da was my coach," I start, feeling the wind pick up around me, lifting the hair off my neck. "We'd always had hopes that I could go on to the Olympics, but shooting was more for fun when I was a teenager. Something we bonded over." I curl my fingers around the hard stone lip of the fountain. "When my brother died five years ago, my father . . . he couldn't handle the loss and—"

"Jesus, Katie. I'm sorry. I didn't know."

"No, it's okay. Really." I smile at him, hoping to erase his stricken expression, but my mouth feels stiff. "My father needed somewhere to throw all his focus and it turned out to be me. My career. The Olympics. He was obsessed with me winning and . . ." My breath slides out little by little. "I didn't have the heart to take away what he needed. Even when it stopped being even a little bit fun, you know? We never did anything but train. Morning, afternoon and night. But I was the only child now, so I was trying to fill that space my brother left behind, as well as my own."

Jack slides closer and after a small hesitation, puts an arm around my shoulder. "So this adventure list . . ." His fingers skim my arm, just a brush, but goosebumps break out on every available inch of my flesh. "Is it meant to make up for lost time?"

"Yeah."

Those green eyes slide over me and he nods once. "Well we better make sure there's music, then."

Against my better judgment, I lift my head and bring our noses a couple of inches apart. "What do you mean?"

"Look, Snaps." His cockiness is back, but I get the feeling it's more for my benefit than his. As if he wants to distract me. "You probably haven't figured this out about me, but I hate to brag."

All the pain of my confession flies off into

the night sky. I'm battling laughter after talking about my brother and father—I can't believe it. "There are none so humble as Jack Garrett. That's what all the other recruits say when you're not around?"

Eyes closed, he nods sagely. "You bet. And they speak the truth." He stands, bringing me to my feet as well and turns me to face him. "One of the things I never brag about is my singing ability, but I'm going to make an exception tonight." He spreads his arms out to the sides. "I'm fucking brilliant, honey."

"Oh, really?" My cheeks twinge, my smile is so wide. "Did it come naturally or were you classically trained?"

"Neither." Is it my imagination or does a dark shadow cross over his face? I must be mistaken, because he's still smiling like an overly confident pirate. "I did some entertaining when I was younger. No places you would know. But I was huge in the underground scene."

I cross my arms, mainly because I'm worried he can see my heart pounding against my ribcage. Why does he have to be gorgeous and funny? "And how is this talent of yours going to help me dance in a fountain?"

He tilts his head and grins. "Are you all ready to go?"

I look around at the handful of passersby and squeal a little, hopping on one foot. "Yes, okay. I guess it's now or never." Kicking off my runners, I toe them towards my backpack where I've stashed a hotel towel. Then I strip off my jeans. The laugh that's been dying to escape finally erupts when Jack's eyebrows shoot up. "Relax, I'm wearing shorts underneath."

"I wasn't going to complain." His eyes are fastened on my legs and doing that melting thing they did last night. "But it was going to be a lot tougher keeping our agreement if you started dancing around in nothing but panties."

"Sorry to disappoint."

He makes a pained sound, but appears amused as I stuff my jeans into the backpack. "You really thought this through, didn't you?"

"I know what you're thinking. You didn't know planning could be so sexy."

There's a breathtaking glint of mischief in his eye. "Do you really think planning is sexy?"

"The sexiest."

"Then get ready to swoon, honey." He reaches into the inside pocket of his jacket. "Told you I had a feeling this fountain dancing adventure was *Friends*-related, didn't I?" He pulls a small umbrella out and hits a button, making it bloom. A red one, just like Rachel held in the opening credits dance. "How's that for planning?"

It's another sign from the universe, but this one isn't so easy to write off as a fluke, is it? This moment—Jack smiling under the moonlight and holding out a red umbrella for me—it feels important. Like I shouldn't just brush it off and move on. But Jack's smile is beginning to lose some of its power and I don't want that. I don't want him to think I'm not grateful that he thought to bring along the umbrella for me. "Thank you, Jack." He nods, relief making his cheek tick. "Total Ross move."

He scoffs. "We both know I'm a Joey."

Joey wasn't near as hot as Jack, even in the first couple of seasons, but I'm keeping that to myself. Besides, he already knows. "Okay, here goes nothing."

Jack takes my arm and helps me into the fountain. The water is a lot colder than I was expecting, but I don't mind. Exhilaration climbs up my calves, making the night real. I'm standing in a fountain in Central Park, the sky above me looks massive and I'm free. Right now, I'm completely free. I'm creating a snippet of time, all for myself. No one else. And then Jack starts to sing and I'm pretty sure it's one of the greatest moments of my life, right up there with the Olympic podium.

"So no one told you life was gonna to be this way . . ."

Someone behind me, one of the milling strangers, does the clap-clap-clap-clap with perfect timing and I double over laughing. I'll probably die in a fit of giggles about it for years to come, but right now I have to grab the seconds before they pass by—or I get arrested, whichever comes first. Jack's voice is rich and low, sweeping along the courtyard as I dance around the center statue in circles, twirling the red umbrella over my head like I'm leading a parade. When I circle back around to Jack, he's launching into the second verse and he's looking at me the funniest way. As if I'm an amusing puzzle he can't decipher.

Cushy abandon whips up inside of me. But memories of my brother linger, too, making me twirl even faster, kicking a splash of water into the air, because I'm living for two of us. The gravity of that, coupled with the unfamiliar flying around me is too much, stunted energy making my insides seize. I've been forced to dwell on the past so long, the future burns too hot and overwhelming. I need an anchor before I fly into the bright flames and I don't think, I simply step out of the fountain and drop into Jack's waiting arms. And they were waiting, like he knew I was going to need them. Even when I didn't?

"Sorry about this," I mumble into his neck, pressing my nose against the warm leather of his jacket. "Thank you for singing. Your voice really is lovely. In a manly way, of course."

His arms close around me slowly. Closing and closing until they're airtight. "So why did you stop?"

My knee-jerk reaction is to make a joke, but I'm already being cradled like a baby with my feet dangling in the air, so I might as well go for broke. "I was supposed to dance in this fountain with my brother. He was the reason those *Friends* reruns were so comforting. We used to watch it together."

Slowly, he sways us side to side and I close my eyes. "What happened to him, Katie?"

I blow out at breath. "Drunk driver."

All at once, he's stiff. We've stopped swaying and his heart has ramped up double time against mine. "That's why you don't go into bars."

The tension in his voice causes me to look up. His brows are dark slashes over burning green eyes and our earlier conversation comes rushing back. "Oh. I didn't . . . yes, Sean is why I don't go into bars. Just the smell of booze and wondering how everyone is getting home. Seeing people lose control of themselves. It makes me feel . . . resentful and angry and . . . I hate that. Maybe someday I'll be able to go into a bar and relax, but not yet." Jack seems to be holding his breath and I think I know why. "I wasn't judging you this morning because of my hang-up, though. That isn't why I asked you not to participate. It's not as if you do that regularly or anything, right?"

Several beats pass during which I can hear the leaves rustle above our heads. "No. Not a regular thing." His lips barely move. There's a prickling along my spine as he says it, too, putting me a little on guard. "I won't drink around you again, Snaps."

"Don't change anything for me." We're swaying again. "You would just have to rearrange yourself right back, since I won't be here very long."

The reminder seems to jerk him out of a trance, but his expression remains troubled. "Right. And you've got a list of adventures to complete before you head back to the motherland. What's up next?"

"There are only four items on the list. Visiting my famous mob hit sites, fountain dancing . . . and I'm not ready to reveal the other two yet."

"You're killing me here." He rolls his tongue around his mouth, dropping his attention to where our bodies press together. "But I'm going to let you slide for now. On account of me getting to hold you when I didn't think you'd let me within two inches tonight."

"I really shouldn't, recruit."

His teeth flash white across his shadowed face. "Don't give me that disapproving frown, instructor. I'm being a good boy, keeping my hands above your waist and everything."

I peek to the side to judge how high off the ground he's holding me. "Aren't your arms getting tired?"

"Nope. I can hold you up as long as it takes."

"As long as what takes?"

Hunger sparks in his eyes. "Tell me the no making passes at Katie deal is off and I'll demonstrate."

That awful, terrific clench happens between my thighs again and I bite back a moan just picturing what Jack means. Sex standing up. With me. As long as it takes for me to . . .

Right. "Well if dancing in a fountain didn't get me arrested, that definitely would."

Jack presses our foreheads together on a pained laugh. Up close, he studies me, lips parted. I can practically feel him needing to move, to touch me everywhere. Not acting on those impulses is like denying his second nature. "Come on, Katie. We can fly under the radar for two weeks." His gaze is searching. "I like being with you."

"I like it, too," I murmur, honesty escaping against my better judgment. Probably because his erection is pressed to the front of my shorts and maybe it's ridiculous, but I swear he would feel a lie if I told one. And I keep snagging on that tingly premonition from before. When he told me drinking in the morning wasn't a regular thing for him. My body's intuition might be the only thing forcing me to keep a level head here. Hello reality check. "I'm not a rule breaker. I made the plan for tonight before we knew I'd be working at the academy. Now that we know . . ."

His breath coasts over my lips. "Nothing has to change."

"See, this is no big deal to you. Because you're the Big Bad Wolf."

"I'm what?" His laugh is full and aching. "Ah, Katie. Is that just because I want to eat you so bad?"

My mouth drops open. "I definitely feel like Little Red Riding Hood when you say things like that."

Jack turns serious. "Look, I didn't hear a lot of fairy tales growing up, but I know the wolf is dangerous. Whatever I might sound and look like to you . . ." He shakes his head. "I want to protect you from danger while you're in town. Not be the danger."

"We might have different definitions of danger," I murmur.

"Maybe." He searches my eyes. "You're not scared of being alone with me, are you?"

"Terrified." I wish I could snatch back my answer when he flinches. "You said it yourself. Most girls don't want heart-to-hearts in the park with you. What if that's all I can offer?"

"Then that's all I'll take." He's vehement. "But I know we both want more."

My stomach hollows out and it takes me a beat to respond. "I have to give you a grade, Jack. It's a conflict of interest."

Slowly, he sets me down on my feet, but keeps me gathered close. "The only interest I have is this. Right here." He licks his lips and moves in, all slow and seductive and full of gruff whispers. "Talking to you about everything and nothing in the park at night. Watching you dance around like some kind of hot fairy princess. Having those eyes on me and nobody else." His throat works. "The academy is conflicting with *our* interests is how I see it."

It's a good thing he has hold of me, otherwise I might do something undignified. Like fly away on a winged team of hormones. But his sweet confession also reminds me what he said before. How much it contrasts to him saying he enjoys talking to me, watching me dance. And my pointless quip gets stuck in my throat. The possibility he lied to me earlier rears its head and I'm a little too distracted by it to flirt. Hands on his chest, I move free of his hold and he lets me go, though I can see it costs him an effort.

His hands drop with a curse. "Look, is this really about the academy finding out about us. Or me being the Big Bad Wolf?"

There's that insecurity in the lines of his body again. The one that messes with my equilibrium. "A little of both."

He levels me with a look. "You ever stop to think the wolf is a little scared of Little Red Riding Hood, too, honey?" When I can only stare, he stoops down and pulls my jeans free of my backpack, kneeling down and holding them for me to step into. His forehead wrinkles in concentration the whole time and while he does sneak longing glances at my legs, he seems more concerned with getting my pants on correctly. His knuckles warm me there as he slides up my zipper, his chest rising and falling quickly, fingers skillfully locking my button in place while I hold back a whimper. When the task is complete, he slides my runners onto my feet and ties them tight, surveying his handiwork and nodding with approval. Then he stands up, reaches out and takes my hand. "Come on, Snaps. I want to make sure you get home all right."

We walk a few yards before I finally find my voice, my heart is pounding so loudly in my ears. I have the sense I've hurt his feelings and it doesn't sit well. At all. "Jack?"

"Yeah?"

"Either way . . . whatever happens, you need to make up the class you missed." I don't miss the leap of his dimples, but I pretend not to notice. "On Wednesday after you're finished, I can meet you to make up the range time."

The smile he sends me is blinding. Outwardly, at least. Maybe it's my imagination or the earlier tingle still cooling my spine, but I swear I detect just a hint of uncertainty . . . and nerves . . . beneath his perfect veneer. "I'll be there."

CHAPTER 7

Jack

W hen my roommates walk into the kitchen Wednesday morning, they stop in their tracks and stare at me as if Jesus Christ Himself has descended to make them pancakes. To be fair, me getting up early and making breakfast is as regular an occurrence as a solar fucking eclipse, but they don't need to rub it in. I pull my weight in other ways, don't I? When Charlie was messed up over Ever, who was the wingman who helped him drown his sorrows? Jack. When Danika needs something off a higher shelf? You guessed it. This guy.

All right so maybe me making pancakes is a tad unusual, but I'm on a roll in the unexpected department. I haven't had a drink in two days, since Katie was introduced at the academy. It's no secret that I'm the least dedicated recruit and yet, getting asked to leave a training exercise was kind of a gut punch. Even then, staying sober wasn't the plan, but . . . it's weird. I can remember ever single second of being in Central Park with Katie. Every word spoken, every gust of wind is still so clear in my mind. It doesn't take a MENSA member to realize the clarity came from being sober. I liked it.

Not that remaining this way has been easy. My skin feels too confining, my throat has an itchy soreness going on, even though I'm not sick, and I can't seem to relax. This anxiousness isn't like me. At least, I don't think so. It's been a long time since I allowed the numbness to wear off for such an extended period.

Lying there in the darkness last night, I was too aware of my thoughts. Without the benefit of passing out, too many memories bombarded me until my stomach began a sickly clench. My head drummed. The bedclothes beneath my tossing and turning body felt like sheets from a different time and place. Sweaty, scratchy ones that rubbed redness into my back and arms. Echoes of feminine laughter and the smell of stale, floral perfume made the half a bottle of Ketel One under my bed seem like a land mine, just waiting for me to step on it. At least if I blew myself to pieces with the contents, I wouldn't have to think anymore, right?

Not knowing how Katie has spent the last

day and a half has not helped whatsoever. I've cursed myself a hundred times for not getting a contact number for her in the park. If that oversight doesn't tell you my game is missing in action around this girl, nothing will. The way she knocks me off balance already has me at a disadvantage without adding booze to the equation. This jumpy, anxious state I'm in will be worth not having to retrace my steps tomorrow or attempt to recall things I said. I made a promise to Katie, too, and I can't fuck that up.

Those old memories aren't going anywhere, though, making this new clarity a double-edged sword. The more my interest in Katie grows, the more worried I get over the prospect of sleeping with her. Does thinking about it get me hot? Better believe it. Hotter than I've ever been for a girl. But will I feel shitty afterwards? I really don't want that to happen with Katie.

Bottom line? I need somewhere to funnel my energy. So. I'm making some fucking pancakes. And if Charlie and Danika don't rave about them, I might move out.

"Ever," Charlie calls over his shoulder towards the bedroom. "You have to come out here and see this. Jack appears to be sleepwalking."

"Funny, dickhead," I say. "Guess who's getting the burned pancake."

Charlie's girlfriend, Ever—a catering chef—hops out of his bedroom while putting on a sock. "Need a hand? I have macadamia nuts in my bag."

"Oh my God." Charlie slaps both hands over his face. "That's so cute, I can't stand it."

"Those aren't the only nuts she's carrying around," I remark.

Ever lays a smacking kiss on Charlie's cheek, then slides towards her purse, courtesy of her socks on the hardwood floor. She joins me in the kitchen a moment later, using the end of the knife to crush the nuts on a paper towel, since we don't have a chopping board. I notice Charlie's eyebrow raised in my direction from where he sits—arms crossed—on one of the kitchen stools, beside an observant Danika. That eyes-off-my-girl expression gives me the urge to fling some batter at him. "Jesus. If you want me to put on a shirt, go grab one off my floor."

Until now, with all this annoying clearheaded thinking I've got going on, I've never really stopped to wonder if Charlie actually thinks I'd make a play for his girlfriend. It started as kind of a joke, but right now, his usual territorial pissing around Ever makes me kind of . . . uncomfortable. Look, I get it. Everyone and their mother views me as nothing more than their guide to a sinful good time. But ever since Katie called me the Big Bad Wolf, I'm not sure I find that label so harmless anymore. Not that I haven't earned it. I'm just not sure I like it now. Especially when it keeps sending my redhead running in the opposite direction.

Or maybe my lie did that.

To hide the discomfort over the reminder that I lied to Katie about how often I drink, I catch the T-shirt Charlie lobs in my direction, yanking it down over my head. When I can see again, I notice Danika watching me funny and turn my back. "You have any syrup in that magic bag of yours, Ever?"

"No dice, but butter is fine, right, guys?"

"Considering I was planning on scarfing down a granola bar on my walk to the academy? Damn right butter will work." Danika pauses and I can all but hear the gears in her head turning. "Why the sudden urge to cook, Jack?"

Ever dumps a handful of nuts into my batter and I begin stirring them in. "I had a sex dream about Rachel Ray last night," I lie smoothly, winking at my best friend over my shoulder. She stares back, tapping a fingernail against our high, square table. "Woke up feeling inspired."

Charlie appears to my left—the guy can't sit still for long—and he begins to make coffee with our old, taped-together, secondhand pot. "I guess we should be thankful it wasn't a Guy Fieri sex dream or we'd be having chili dogs for breakfast."

"Thanks for that image," Danika mutters. "Can you take a nap this afternoon and have dream sex about Giada? I'm in the mood for Italian tonight."

My hands slow their whisking motion, because I definitely just felt a bolt of guilt over hypothetical dream sex with a Food Network star. No further proof needed that I've got it bad for Katie. "I won't be around for dinner," I say without thinking.

Normally my roommates would probably just assume I'd be out drinking in the old neighborhood, but these are future cops I'm living with, so the brittle tension in my tone piques their interest. I can practically feel them circling me like beat detectives, looking for an alibi. "No?" Charlie does not pull off casual by any stretch. "Where are you going to be?"

"Yeah." I hear Danika hop off her stool and approach from behind. "What are your plans?"

"Looking for new roommates." I pour pancake batter onto the pan and a slow sizzle invades the small kitchen. "Ones that appreciate my attempts to feed their sorry asses and mind their own damn business."

Charlie's head ticks back and forth as he scrutinizes me. He's lucky I like him or he'd have a face full of Bisquick by now. "Been something different about you the past couple days."

"Noticed that myself, Burns." Danika props a hip on the stove. "Right around the time a certain redhead with a cute accent showed up."

Ever reaches around Danika with the spatula and flips the first pancake. "If you guys are teasing him over a girl, at least wait until we've all been fed so it stays civil."

Funny, I actually don't mind them ribbing me about Katie. It's kind of . . . nice. Really nice. She could very well decide I'm not worth risking her job over, but for this moment in time, I'm being linked to her. As if we're an actual thing. I haven't been part of a thing since high school and even then, calling someone my girlfriend—for a day or two—was just a formality. It never made me prideful the way being paired with Katie does. "McCoy is letting me make up the first class tonight. Happy now?" Remembering who Charlie is related to makes me backpedal. "It's . . . there's nothing weird or hush-hush about it. She's a professional."

Danika frowns. "Why do you have to make up the first . . . oh."

I don't like the way she trades a look with Charlie. Like they're lab partners and I'm the bug under their microscope. My skin stretches tight, making my neck muscles feel like they've been wound around a fist. "Could you drop it now? You got me. I have a thing for the shooting instructor." I stick a fork in the first pancake and drop it onto a waiting paper plate. "Not sure if you noticed, but so does everyone else."

"Except me," Charlie qualifies, cutting a slice off my finished, golden brown pancake.

I smack his hand away with a stern look.

"Or me," Danika echoes. "Even if she does have great boobs."

A chuckle escapes me. "I knew there was a reason we stay friends even though you nag me to death."

Danika's features cloud over for a split second, making me regret my choice of words. She only gets on my case about the drinking because she cares about me. After witnessing my body's reaction to being without alcohol for less than two days? I don't think I can deny anymore that she's right and I might have a problem. The question is whether or not I want to do something about it. Two nights with a clear head was hard enough, but imagining an endless cycle of staring at the ceiling and remembering the past sounds like a nightmare I'd rather avoid at all costs.

All I can do is focus on the next hour. And the hour after that. When the craving starts to bombard me, I'll remember the fountain spray hitting me in the face the other night. The feeling of Katie in my arms. Walking home without stumbling or feeling like I forgot something. How vivid those experiences were. Katie is in town for only a short window of time and I want to remember every second. Breaking my promise to her is the only thing that sounds worse than tossing and turning in my bead, haunted by memories.

"Hey." Charlie elbows me and I glance over, surprised to see him looking slightly offended. "You know I don't run to my brother with gossip, right? If you want to see the instructor, it stays between us. What happens on the East Side, stays on the East Side."

I elbow him back by way of apologizing for my assumption. "Good to know." Ever pours twin pancakes onto the pan and the sizzle nudges me back to the present, forcing me to shake the weight off my shoulders. "Anyway, it might not work out. Apparently there's something in the Irish water that makes their women immune to me. It's an international conspiracy and I have calls in to the United Nations, so . . ."

"Oh shit." Danika backs away from the stove laughing. "Don't tell me Jack Garrett got turned down."

I hold up the fork and mime jabbing it into my eye. "Twice."

My best friend snatches up a marker and begins writing on the dry-erase board fastened to the kitchen wall. "I have to make note of today's date."

"I'm glad you find my blue balls hilarious."

"Not even Rachel Ray could take care of those?" Ever asks, flipping a pancake. "Man, they say to never meet your heroes . . ."

Charlie comes up behind his girlfriend and wraps both arms around her waist, watching over her shoulder as she tends to our breakfast. For the first time, I'm not completely eye rolling their coupledom and taking mental bets on how long such a thing can last. I'm kind of envious, actually.

Christ, being sober is a mind fuck.

"Don't count me out just yet," I tell the room at large, trying my best to sound confident even though for once, I feel no such thing. "The third time will be a charm."

"Word to the wise," Charlie says, his chin resting on Ever's head. "Don't piss her off while she's holding a firearm."

Being shot by the woman I want to sleep with would definitely be a first. In that moment, I had no idea exactly how many *firsts* were on that night's agenda.

My STOMACH BOTTOMS out hard when I see Katie for the first time in two days. She's in stretchy-looking black pants and a gray tank top. That red hair in a swingy ponytail, the ends brushing against her neck. And her eyes are full of awareness. For me. As I approach her in the dim empty gym, she's balanced on the balls of her feet, like a cat. Like I give her a need to move somehow, some way or she'll pop. I know the feeling, because that's what she does to me.

And look, I'm a man. A horny-as-fuck man who's stone-cold sober. Lust punches me in the gut hard around Katie, but it's noisier now. It doesn't raise a hand and wait to be called on. It just speaks up and it's loud, more purposeful and *right*. I've grown used to feeling like garbage because of the one time I wasn't in control of my body. The situation. Katie doesn't make me wish for hell, though. I'm more than a means to a satisfying end around her. She's here, right now, because she believes I should be given a chance to make up a class, isn't she? I mattered enough. She's hung out with me three times because she likes me. Likes Jack.

I'm relieved as hell to see she's safe. So much that I make a hoarse, embarrassing sound in my throat that has no place coming from someone with a scrotum. She's survived two days alone in the city and my hands still want to run over every inch of her body, looking for injuries.

There's also the fact that I want to fuck her so hard she slaps me across the face afterwards.

"Hi, Jack," Katie says in that amazing voice. "You're even early. I'm impressed."

"Don't tell anyone. They'll start calling me teacher's pet." I'm not sure how she'll let me greet her. A hug, a kiss. A handshake, for chrissakes. My question is answered when I reach her a moment later and she turns in a fluid motion, heading towards the stairwell that leads down to the firing range. Not a great sign, but I'm in an optimistic mood, so I shake off the disappointment and follow. "How have you been keeping busy the last two days?"

"Touristy things, mostly." She hands me goggles and headgear as we enter the range, but neither of us puts them on just yet. Apart from a sharp intake of breath when her fingers brush mine, she's not giving me any sign of what she's decided. About us. "I went back to Central Park and had my caricature drawn. Have you ever gotten one?"

"Sure."

"Tell me about it?"

Satisfaction spreads down my limbs at her interest. "You know customers are more likely to stop at a caricature booth when they see someone is already having their picture drawn?" She shakes her head and waits, interested. "When I was a kid, I was looking to make a few extra bucks and found myself up by the park. One of the artists paid me to sit there all day. He would just retrace what he'd already done, but sure enough, tourists would stop to ooh and ahh. He gave me a cut every time I lured someone in."

"The cheek of you." Her lips tug at one end. "What was the picture?"

"Me holding a lightsaber."

Her hum makes me want to get closer. "Well, I didn't get a cool Jedi weapon. They gave me a giant nose, so I've been spending a fair bit of time today worrying about it. I always thought it was my ears that were too big, so I'm reevaluating every truth I've ever known."

"Your ears and nose are perfect, Snaps. It's your eyes that are too big."

She blinks a couple of times. "Too big?"

"For my sanity, yeah." Following instinct, I lean down and drop a kiss onto her cheek. "Hi, Katie."

"Didn't we say hello upstairs?" she asks softly, her breath hitting my cheek.

"Yeah, but that was the kind of hello you give your third cousin."

So subtle I almost miss it, she turns and inhales, clearly testing my breath for alcohol. "Hello, Jack. It's nice to see you again," she murmurs. "Is that better?"

I give an uncertain hum on my throat. "Maybe we'll be better at saying goodnight." Her look of reproach makes me hold up both hands. "I meant an innocent goodnight outside on the sidewalk. Man, a couple days roaming the city and your mind is already in the gutter."

She pokes me in the stomach. "I think it's you putting it there."

"Yeah?" I let my mouth hover an inch from her temple where wisps of red hair curl. "What other bad thoughts am I putting in that head?"

Her breath escapes on a shaky laugh. "I swore I wouldn't let you knock me off balance, yet you manage it in under a minute. Honestly, rambling on about my ears and nose. It's so embarrassing."

Something tightens in my chest. "It's the cutest goddamn thing in the world. I like when you say anything at all. Anything."

"Jack . . ." She pushes away from me, her fingers messing with the hem of her tank top. "I can't tell if . . . are you so persistent with all your women?"

"What do you mean 'all my women'?" I ask the question louder than intended, so I sigh and soften my voice, even though my stomach is pitching. "Explain what you mean."

Katie looks at me quietly. "You know what I mean."

There's no denying we're on the same page. Katie is too smart and perceptive to think I'm some kind of monk. Hell, the night we met I admitted I didn't know how to have a conversation on a park bench without the expectation of something physical. Is my past with women what's going to screw me over here? Or the drinking? God, I must be a checklist of things Katie doesn't want in a man. Which means, I have nothing to lose here. And I think that's why the honesty slips out. "No, I'm not usually this persistent, Katie. Most of the time, I can barely stand how women look at me long enough to close the deal."

Her face goes pink. "And by close the deal, you mean—"

"Sex." The word tastes sharp on my tongue. "And afterwards . . ." My laugh is missing any trace of humor. "Afterwards, I can barely stand to look at myself." Concern moves into her expression and I know she's going to ask me to elaborate. To explain why sex doesn't have the usual dude effect on me. Most guys fall into a coma afterwards or make a ham sandwich, while I just need to be as far away from other humans as possible. But I'm trying to win this girl over and I don't want to appear any more freakish to her than I already do, so I divert her attention.

"Look, Snaps." I sling on my goggles. "Sex is how my mother made money when I was growing up. It's just something that's a part of me. It's not a big deal."

Silence passes. "If it's no big deal to you, Jack, then why can't you look at yourself afterwards?"

Christ, had I really come here feeling optimistic? I hate everything I just said out loud to this sweet girl. Telling her sex is no big deal, being flippant about my mother's profession when it was anything but inconsequential. I wish I hadn't even come here. Why am I bothering to pursue Katie when she's obviously turned off by everything about me? Maybe she met a chef or a graphic designer since the last time we were together and this whole makeup class is a chore for her. "Look, Katie . . . let's just get started, huh?"

Her movements are slow as she puts on her goggles and stoops down to pick up a nylon gun case, setting it down on the carpeted hatch that serves as the barrier between us and the range. I catch her peeking over at me from beneath her thick eyelashes as she unpacks a rifle, complete with scope. When I was in the range on Monday, I didn't pay attention to the weapons being used, but compared to the standard issue Glock we've been training with, it's a monster.

"I didn't mean to bring up something uncomfortable," she says quietly. "Or to make you feel bad."

"I know you didn't, Snaps. It's fine."

She doesn't look even a little convinced, but suddenly I feel completely unequipped to reassure her of anything, especially myself. So I just wait for her to ready the rifle, listening as she explains the features and functions, her voice matter-of-fact. The musical tone draws me in, despite the fact that the night was fucked from the word *go*. What did I think? I'd swagger into the gym and this beautiful Olympian would throw herself at me? I am an idiot. The painful tick I've been experiencing in my head since Monday is back, making my right eye throb. My throat feels like sandpaper and I know what's going to happen, soon as I walk out of this place. I can already feel the glass in my hands and I resent my last two days of trying to abstain. Trying only led to confirmation of the problem.

When Katie slips on her headgear, I follow suit, stepping back while she demonstrates firing at the target, hitting it with no problem. God, she's so damn incredible. It never occurred to me I was going to be testing myself in front of an expert, but I might as well make tonight's shit show complete, huh?

After setting down the rifle, she turns solemn eyes on me. "Ready?"

Ready as I'll ever be. I nod once and step into the booth, lifting the gun and propping the butt of it against my shoulder. I'm surprised how natural the weight of it feels, even though I've never held a weapon this heavy before. The metal is cool in my hand, smooth against my cheek. When I close one eye and focus on the target through the scope, the throbbing in my head lessens, which is most surprising of all. There was a small tremor in my hands this morning upon waking, but it's tapered off through the day and it's gone now. Gone. Everything is so . . . steady. That balance finds me right in the middle, evening me out until I can't hear anything in my ears. Just the whisper of my shirt against skin as I adjust to the left, bringing the target into better focus. A breath. Another breath.

I fire and hit the target.

For a moment, I can only stare straight ahead, positive my eyesight is at fault. But when the sound rushes back in, I hear Katie's shocked exhalation to my right and realize I'm not mistaken. "Beginner's luck," I mouth at Katie. "Next time I'll probably hit the ceiling."

She shakes her head. "Go again."

The astonished pleasure she's directing at me is so new and unexpected, I stare at her until my throat starts to tighten. Ducking my head, I reload the rifle, feeling the pop and slide in my veins. I'm almost eager to have my focus narrowed down again, it was so fucking nice last time. And it comes quick the second time around, like the silence was waiting for me. There's the familiar stillness, like I've had amnesia and I'm finally recognizing an old friend. Katie is helping, too. Her confidence is radiating from her and infecting me with heat. My spine feels straighter by the second, my bones more substantial, purposeful. It takes me a moment to realize I feel . . . encouraged. This is what encouragement feels like.

This time when I fire, I hit slightly to the right of my mark, but I hear Katie's laughter through my headgear, so the disappointment is short-lived. Especially when she eases the gun from my hands, sets it down and motions for me to remove my headgear. "Are you telling me you've never handled a weapon like this, Jack?"

"Yeah . . ." Realizing I'm jerking my shoulders like I've had an electric shock, I force myself to stop. "I haven't."

"Well . . . shite." She's sputtering a little and it makes me desperate to kiss her. "No one hit the mark at the first session on Monday. Not even close. And you've basically just done it twice." A beat passes while I just stare at Katie, trying to sort through the pounding in my chest. "And it's not only the accuracy, it's the way you shifted your weight to accommodate the feel of the rifle. It was so natural and I didn't prompt you once. I—Jack, I think you have a serious talent for marksmanship."

I scoff while taking off my goggles. "No."

"Yes. I'm the instructor and I say so." She stamps her foot, then seems surprised at herself for doing it. "Oh, you confuse me so bloody much."

"How?"

"I don't know." She chews her bottom lip while

scrutinizing me. "When I say you're good at some-thing, I kind of assume you would expect to be. Good at things. Don't you have high expectations for yourself?" Her voice softens. "Or have I judged you completely wrong and I should just go stick my head in the toilet or something?"

My wink and a smile happen on command, but for the first time, it feels wrong on my face. "I think we've established what I'm good at."

I think Katie gets me, right here in this moment. Or comes really close. She's looking through her own personal rifle scope and seeing my target. Truthing me, the way only she has ever done. I'm stripped down and defenseless because of one transparent comment and I watch as knowledge trickles into her gorgeous eyes, see it soften her mouth at the edges.

Katie thinks she knows why I default to sex. And with her standing two feet away, so pres-ent and breathtaking, I want more than anything to hand her those confusing pieces of my puzzle and see what she can do with them.

Take them. Take them.

I don't have a chance to say the words out loud, though, because she speaks first. "You're show-ing me your teeth on purpose. The Big Bad Wolf doesn't do that. He doesn't bring secret umbrellas or carry backpacks, either. I shouldn't have called you that." She tips her head towards the range. "It's up to you to establish what you're good at. Not me. But I know you're more."

She blinks, as if coming out of a trance and starts to turn away. I'm paralyzed on the outside, but my chaotic insides are the exact opposite. How am I so . . . elevated when I'm stone-cold sober? I feel every breath that scrapes out of my lungs, the whiz of life rushing in my ears. I'm clearheaded enough to realize I can't reach for Katie the way I reach for a bottle. Can't use her to drown out this crushable optimism and numb myself instead, where I'll be safer.

She's given me this gift, though. Even if believing I'm good at something only lasts a little while, even if I wake up tomorrow and it's all a dream . . . I need to thank her. Need to share how I feel with her. It's an urge stronger than anything I can remember.

Above us, one of the fluorescent lights buzzes loudly, then goes out, dimming the room. Katie turns towards me with wide eyes and my body releases me from paralysis, allowing me to pull her into my arms.

"Thank you," I whisper against her mouth, before we moan into the most insane kiss.

CHAPTER 8

— Katie —

Timid Katie isn't available at the moment. This is bold, tries-new-things-like-kissing-very-attractive-boys Katie. And I like her. She gets to do things like wrap her legs around Jack's waist and kiss him like her lips will vanish into thin air at midnight. Poof.

Oh my God, how did I hold off kissing him again so long? I'm like a child bingeing on sweets, except I'm an adult woman and instead of Mars bars, I'm desperately trying to get my fill of Jack's mouth. He's delicious and that's putting it mildly. Last time we kissed, I detected something bitter on his tongue, but this time, he's all hungry, manly, minty goodness and he's giving it all to me. Tipping his head back and letting me taste him however I want from above, my legs cinched around his body like clamps.

It would be wise and cautious to tread slower with Jack. There are so many unknown things twisting under his surface, I can't count them all or give them names. Am I crazy to think he wouldn't mind it if I tried, though? This man, this devastatingly hot man, thought he'd blown his chance with me about five minutes after arriving. Unbelievable. And I could see plain on his face that he cared about that. That he'd let himself down somehow.

I can barely stand how women look at me long enough to close the deal.

So why does he close it? Does he think sex is all he's good for? After the way he blew off my praise of his shooting skills, it seems like the only conclusion. I don't like it. At all.

Pulling away is torture. "Jack, stop—"

"Aw, honey." His hot groan bathes my lips. "Don't say that."

"I didn't just come here for the kissing," I say in a rush. "I . . ."

"What?"

I squeeze my eyes shut. "I wanted to see *you*."

His swallow is loud enough to hear. "I . . . know. I think that's why this feels so fucking good." His expression is searching, a little incredulous. "And trust me, I wanted to see you worse."

There's no telling who dives back in first, but I can't stop kissing him now that I've started again.

Fully recovered from me vaulting onto his body, Jack's skilled mouth begins knocking loose oxygen and brain cells, sending them scattering on the ground. Already, this is the closest I've come to sex and we're fully clothed, but that's not how Jack kisses me. He thrusts his tongue into my mouth like we're naked, tasting every corner of me in one long lick, before drawing out and lapping at my bottom lip. Nipping it. Diving back in to divest me of anything resembling sense. One big hand invades my hair, the other slides down my back like it owns me. And very slowly, he rocks me, rocks me on the ridge behind his fly.

The flesh between my legs clenches—a hot, insistent squeeze—and it's like Jack knows I've just been hit by a massive lust tidal wave. While his mouth continues to devastate me, his eyes open and lock with mine . . . and he rolls his hips. Rolls them twice, three times, dragging his bulge up and back underneath my quickening heat.

I tear our mouths apart with a gasp. "Wow."

His mouth is wet, jaw slack when I pull away. Even his head pitches to the right, like he's drunk on need. "Fucking right, wow. Get back here."

"Brilliant."

I catch the barest hint of his lips curving into a smile before I part my mouth against his, tempting him to taste me even deeper than before. And he does. His fingers twist in my hair and waistband, growing more aggressive by the second, his breath harshens, growls kindling in his throat. His upper body plows into my space, bending my top half backwards, while dragging my hips closer to his hardness. Grinding against me. God, I'm almost horizontal, my thighs wrapped tight around Jack, restless and writhing. And all the while his mouth is bruising mine, our teeth occasionally bumping in our haste to take.

"Fuck, Katie." He breaks away from my mouth, dipping his head to plant a bite between my breasts, jerking my whole body with a moan. "What the hell are you doing to me, honey?"

"You took the words right out of my mouth," I wheeze, the room spinning around me. "Must have been while you were kissing me."

Jack's eyebrows shoot up. "Did you just quote a Meatloaf song?"

"Yes." I dive forwards and bury my face in the crook of his neck. "Kill me. Kill me now."

His chest shakes with laughter. "I've got a better idea, but it's not happening here." He turns in a circle, totally unaffected by the weight of me clinging to him. "I finally get you kissing me like you don't want to stop and there's not one damn surface around that isn't made of concrete."

"Why do you need a surf—I'm going to stop talking now." Still hiding my face in his neck, I pat his shoulder. "Find a surface. I'll just wait here."

Jack groans. "So damn cute." I'm jostled as he leaves the range and climbs the stairs, using an unbreakable forearm to keep me plastered against him. The faded scent of shampoo and aftershave is mouthwatering so close and I can't help pressing my lips to Jack's neck, teasing his flesh with my tongue and feeling his steps falter. "Just so we're clear, this means you've decided the rules aren't stopping us from spending time together while you're here?"

The hopefulness in his voice tugs at me. "For once, I didn't make a decision. I'm acting out of total spontaneity." I snuggle closer and drag my tongue down the cord of his neck, smiling when he moans. "Is that okay with you?"

"If it's your decision, I have to be." A muscle jumps in his cheek. "I just hope you won't change your mind tomorrow."

We've reached the upstairs gymnasium now and Jack wastes no time dropping onto his knees, then laying me back on one of the leather mats. God, he's extraordinary above me, propped on his hands and knees. Waiting. Waiting without breathing, as far as I can tell, his eyes an intense green. How could I resist spending time with this man? Walking away without getting to the center of him and exploring—maybe letting him explore me in the process? I don't think I could stand letting the chance slip away.

"No, I don't think I will change my mind." His breath leaves him in one fell swoop, his smiling face dropping towards mine. "A mad love affair."

Pausing, he sucks the breath back in. "What?"

"That's one of the items on my Katie Conquers New York list."

His head tilts, just a touch, but it might as well be earthquake fallout. "And before tonight, you actually thought that might happen with someone other than me?"

His arrogance is back and it makes me want to smile, but I purse my lips instead. "I still have a choice in the matter, don't I?"

A short laugh. "You're really testing the bonds of my feminism here, honey." He curses. "I'm going to kiss you now, Katie. Consider your mad love affair checked off the list."

I should protest, right? That high-handed male attitude is why I spent the last four years in solitude with nothing but Ross and Rachel to keep me company. But I kind of love it coming from Jack. His possessive growl as he melds our mouths together makes me feel free, instead of confined. Lust whips the heat in my stomach like an eggbeater until it's liquid fire, spreading to the insides of my thighs and coating my belly. His weight presses down into me, like he's testing to see how much I can take. More, more. And when he lets me have every ounce, we both gasp into the kiss. Because there's no mistaking what the thickness nudging the juncture of my thighs means. When we were standing, the pressure was suggestive. When he rolls his hips and our lower bodies grind together, however, that is not a suggestion. It's need. That first drag of his erection over the seam of my pants is slow, but the next pump is desperate, Jack breaking away from our kiss to grunt my name.

Oh my God. We're still in our clothes. I imagine Jack naked, gritting his teeth and thrusting his hips and the most embarrassing whimper falls out of my mouth.

Or maybe not so embarrassing, because Jack zeroes in on me like I said something completely genius. "You're right here with me, aren't you? You're feeling how good this is?"

"Yes."

His amazing lips part mine, his tongue delving in to taste me and I feel that lick everywhere. Everywhere. "What do you want tonight? My mouth and fingers?" Those magic hips twist and drag between my splayed thighs, rubbing the fly of his jeans against my clitoris. "Or do you want me to unzip my jeans and fuck you here and now, honey? We can deal with that first rough one, so I can take my time with round two."

Oh, okay . . . wow. My muscles clench, toes curling into the denim covering his calves as he pumps against the damp juncture of my thighs. I don't think there is anything that can steal my focus when Jack is absorbing every ounce, but his words in the firing range trickle into my consciousness.

Afterwards, I can barely stand to look at myself.

Maybe I don't understand why yet, but I know it would gut me if that happened.

"I want more, but . . . not that. Not yet." I take a deep breath and push out the final bit of truth I've been keeping to myself. "Jack, I'm a virgin."

His expression is almost comical, before he catches himself and clears the disbelief from his face. "A v-virgin. Okay." It's like I'm a lake of fire all of a sudden, prepared to scorch and possibly kill him, but his hungry expression says he still wants to jump in and confirm. Finally, he runs a warm hand down the side of my body, squeezing every few inches like he's searching for something. "Do you guys come with a manual or what?"

My giggle catches me off guard. "Jack."

"I'm kidding, Snaps. I know . . . I know someone's first time needs to be special." He plants a kiss on my nose, my forehead, but I think he's trying to distract me from his concern. "Do you trust me?"

I'm astonished when the answer is clear right away. "Yes."

And there it is. It's the most incredible way anyone has ever looked at me. Jack's eyes are still glazed with hunger, but when I say yes, appreciation warms his features, too, and he's now a lovely combination of male lust and sweetness. My nerve endings clamour and sing with pleasure. All I want to do is soak him up, soak up everything he gives me. "Not a lot of people do, you know. Not the other instructors. Hell, not even my friends sometimes." His eyebrows draw together. "Why would you?"

"Because you asked if I trust you, instead of telling me to. Classic tell." I lick my lips and taste Jack. "And I really want to."

"I really want that, too." He shakes his head. "Jesus, you're something."

Every cell in my body shakes wildly when he hooks a thumb in my waistband, keeping thoughtful green eyes locked on mine as he tugs down my pants. Lower, lower until they're bunched at my knees. Then . . . oh Jesus, then, he drags just the barest hint of his fingertips up the inside of my thigh, before giving the opposite leg the same treatment. By the time he finishes with both sides, I can feel slickness building between the folds of my flesh. My belly is shuddering up and down and I can't look away from him. He's trapped me.

"I can get on board with this," I whisper.

Jack's lips tick up at one corner. "I'm showing you where my mouth is going to go."

Self-consciousness snags me, but I nod through it. "Oh, sure."

"And trying to figure out if you've gone this far before."

"Nope."

"Hmm." His eyes run over my face in the silence. As if maybe he's awed by this awkward creature that's fallen into his lap. But I know that's not true when he speaks again in a patient tone. "Talk me through why you're nervous."

If he thinks I don't notice him sliding down my panties, he's dead wrong, but I try to focus on answering. "Well I don't have a lot of girlfriends, so I haven't really talked to anyone about this, but I think every girl probably has the same worry. At least the first time?" It's either the mortification or the slippery glide of his fingers along the seam of my sex turning me red. I don't know which. "And I think maybe I'm worried I'll be . . . wrong somehow. Or you won't like how it looks. Down there."

Jack arches an eyebrow. "Does it look like your pussy?"

A hiccuping laugh escapes. "I'm fairly sure."

He hits me with that pirate smile. "Then I'm already in love."

Something sharp turns right in the center of me, like a key opening a door. All I can do is gasp through the emotion shivering through my insides as Jack eases up my tank top. Giving me a final reassuring kiss on the mouth, he starts moving down my body, like a prowling sex god. His tongue skates between my breasts, one of his palms abrading my nipple through my thin sports bra, the touch so light and yet it yanks an invisible wire inside me. My back arches like I have no control, lifting right into the descent of Jack's mouth, his greedy licking tongue.

When his hands bracket my waist, squeezing,

his thumbs pressing into that sensitive spot just inside my hip bones, I jerk upwards, my body smacking back down onto the mat.

"Goddamn, Katie." Jack whips off his T-shirt, revealing a tight, golden climbing wall of muscle, dropping my mouth open. "If my thumbs are making you shake, you're going to love what I can do with my tongue." In one fluid motion, he removes my pants and underwear the remaining distance and drops down onto his stomach. I feel his breath on my damp flesh and—"Uh-oh," he says, his voice gravelly.

My fingers dig into the mat. "What?"

"Your pussy." His tongue slides through my sensitive lips. "It's too perfect."

Relief swoops in. For a split second. Then another swipe of Jack's tongue turns me into a writhing jumble of sensation. "That doesn't s-sound like a problem."

"Hell no, it's not a problem," Jack rasps, nudging my clit with his upper lip. "I just hate to make a mess out of something so beautiful." Another nudge. Another. Followed by a long, fluid lick. "Actually, fuck that. I'm going to love every fucking second."

Maybe I'm not so afraid of the Big Bad Wolf side of Jack, is the ridiculous thought that tumbles through my mind. But it's sideswiped and run off the road when Jack tosses my legs over his bare shoulders and essentially begins making out with my already tightening flesh. His forehead is creased, eyes clamped shut as he works his lips and tongue against me, over and over, reminding me of the treatment he gives my mouth when we kiss. Complete and utter dedication to tasting every part of me he can reach, and then some.

My fingers find the edges of the mat and cling, my head falling back as I cry out at the ceiling. Oh God. Oh God, the texture and roughness of his tongue makes me quake in a way I can't control. My mind barely manages to wrap itself around one sensation, before Jack introduces me to another. I don't know whether to let my thighs drop open, or to tighten them around Jack's head. I have a different impulse every time he licks me. Jesus. Jesus.

And all that is before his middle finger slides inside me, careful but insistent. His every movement is confident, as if he's been created to please a woman, but when I glance down, he's watching me with a mixture of heat and concern. "Tell me I can call this mine." His knuckle turns and grazes my clit, making me moan. "Tell me when we're in this room tomorrow and everyone wants what I got, I'll know this tight spot is for me. Only for me to treat so fucking good. Katie, tell me."

I have no idea what he means about everyone wanting me, but I'm willing to agree to anything right about now. Especially Jack referring to me as his. I am his in this moment, my flesh quickening around his finger, his tongue lapping at that bundle of nerves with such reverence. "Yours. Yes, yours."

He falls into me with a savoring groan, sliding his tongue inside me to replace his finger. My hips shoot up off the ground, a scream trapped in my throat. Somehow he manages to keep his upper lip against my clit as he saws his tongue in and out of me. Heat engulfs me like I just plunged into an erupting volcano. My body twists on the floor, sweat beginning to form at my hairline. I'm whimpering like a cheesy porn star—but my cries of Jack's name seem to only encourage him. The muscles in his shoulders shift under my legs, his body crawling closer and closer, as if he can't get enough of me, those growls vibrating along my inner thighs.

When I hear the clang of metal, I peer down between our bodies and find Jack reaching into his jeans. "Honey, I just need to. I need to." His words are pushed past stiff lips, like it's costing him an effort to speak. "It's just . . . sweet fuck. You taste too goddamn good. Need to stop it hurting so bad, okay? Not going to fuck you, I swear. It's just my hand . . . ahhh."

I make a sound of protest when he drops his head again and begins polishing my clit with his tongue. Not because it doesn't feel like a miracle, but I wanted to watch his hand move between his legs. From my angle above, I can only see his cut triceps flex, his elbow bobbing, so I close my eyes and picture him stroking his erection. And oh . . . oh God. Combined with the relentless rubbing of his tongue, the image shoots me past my breaking point.

My inner walls clench so hard, I think I make a sound of pain, but the crest that follows is so blissful and thorough, I forget what pain even feels like. Maybe I'll never remember. I don't know, but my core continues to milk Jack's tongue, again and again, my stomach spasming in seismic ripples, my fingers ripping at the mat on either side of my hips.

"Jack. Please. Jack."

The orgasm is so intense, I'm almost relieved when my body depletes of tension and I'm left sucking in giant gulps of breath. Jack appears over me, his mouth finding mine in a hard kiss as moisture lands on my stomach. He breaks away with blind eyes and my name growling from his lips. I don't think, I just follow instinct, reaching down to cover his hand with my own, holding tight and helping him work through his release, same way he gave me mine. "Yes, Katie. Jesus, yes. Touch me. Feel what you made me do."

He falls to the mat beside me once his climax passes, our rapid breathing echoing in the gymnasium. I'm wondering what happens next when his fingers slide through mine, lacing us together. "How long do we have, Snaps?"

Something sticks in my throat, because I know he's not referring to tonight. "Ten days. Nine, really, because I fly back to Dublin on the final morning."

"Nine." He brings my hand to his mouth, kissing my knuckles. "I'd be grateful for one, so I won't complain."

It sounds as though he's speaking to himself, but when I glance over, his pirate smile greets me. "'Do you guys come with a manual?' Did you seriously ask me that?"

His laughter and my yelps ricochet off the walls of the gym as Jack wrestles me into his arms, planting kisses on every inch of my face.

CHAPTER 9

— *Jack* —

Field trips aren't as fun when you're an adult. Especially if you're a lifelong Manhattanite. We don't like to leave the borough unless it's on fire, with the exception of your standard vacation. Or when a friend drags you to Brooklyn for craft beer and an outdoor concert. Today, however, I'm more than willing to endure the trek because Katie is two rows ahead of me on the academy-chartered bus and she can't stop turning around, peeking at me through those eyelashes. Pretending to take pictures of the passing scenery. Adorable.

There is only so much we can learn at the indoor firing range, so we're traveling to our sister academy in Long Island to train outdoors. It's Friday morning and I haven't seen Katie since

Wednesday night when I got her pants off in the gym. Meaning I'm desperate with an ache in my pants that won't quit. If I had my way, yesterday would have been spent with my mouth attached to her pussy, but since she's here with the exchange program, she was required to meet with some Irish community leaders and members of the NYPD brass. Meetings that ran late into yesterday evening.

I want her to myself. Yesterday. Now. Tomorrow. I don't like her meeting other dudes without me around. Hate having gaps between the time we spend together. We've got so little time and I want to make the most of it.

Am I crazy to have this new, quiet voice in the back of my head whispering that . . . Katie could stay in New York? Yeah. That's exactly what it is. Batshit crazy. She has a life in Dublin. A family that loves her. A badass job. Shit, though, I would miss the honesty in her voice when she speaks to me. Looks at me. It makes me want to be honest, too. Not only for her, but for myself. Like I'm finally wondering if I owe it to myself to try harder. At the academy. Hell, at life.

Jack, I think you have a serious talent for marksmanship.

What if that was actually true? Before Katie showed up, I never would have thought an opportunity existed for me outside of a daily grind on the way to a bottle, but . . . the conviction she delivers while looking me straight in the eye? It makes me want to believe. In everything. Myself. Magic. Rainbow-colored unicorns.

I've been sober since Monday. Yesterday was difficult. I woke up sweating and actually went for a run along the East River with Charlie to exhaust myself. My bedroom is cleaner than before I moved into it and I even volunteered for the grocery run. My roommates are still reeling. And hell, this morning isn't easy, either, but when the bus pulls to a stop and everyone begins to get off, I'm sure as shit not thinking about vodka. I'm thinking about getting close enough to Katie to remind her we're still on. Jack and Katie are a thing for the duration of her stay. I'm determined to be sober for every second of it, so I won't forget a thing.

Almost everyone, including the instructor who came to assist Katie, heads out of the parking lot and towards the outdoor range, packs thrown over their shoulders. Three recruits hang back like diseases to help Katie carry the heavy cases she brought, but I send them on their way with a jerk of my head. "Fuck off, yeah?"

One of them thinks about mouthing off, but his friend tugs on his elbow. "No offense, but pick your battles, bro."

"Good advice," I say, winking at the trio. "Better listen to him."

Katie stands at the bus's luggage compartment. Looking over and seeing me waiting, she sends me a cute, disapproving frown and, fuck, my tongue feels unnatural inside my mouth. Like it doesn't know how to exist without kissing her anymore. "Just helping out my instructor . . ." I slide a look down her body and wink. "With her equipment."

The sunshine highlights her flushed skin. "Just for that, you can assist me in a demonstration."

"Yeah?" I pick up a heavy case in each hand and waggle my eyebrows at her. "You didn't seem the type to like an audience, but I'm game if you are. Kinky." She sputters and marches off ahead of me. I follow with a grin on my face, not bothering to hide my appreciation of her tight, twitching ass. How'd I miss her so much? "You don't really plan on having me help you with a demonstration, right?"

"Oh, but I do." She tosses a triumphant look over her shoulder. "How does it feel to be thrown off?"

"I've been thrown off since we met, honey." Her step slows down long enough for me to catch up with her. Blocking us from the moving pack of recruits with my turned back, I drop my voice low. "Come out with me tonight, Katie?"

"I have a fundraiser dinner," she whispers. "At the Irish Consulate."

I can't hold back a frustrated sound. "Tomorrow."

She hesitates, before giving me one firm nod.

My smile is dopey as fuck over gaining her agreement, but ask me if I care. "I'm not taking you just anywhere." As I quell the urge to kiss the life out of her, I'm also kind of marveling over how good it feels to be clearheaded and have a plan. I could get used to this. Even as I have the thought, there's a twinge in my throat, a tightening in my spine, but I ignore them both. "Any idea why I'd want to take you to Bensonhurst?" I hum in my throat, like I'm trying to come up with a reason. "Maybe to a little place called Sal's Steakhouse?"

"Shut up. Bensonhurt, Brooklyn?" She smacks me in the chest, but her smile could make a man want to move mountains. "You're . . . that's where crime boss Joey Big Time was taken out. No way. You're not taking me there. Yes, you are. Oh my God."

"You're a little sick, honey, you know that?" My laugh feels strange climbing my throat because it's so real. "I love it."

She stares at me for a beat, the wind dragging a strand of red hair across her mouth. "Thank you for thinking of that. Thinking of . . . me."

My heart is knocking against my ribs. "Don't mention it, Snaps."

"We should go," she whispers. "Before they send out a search party."

Katie turns and starts to head in the direction of the firing range, but spins and plants a quick, forbidden kiss on my mouth. We stare at one another a moment, before she gasps at her own behavior and jogs off.

Afterwards, I stand there and remember that open, carefree look she hit me with right before our lips connected. A lot like how she looked at me when I hit that target in the firing range. I love it. I want her to keep looking at me like that. A girl like Katie wants to spend time with me and I should be on cloud nine. A man *earns* a girl like her.

Have I earned a night out with her, though? Would she still want to go out with me if she knew I'd lied about my drinking?

KATIE WASN'T KIDDING. I'm actually helping with a demonstration.

When she calls me—by my last name—to come forward, no one is idiot enough to say shit about her odd choice, but there is a definite ripple of skepticism through the ranks. Charlie smacks me on the back, wishing me luck and I don't have to look at Danika to know she's enjoying every second. One of the other two instructors smirks, leaning back against the low concrete wall to watch the show and I hate how it gets to me.

Not that I care what *he* thinks, but I'm already beginning to sweat, wondering if the night with Katie in the range was a fluke. I'm barely getting used to Katie believing I have potential, now I have to prove it in front of these assholes, none of whom take me seriously. Unless you count my ability to clean their clocks or win a battle of insults.

A tremor snakes through the veins on the

backs of my hands. It's been happening a lot over the last five days, but not now, though. *Not now.* As if one symptom tempted the others to life, I feel like I'm sucking sand, the grains flying to the back of my throat and causing abrasions. Katie waves me forwards, but I catch the uncertainty in her eyes, as if she's wondering whether she made a mistake, testing me too soon.

No, I won't let her think that.

Willing the shaking to stop, I shove my hands into my pockets and saunter forwards.

"Put me to work."

I feel, rather than see, Katie's relief. "Right," she says, addressing the recruits. "So in our first session, we fired with bladed-off stance. Today we'll be utilizing the athletic position, which is more for tactical shooting or a situation where rapid fire is required." I can hear every intake of breath in my ears as Katie approaches the firing point and goes over safety instructions, the proper technique for holding the weapon. Every recruit is glued in and I want to be, too, but that goddamn tremor is still going through my hands, making all her words bleed together.

Before I know it, Katie is turning and calling me forwards.

When I sidle up beside her, she glances at me, then down at my pocketed hands, giving me no choice but to draw them out. And I call on something deep inside myself to stop the fucking shaking. I think about the fountain spray on my face, the sound of my footsteps while walking through the crosswalk after putting Katie in a cab, the sizzle of pancakes in a pan. All the clear thoughts I've gathered over the last five days and shit, I can't believe it, but the rightness of going without a drink stills the tremors.

"Ready?"

I nod, taking the weapon from her, making sure to keep it safely pointed away. Just like in the underground range back in Manhattan, the weight of the rifle makes my blood slow, brings everything into sharp focus. Calm slides beneath my skin and spreads out like warmed-up peanut butter. Katie is at my side, talking to the recruits about the proper stance and I listen to every word, while somehow already anticipating what she is going to say. Feeling her instructions, interpreting them faster than I would have thought myself capable.

Recalling Katie saying not to rest my finger on the trigger until I've made a conscious decision to shoot, I breathe and slowly press digit to metal. The sound of shuffling, the wind, traffic on the nearby road fades out. By the time I fire, I'm not even surprised when I hit the target. In my stomach, it was a given. A certainty I'm stunned by.

My mind goes back online, hearing Katie's breathless encouragement first, then everyone else. There's actual whooping of my name, high fives going on behind in the viewing area. I set down the weapon carefully and turn, trying to bite back a smile when Charlie gives my shoulder a shove.

"You been holding out on me, man?"

I try to shrug it off, but my roommate is like this massive, unmovable barrier of positivity *most* of the time. Right now? He's The Great Wall of Charlie. "Some things I save for the privacy of my diary, all right?" I shoot a glance at Katie and she's smiling to herself, preparing the weapon for the next recruit. God, I want to scoop her up and hold her so bad, my arms feel like empty vessels. This. Shooting. It's something I share with her. We share this.

She gave it to me. I need to give her something back.

My knee-jerk answer is sex, but . . . she needs and deserves more. I have to find out what I'm capable of giving and right now, right *this* minute, I'm looking forward to the challenge.

"Hey." Charlie steps into the firing point, the rest of the recruits fanning out down the row facing the target area. "Help me out?"

"Me?"

The question is barely out of my mouth when another guy I've only spoken to once in the locker room calls my name, farther down the row. "I'm next."

"I've known him longest," Danika says, holding up a finger. "You can all wait."

I'm dumbfounded by the sudden requests for help, and my gaze zooms to Katie. And my little Irish honey winks at me, so fast I barely catch it.

Tomorrow night can't get here fast enough.

CHAPTER 10
— *Katie* —

Nighttime sounds rush in from my open hotel window, lifting the curtain and sending it fluttering into the room. I haven't bothered turning on lights, because the moon is bright enough and the shadows it casts in the room feel dreamlike.

It occurs to me as I stare back at my reflection in the mirror, I have no idea what American girls wear on dates. My dating experience is literally just what I've seen on the telly and I'm not so naive that I think real-life people wear designer clothes on a regular basis. There must be a happy medium and I'm praying I've landed on it. At the fundraiser last night and most of the events I've attended, I've been required to wear my proper Garda dress clothes for endless rounds of photographs with high ranking NYPD brass and officers from other countries traveling with the exchange program. Finally being out of the starched uniform makes me feel like Cinderella heading to the ball. Although, she was dressed by a fairy godmother and I've been left to my own awkward, unskilled devices.

Worrying my lip, I turn to the side and wonder why everyone doesn't just sign a pact to wear leggings all day, every day and do away with the angst. Jack seemed to like me just fine in my workout gear, hadn't he?

Remembering the way I kissed Jack yesterday in plain view of anyone who might have turned around, my cheeks flush bright red and I press my hands there to cool them down. What an utterly reckless move and—God help me—that was part of the reason it was so thrilling. Concentrating during the shooting lesson had been more difficult than the Olympics. Watching Jack help instruct his fellow recruits, I'd checked the urge to touch him several times. Just rub a circle into his back or squeeze his hand. I won't have to hold back tonight, though.

When I realize I'm smiling in the mirror, I up the stakes and dance in a circle, kicking my legs like a showgirl. This is what it feels like to have no restraints. Apart from the sexy stuff, I think my brother would be proud of me right now. I'm really living. By going on a date with Jack—by going to Brooklyn!—I'm having the adventure we'd promised ourselves.

An image of my father's weary face pops into my mind. Am I trading my father's happiness for my own? What is he focusing on now that he doesn't have me to train? With a large helping of guilt, I stow the worries away for the evening, promising an extra-long phone call to Dublin in the morning.

I take a final look at myself in the mirror, smoothing a hand down the front of my rather snug green dress. The tall, black leather boots were the only special purchase I made before coming to New York and they feel so daring, with their three-inch heels. No more obsessing over what American girls wear, I decide with a nod. Maybe I'll be the trendsetter.

My cell phone goes off with a series of complicated xylophone jangles and I nearly hit the ceiling. Jack's name blinks on the screen. I bounce and squeal a little, then calmly answer.

"Hello?"

"Snaps." His low voice turns my knees to butter. "Nice place you got here."

"Where are you?"

A piano tinkles in the background. "Downstairs in the lobby."

I look around at the room I'd tidied after my shower. On the bus ride home from the field trip, Jack texted me and asked for my room number.

Answering him in the middle of the other recruits had charged the air around me, made the secret situation feel so real, but I'd responded fast enough to break land speed records. "Oh, I wasn't sure if you were meeting me at the door."

His low hum travels through the phone and makes my stomach lining feel heavy. "I was going to. You deserve to have me pick you up at the door." He sighs. "But I'm not sure we'd make dinner if I got you that close to a bed."

Reaching down, I smooth my palm over the fluffy white comforter. "Why does that sound like it embarrasses you?"

"It does and it doesn't." His words are stilted, like he's trying to work an explanation out in his mind. "I want to get you underneath me, Katie. Bad. And I'm not embarrassed by that. But it's not the only reason I'm here. I don't want you thinking I'm the Big Bad Wolf, you know?"

My hand presses to my stomach to chastise the butterflies. Needing to see his face and reassure him, I stuff my room key into my clutch bag and head for the door, closing it behind me. "I wish I'd never said that to you. It was silly."

"Was it?" The strain in his tone makes me super aware of my femininity. More than I've ever been in this lifetime. "I think about mauling you pretty frequently."

Bloody hell. "There's a difference between you and the wolf, though." I hit the call button for the elevator and silver doors slide open to my right. "You'll always stop if I ask you to."

"Damn right I will, Katie."

Not for the first time, I'm struck by how serious he takes my consent. As it should be. But I'm not sure most men are so vocal about the importance of it. "I loved the way you've touched me so far. Kissed me. There's nothing bad about any of it."

The doors roll open and the elegant lobby spreads out in front of me. Gleaming floors, pleasing piano music, lush greenery and so-phisticated guests rolling luggage in crisscross patterns. There's Jack. Leaning against the wall, just inside the entrance, as if he couldn't go any farther than one step inside. And oh Jesus, he's wearing a hat. One of the brimmed types that make him look like a young Sinatra. The hat is pulled low over his brow and his shoulders are hunched protectively. Beneath the brim, he looks so deep in concentration over our conver-sation, my mouth goes dry.

"I know you loved it." He shifts against the wall. "But sometimes we don't get a choice in what our bodies like. Sometimes it's confusing. And I don't want you to be confused by anything I make you feel. Does that make sense?"

Desolation ghosts through his tone and I walk faster, stopping in front of him and hanging up, searching his face frantically for an explanation of what he means. But as soon as Jack sees me, he appears to snap out of some trance, hanging up his phone, straightening off the wall and . . . freezing. Not moving a muscle as he looks me over, head to boots.

"Damn, honey." He drags a hand over his open mouth, a low growl rumbling in his throat. "Is it too late to pick you up at the door?"

Feminine pleasure prickles every inch of my skin. "You had your chance." I force myself not to fidget as he eats me alive with green eyes. "I tidied up and everything."

He deflates against me with a gruff sound, pulling me into the bubble of happiness that is his worn leather jacket. I just kind of bask there as he buries his face in the crook of my neck, sucking in a heap of my scent through his nose. "No. This is better. I want to take you out." He nods as if trying to convince himself. Threading our fingers together, he pulls back and plants a kiss on my forehead. "But I'm walking you to the door later, so start thinking about whether or not you're going to invite me in."

With that warning echoing in my head, Jack leads me out of the hotel. Night has landed and the air is crisp, but I'm enjoying the feel of it on my arms. I've ventured out of the hotel at night for quick bites or a turn around the block, but it didn't feel like this. Like possibilities. Going out. Way outside of my comfort zone. None of it seems daunting with my hand enfolded in Jack's, though.

"Are we taking the subway?"

"Thought I'd give you the full New York experience." He grins down at me. "Are you up for a short walk in those boots? Or do you need a piggyback ride?"

"Tempting, but I can manage."

He throws an arm around my shoulder, guiding me through sidewalk traffic, which is considerable. "Good. We're going to walk west and catch the N at 23rd Street. It's express so we should be in Bensonhurst in no time."

My cheeks hurt from smiling. "You might as well be speaking in Latin."

His laugh turns every female head on the sidewalk. "Do you trust me?"

"Yes."

Just like the last time he asked, I can sense his awe over my answer. The walk to the train goes by in a heartbeat because I'm caught up in the romance and frenetic pace of the city. Sure, the sidewalk and streets could use a good scrubbing, but the sound of trains rumbling beneath our feet, the colorful shopping bags, dressed-up people signaling for cabs, it's so alive. It's happening now. Strangers are right alongside me having their own adventure and I feel a kinship with all of them. Every block, Jack bends down and whispers about some landmark or another in my ear, using his chin to indicate it.

The subway is packed because it's running late, giving time for the platform to fill up, so we cram onto a train like sardines, rubbing shoulders with people blaring headphones or having conversations about their Saturday evening plans, the screeching of the breaks and hum of the engine gathering together to create a symphony. I'm flush against Jack, the fronts of our bodies rubbing as the train jostles. His eyes are smoky, studying my mouth, that gaze sliding down to my breasts. After only one stop, we're breathing heavily, sexual awareness filling every scant available inch in the subway car.

"Say something to distract me," he murmurs, just above my mouth. "Anything."

"Um . . ." I swallow with difficulty. "Actually, there's something I did want to mention."

His palm molds to my hip. "Now would be a good time."

"Right." Deep breath. Pretend your nipples aren't spikes and they aren't riding up and down his richly grooved stomach. "Yesterday at the range, you proved me right. Jack, you're a natural." His eyes sharpen and shoot down to meet mine. "Everyone tried harder after they saw what was possible. Through you. Did you notice they were looking to you as a leader?"

"Nah, they're just competitive assholes." He pauses to clear his throat. "A few of the guys asked for some help outside training, though."

"And did you say yes?"

A curt nod from Jack. "Told them I'd think about it."

Which was probably as good as they were going to get from Jack. For now. "How did it feel to be asked?"

He thinks about brushing it off or being flippant, but I watch his Adam's apple bob. "Weird, I guess. Not in a bad way. It was . . . different."

"If I recommended you for ESU training—"

His scoff cuts me off. "Come on, Snaps. They would veto that shit with a quickness."

"Why?"

He avoids looking at me for a moment. "Look, you're better off recommending Charlie or one of the other guys." Even as he makes the statement, I can tell hearing the words out loud bother him. "I'm not in the academy to be shaped into Captain Save-the-Day. It's not about that for me."

"What is it about?"

"A paycheck." Eyebrows raised, he seems to be waiting for judgment from me, so I keep my features neutral. "Saving for the day my mother can't work as a receptionist anymore."

I desperately want to ask about his mother, about her experience as a sex worker, but I sense I'm already pushing too hard towards something with the conversation. Not knowing what is opening a pit in my stomach, but I don't want to ruin our night, so I change the subject in the only way I know how. By rambling. "I was worried I wouldn't be dressed to blend in with the American girls. I don't mean I want to look like part of the wallpaper, but I didn't want to look like a parade float coming down the street, either.

And these boots aren't that great for walking, actually. I lied by accident. My feet didn't start hurting until I was standing still."

His lips jump at one corner. "Piggyback ride to the restaurant."

"My toes thank you." Jack seems to have forgotten about the uncomfortable conversation and decided to focus on playing with my hair instead, picking up strands and rubbing them between his big fingers. "I'm kind of a planner. I don't know if you've noticed."

"I have." He pressed a fistful of my hair to his nose and inhales. "And I fucking love it."

"Try to remember that . . ."

Jack drops my hair and tips up my chin. "What's going on in that head, honey?"

"Well . . ." Lord, he's distractingly gorgeous. His smell is wrapped around me, he's seconds from kissing me and I should just keep my bloody gob shut. "My plan is to pay my half of the bill after dinner. If you could just agree to that, I wouldn't be anxious about it."

"Explain why first."

Honesty is always the best policy, right? And it has worked for us so far. "Because when I invite you inside my room later, I want everything on equal terms. So you'll know I want you there whether or not you bought me a nice dinner. Is that crazy?" Slowly, Jack shakes his head, his brow furrowed. "Are you less anxious knowing I'm going to invite you in later?"

"Fuck yeah."

I smile. "That worked out nicely for the both of us, then."

The amusement in his eyes makes them twinkle, but there's a hard layer of lust underneath. He leans down and presses his lips to my ear. "You're in trouble later, Katie. I remember those sexy thigh shakes of yours from having you pantsless on the gym floor. I won't stop until they're too tired to move and I have to hold them up around my waist." His tongue treats my lobe to the barest of grazes, before he eases back. "What if neither of us had to pay for dinner?"

It takes a few heavy seconds for my pulse to return to normal, so I can focus on his question. Maybe I should worry about being an accessory to robbery—or a dine and dash—but I can only vibrate with anticipation. "I'm listening."

Jack's pirate smile broadens and almost sends me melting to my knees. With a wink, he plants a kiss on my cheek, then removes his hat. A split second before he begins singing, I cop on to what he's planning and a laugh flies out of my mouth. I turn slightly and find the train car has emptied somewhat while I've been wrapped up in Jack, passengers disembarking at each stop as we make our way farther into Brooklyn. This extra space gives Jack room to walk through the train, singing "New York, New York" at the top of his lungs, holding out his hat to everyone he passes.

Holding on to the silver poles, he swerves

around them, his eyes crinkled at the corners as he throws his head back and hits a high note. By that time, women are actually getting up out of their seats to throw money into the hat, earning themselves such perfect, roguish winks that I can't even be jealous. Every woman should have the privilege of one of Jack's winks.

When he tosses me a devilish smile over his shoulder, I send him one back and quickly take out my camera to snap a picture. We have only seven more days together. And suddenly that doesn't seem like nearly enough time to understand what makes Jack tick, find out what he's been through . . . or convince him he's got potential.

When did those things become so important?

As the train screeches to a halt, Jack jogs back towards me triumphantly—jingling hat in hand—capturing me around the waist and hauling me off the train in a sea of applause.

"I think we made enough to cover dessert, Snaps." He sets me on my feet and spins me in a pirouette with his free hand. "Not bad for one stop, huh?"

"No." I go up on my toes and press a kiss to his mouth, my bones liquefying when he ceases all movement and throws a monsoon of passion into kissing me back, before pulling away with a contented sigh. "Not bad at all, Jack."

He turns around and jerks a thumb in the direction of his back. "Hop on, honey."

CHAPTER 11

Jack

I've been on a few dates, but I've sure as shit never been nervous. Then again, I've never taken out a weapons expert with a mob hit fetish. That level of awesome might intimidate other guys. To which I say? Good. Unfortunately, when we walk into the restaurant, every male head that turns in her direction sees only tits and legs. One week ago, if you'd told me I'd be wrapping my leather jacket around a broad and hustling her through a restaurant like a bodyguard, I would have called you a filthy liar. But here I am. Doing just that.

When we walked into the place, the hostess kept trying to give me a secret signal with her eyes, but I think my reaction to other men checking out Katie put an end to it. Something sharp inside me dulled into a rounded edge when the hostess's interest faded to aloofness. Comfort spread from the base of my spine, around into my stomach, resting there. I . . . love claiming Katie. Or being claimed by her. I'm not sure which is better.

For a long time, I've been surfing this weird balancing act. Prove I'm worthy. Then get hit by the reminder that I'm not. A reminder that I *allowed* what happened to me.

That's where the nerves are coming from. Do I want to spend the night in Katie's cushy hotel bed, delicately taking her virginity, then fucking her motherloving brains out? Yes. Hell yes. I want that so much, my cock has been at full mast behind my belt since she walked into the lobby in those boots. God, I want to please her. Want to please her so bad. I know, though, if I can't be one hundred percent what she needs afterwards? If I fuck off into mental no man's land like always? I don't know if I can bounce back from that kind of failure. If I can't keep it together for Katie, this sickness of mine is definitely a lifelong affliction.

Not with Katie. Please not with Katie.

The hostess stops at our candlelit table, setting menus down as I pull out a chair for Katie, scowling at the old men in our wake—clearly regulars—having a laugh at my expense. With a mammoth case of reluctance, I unspool Katie from my jacket and hang it on the back of her chair, taking my seat.

Her eyebrows are halfway to the sky. "What was that about?"

"You being a fox is what that was about."

Pink climbs her neck, but in the glow of the candle, it looks more like rose gold. I'm going to paint every inch of her with my tongue later, swear to God. "Fair enough. Just checking." She picks up her menu, sets it back down. "Actually, you going all hulking caveman just gave me an opening. So I'm going to be more of a dainty, coy cavewoman for, like, two seconds, okay?"

I lean forwards on my elbows. "Hit me, honey."

She squints one eye. "You and Danika—"

"Friends. Best friends, but only ever friends." If I didn't have this stupid, mandatory crew cut, I would be yanking on the ends of my hair about now. Not because I mind her asking, but because I hate knowing there might have been a roadblock between us I wasn't aware of. "I really don't want you to have more doubts about me than you already do, so let's clear this up. All the way."

That seems to trouble her. "It wasn't a doubt, so much as . . ."

"What?"

"So much as I didn't like the possibility that she was ever your . . . girlfriend. Or could be again." She eyeballs the water glass on the table as if willing it to be full. "I'm already on a date with a recruit. I don't want to add home wrecker to my list of sins."

"She has never been my girlfriend. Never will be." Damn. Now Katie is claiming *me*? I'm king of the world. Unrealistic as it is that me and Danika will ever be a couple, if Katie is jealous of it happening in the future, she must be here for more than what I can do in bed. I can't relish the satisfaction climbing my insides, though. Not just yet. "Charlie, Danika and I live together. I should've been upfront about that."

Her nod is kind of jerky. "Oh. Okay."

We're losing ground, shouts a tiny war general in my head. Panic prods the back of my neck, so I take the menu out of Katie's hands and grip them inside my own. Tight. "Look, if you were living with a guy, I wouldn't like it, either. I'd goddamn hate it, actually, and I'd probably guard your bedroom door with a meat cleaver. But I think if I explain the way things were growing up, you won't worry at all. You shouldn't."

Of course, the waiter chooses that moment to show up, coughing discreetly to get our attention. Taking her hands out of mine, Katie switches into charming mode, asking the older, red-vested man about his favorites on the menu. In seconds, she has his heavy cheeks lifted in a grin, the kind people only get when presented with a basket full of kittens. His second cousin, twice removed was from County Kerry and so of course, that topic segues into his dream vacation. By the end of it, Katie has invited the waiter and his wife to stay with her next time he travels to the Emerald Isle. And the guy hasn't even taken our order yet.

Normally, my eyes would be heart-shaped watching Katie work magic on the waiter—and anyone within ear shot—but I'm eager to get back to our conversation. A little jealousy coming from either of us is one thing, Katie having valid concerns about Danika is another. I don't want Katie to have any doubts that I'm all about her.

Unfortunately, explaining my friendship with Danika means talking about my past. I already told Katie my mother worked in a brothel, but she doesn't know I lived there. Doesn't know my life has revolved around sex since I can remember. The details of my past are the nasty part. Will she look at my differently if I tell her everything?

In the back of my mind, I hear a door slamming. Hear the sound of bedsprings rebounding, creaking, rebounding. Feel my clammy hands on slick skin—pushing away or pulling close? I can't remember. Pushing away, I think. The door opens again and someone else comes in. A friend of my mother's, just like the other woman who brought me into the room. The door is locked, tested. There's laughter and the smell of whiskey. Strong. So strong. It's pouring down my throat. Everything that's happening feels good, but it feels fucking awful at the same time—

"Jack."

Katie's voice cuts through the images and sounds crashing in my head. Both she and the waiter are watching me with concern. "Oh . . . uh." My gaze drops to the menu and it's all a blur. Except for the beverages section. There's a list of liquors and they stare back at me like old friends, clear as crystal. "Whatever she's having is great," I force out. "And a Coke. Thanks."

Katie

That same thousand-yard stare Jack had earlier in the lobby is back, but just like before, he snaps right out of it. His recovery is so immediate and drastic, I wonder if I imagined the whole thing. As soon as the waiter leaves with our order, he's back to toying with my fingers across the table, telling me I look gorgeous, generally distracting me from my worry. I don't want to be distracted, though. There's a dull throb in the center of my chest that gets worse the more he attempts to change the mood.

"Is everything all right?" I ask, cutting him off midsentence. When he only shakes his head and furrows his brow, like he's not sure what I'm asking, I try another tactic. "What were you going to tell me before? About growing up."

"Yeah." His throat muscles bob. "I think maybe we can leave it for another time."

I smooth my palm over his, notching our hands together. My calluses match up with the ones he's probably been forming since I arrived, thanks to the training. "If you're sure that's what you want, okay."

Green eyes snare me across the table, holding me there so long, I forget to breathe. "One year, my mother and a couple of her friends chipped in and bought me a Game Boy Advance for my birthday. You know, the handheld game?" I nod and he pauses, looking away. "When my mother had a customer, I used to go play it in the stairwell of my building."

A wretched sound tries to escape me, but I hold it in. I think I don't move at all.

"Depending on when the customer showed up, that could be in the middle of the night. Or during dinner." His voice has turned rusty, so he clears it. "There were four bedrooms and a communal kind of living space with a table and chairs. That's where I ate. Most of the time it was fine. I think they tried to send me outside as much as possible, or wait until I was at school to have johns over. But it didn't always work out that way. And I saw and heard . . . everything."

The waiter drops off our drinks and Jack drains half his Coke in one swallow, but I'm so frozen in place, all I can do is wait and hope/dread he continues.

"We moved into the brothel when I was six, after my mother's boyfriend left. Danika moved in downstairs right after I turned eight." He shrugs. "After that, I didn't have to play Game Boy in the stairwell anymore. Her mother let me eat dinner at their place. They even gave me a key so I could come inside at any hour of the night and sleep on their couch." He sees how devastated I am to know a child had been forced into such an awful independence, because he sighs and squeezes my hand. "I'm only telling you this because I want you to understand Danika and I are sister and brother."

"That's the only reason you're telling me?"

"No," Jack says quietly. "No, I want you to understand me, too. You said you felt like Little Red Riding Hood around me and it wasn't your imagination, honey. I wanted to bring you home and get you naked two minutes after we met. That was the only outcome I could imagine. Never this. I couldn't have pictured you sitting across from me, talking to me, if I'd tried."

"Oh," I whisper. "But here we are."

"Yeah. Here we are." Picking my hand up, he runs his lips over my knuckles, before setting it back down. "When customers showed up early to see one of the women, I entertained them with card tricks or singing. Sometimes they would be drunk and talk to me about things they shouldn't. Or talk amongst themselves. I knew what they were there for, what they wanted and . . . how. Sex . . . I guess it became a given for me. I'm physical without thinking."

Fire crawls up the inside of my throat when I remember referring to him as the Big Bad Wolf. I want to go back in time and slap myself now that I know how he grew up. The sexual energy I'd found so intimidating? I think deep down it intimidates him a little as well. He wasn't born a wolf, he'd been encouraged by his environment to be one. "I'm sorry you went through that. I'm sorry for your mother, too."

He's surprised I said the second part. Surprised and grateful. "She didn't have a choice, Katie, you know?"

"Okay." I nod. "Okay, I'm sure she didn't."

The smile he gives me twists my heart into a knot, and it tightens when his expression goes serious once more. "Everything is different with you, Snaps." He reaches across the table and cups my cheek. "It feels right when you look at me. Honest. When you touch me, it's because you're seeing me, same way I see you. Whatever happens after dinner . . . it's important. But it's more important that we both want to be *here* right now." He hesitates, a shadow passing through his eyes. "Can it still feel right for you? Knowing all this?"

"Yes."

If there wasn't a set of invisible hands around my neck, I might have shouted the word. Whispering it was enough, though, because Jack releases a pent-up breath, the light growing brighter in his eyes. "Jesus. We come to this place because someone got murdered here . . . and we're the ones making things heavy?"

My laugh is accompanied by a snort and I slap a hand over my face in embarrassment. But it only makes Jack laugh harder, that pirate smile in mass effect.

"You know . . ." He arches an eyebrow and tips his head down. "You're sitting in the seat where it happened."

I slap my hands down on the table, excitement flaring in my blood. "Get out of here."

"Scout's honor. I nearly broke out in a rash making the reservation for this table." Sharp green eyes scan the restaurant, lingering on a table of suited men longer than necessary. "I don't like having you near danger, even if it happened forty years ago."

"But you sacrificed for me."

He grabs my hand, turning it over and kissing my palm. "Damn right."

Our dinner arrives just in time for me to melt into a puddle.

THINGS ARE GOING too well.

I can count on one hand the amount of times I've gotten that niggling pinch in my stomach, but I have it now. It's warning me I don't know the whole story about Jack. Granted, the things he shared with me at dinner were horrible, which might be the culprit for my niggle. If he hadn't spent the rest of dinner telling me hilarious locker room stories or turning me to mush explaining how Charlie and his girlfriend, Ever, ended up together, I would have dwelled on the reality of Jack's upbringing much longer. He didn't let me, though. Before I knew we'd moved past the difficult subject, it was in the rearview, Jack prompting me with questions about the Olympics and inside secrets about my competitors. Not that I resorted to petty gossip. Much.

As soon as dinner was over, Jack and I paid the bill—him throwing me a conspiratorial look when he used some of the money he earned on the subway—after which, he gave me another piggyback ride to the train. And here we are now, on the mostly empty subway car . . . learning each and every corner of one another's mouth.

He pulls me down into his lap before the doors even smack closed, cupping the back of my head and sliding us into a slow, heated kiss. Immediately, I'm his. The curve of his lips against my mouth tells me he feels the shift. How quickly I hand over the keys to my city, my breathless moan encouraging him to explore every hidden valley and rise. It's a scary thing, the kind of control I lack when Jack touches me. If he laid me down on the subway bench and hiked up my dress, stopping him would cause me pain. His tongue is masterful, his hands touch me like I'm a fragile artifact, his own heartbeat wild against my shoulder.

We've just had this incredible date and now we're going back to my hotel to have sex. It doesn't even happen this perfectly on television—and

I should know. I've watched loads. Because I'm an annoying, detail-oriented planner, I search for an imperfection. Something that makes this moment with Jack more realistic. I need to find something. Something that will keep a section of my heart in check, so that leaving in eight days isn't impossible.

As it has for the last few days, my mind circles back around to that night in Central Park. When I got the feeling he was lying to me about how often he drinks. But my heart must be on Jack's side, because it boots my concern across the train car. That morning at the academy when he showed up drunk was just an anomaly. As far as I know, he's been sober ever since.

Everything is fine.

Jack's hand leaves my hair and coasts down my front, journeying through the middle of my breasts. His knuckles drag over my stomach, shooting my thighs together, before he rests the hand on my hip. Then down to my thigh. Kneading. My whole body is tingling, waking up for the first time and dancing for Jack, its puppet master. I've never had sex and yet, when he touches me, these images rip through my head. Naked, sweaty, rolling bodies. Thrusting. I'm craving and missing something I've never had before. Only Jack could accomplish that.

He pulls away with a reluctant groan, lust making his eyes a bright, vivid green around dilated black pupils. "I have to stop kissing that mouth or we're going to give these people a show they'll never forget."

"We could set your hat out on the seat." I say, hypnotized by the way he licks his lips. "I bet we could make enough for our next five desserts."

Jack dips his head to meet my eyes, giving me an incredulous look. "What happened? Did Brooklyn rub off on you or something?"

My smile springs to life. "Maybe. Are you going to rub it back off?"

His booming laugh echoes around the subway car, his fingers digging into my ticklish thighs. And I squeal. Squeal. "That is enough sass out of you, Katie Snaps McCoy. Our next date is going to be Sunday mass, if you're not careful."

"You sound like my father," I tease, poking him in the chest.

"If you want to call me daddy, just say so."

My groan makes him laugh harder. "I walked right into that one."

"Sure did." His mouth finds mine and he kisses me hard. "Our stop is next." He searches my face with his eyes, those talented fingers stroking my hair. "I can walk you to your hotel room door and leave, Katie. You know that, right?"

"Yes." I turn and slide off his lap, gaining my feet. "I also know I don't want that."

Relief and anticipation meet on his face as he takes my hand, leading me off the train.

CHAPTER 12

Jack

The hotel room smells like Katie. Minty and girly. Scarves are draped along the backs of chairs, lotion bottles are arranged on the nightstand, her suitcase lays open in the corner. I want to pick up every item in the room, feel it in my hand, smell it and commit it to memory. Especially Katie. God, this girl has me by the bones. I don't want to get away.

She was bouncy and courageous on the train, but as we got closer to the hotel, I could feel the growing tension of her body from its perch on my back. Which is why I'm halfway across the room, hands shoved into my pockets. I might want to tackle her onto the bed and strip her down to the skin, but tonight is her first time. I'm lucky as shit she's letting me have anything to do with it. So we're going to take this slow.

Out of the corner of my eye, I spot a second suitcase in the slightly ajar, mirrored closet alongside the bed. "I wouldn't have taken you for a heavy packer."

"Actually." She winces, probably because her voice came out ten octaves higher than usual. "Actually, those aren't clothes or shoes or anything."

"What is it?"

Avoiding my gaze, she bends down to unzip her boots, stepping out of them. "Inside that suitcase . . . is the fourth item on my Katie Conquers New York list."

"Yeah?" I shrug off my jacket and hang it on the desk chair. Then I slip my hands back into my jeans pockets. She watches me all the while and I think she understands what I'm telling her. One thing at a time. No rushing. "If you don't want to show me what's inside the suitcase, that's okay. But if it's a dead body, I'd help you bury it. Might want to take advantage."

Some of tension leaks from her shoulders. "You would, wouldn't you?"

I nod once.

The rest of her anxiety would go away if I put my hands on her. I'd disrobe her and distract her so thoroughly, she wouldn't have time for nerves. I want her to feel comfortable before I touch her, though. Who the hell even knows why? Or how come I'm suddenly so goddamn Zen about fucking, but there it is. I want tonight to be about Katie. And I want it to be different for me, too. Different from any other time I've been with a girl. Nothing I've done in the past has any place in this room with us.

Just because I can't touch her doesn't mean I can't remind her what it's like, though. Right? Dipping my head, I watch Katie from beneath my brows and approach her. Slowly. Giving her time to anticipate it. Even in the room's moody near-darkness, I can see her feet writhe in the carpet, see her sucking in a deep breath. But at the last second, I plant a kiss on her shoulder and move towards the window, pushing it open, letting the sounds of Manhattan fill the room. Whooshing wind, sirens, rushing traffic, distant bleating boat horns drifting from the East River.

"I want to show you," she says, her voice mingling with the city noises. "What's in the suitcase."

She's not facing me, which is probably a good thing, because she can't see my eyes close, the gratified smile that ticks my lips up. Before Katie can venture to the closet to lift the possibly heavy luggage, I move past and do it for her, laying it on the bed.

"I'm going to ramble a bit now. I hope you don't mind." She unzips the suitcase, which forces her to bend forwards and give me a great view of her ass, the green material stretching over those works-of-art buns and moments like these, I really think Jesus loves me.

"I definitely don't mind."

Hearing my lecherous tone, she sends me a reproving look that can't quite hide her amusement. "Once a year, my mother brought me to Blackrock Market and told me I could buy one thing. It wasn't for Christmas or my birthday. More like a special girl's day out present. Just one thing, and somehow it was always better than all my birthday and Christmas presents combined." After a slight hesitation, she peels back the suitcase and color explodes across my vision. Yellows, reds, startling whites, robin's egg blues, teals and pinks. "I always chose a purse."

"These are them?"

"No." Her chest rises and settles. "I made these ones."

Look, I don't know the first thing about handbags. Or pocketbooks, as my mother calls them. Whenever I happen to be down on Canal Street, knockoffs are being sold everywhere and I might give them enough attention to spot the newest trend. Buying one has never crossed my mind, however, so my knowledge is pretty limited. Still, I can tell these purses of Katie's are good. They're quality. Without laying a finger on the packed leather bundles, I'm willing to bet they're butter soft. The buckles—silver, shaped in a KM—gleam in the low lamplight. They're organized according to color family, which is so like Katie, I have to swallow.

"When did you make them?" I finally ask.

"During downtime, when I was training." She tucks a strand of red hair behind her ear. "Nighttime mostly, when it got hard to sleep. I ordered the materials from the Internet and had them delivered. Special-ordered the buckles with my left-over graduation money." She shrugs. "I learned what I could online and taught myself the rest."

That'll teach me to think Katie can't get any more amazing. "Can I hold one?"

"Yes, of course." Her hands flutter over the purses, trying to pick one, and she finally lands on a fire-engine red creation with black stitching. I don't miss the way she's looking at me, like she's holding her breath. For my opinion? "Damn, Snaps. These are . . . wow. I know Ever and Danika would rock this. My mother, too. It's beautiful."

"Really?"

"Yeah, really." I give her an are-you-insane look. "Hasn't anyone told you?"

"You're the first one I've shown." She's pink to the roots of her hair. "Well, apart from my mam."

Humbleness closes in around me, making it necessary to gather my thoughts. "Why do you have them here?"

"That's where my list comes in." She takes the purse from my hands, wedging it back into place, and closes the suitcase. "Making bags is the only thing I've ever done just for me. Because I love it. And I thought . . ."

"Yeah?"

She bends over the case and zips it back up, but this time I refuse to look at her ass. I'm too interested in hearing her explanation. "The Olympics was my father's goal; a way to divert his grief. Joining the Emergency Response Unit as an instructor seemed logical, with my skill set." A slow, dreamy breath leaves her. "But bags . . . that's just for me. I thought if I could sell just one or two, it would mean what I love isn't a waste of time."

"I'll buy all of them right now. Just give me a couple hours to sing on the subway," I say without hesitation. Her rush of laughter hits me square in the stomach, heating every inch of me, inside and out. "Nothing you love could ever be a waste of time, honey. Nothing."

I'm a far cry from Shakespeare, but hell if the words I managed to string together don't chase away a little more stiffness from her body. "I have this secret wish to create them on the side, when I have time." A tiny, too-quick laugh tumbles out. "A weapons instructor moonlighting as a handbag designer. Have you ever heard anything like it?"

"No. But I've never met anyone like you, either. That's how I know it's possible."

Another dose of tension leaves her, those pale

blues holding mine for heavy—important? I hope so—beats, before tracing down to my belt buckle, her palms rubbing the fronts of her thighs. I'm used to women wanting me, but I've definitely never wanted to crawl towards them on hands and knees. Never wanted to make every single thing so perfect, she can't forget me, even if she tries. Before I can second-guess my intuition, I take off my hat and my shirt, letting the latter dangle in my fingers a moment, dropping it to the floor. With Katie's wide eyes on me, I climb onto the bed, leaning back against the center of the headboard.

"Come here and kiss me," I say quietly, crooking my finger at her. "I'll kiss you all night until you decide you want more."

Appreciation glows so brightly inside her, my hand drops. Stowing a lock of hair behind her ear, Katie walks towards me on her knees. Her weight barely dips the mattress and I'm suddenly so protective, my fingers curl into my palm with the urge to yank her close. Not yet. Not this time. When she's only inches away, she hesitates, then rests her hands on my shoulders. I hold my breath as she eases herself onto my lap, straddling me.

There's no restraining the moan that flies out of me. No stopping my hands from snagging her waist, holding her steady. Her pussy is hot and firm, pressing down onto my cock, her mouth a millimeter from mine and I beg, beg, beg myself not to lose control. Not to lunge forwards and pin her down. The idea of her being nervous or uncomfortable stops me, calming the crazy boiling of my blood. Somewhat.

"Did I tell you earlier how fucking hot you look in that dress?" My hands glide up her back, tangling in her hair. I tug a little on the strands and her head falls back, exposing her throat. My tongue takes advantage with a hungry lick, right up the middle. "Those boots were just cruel, Katie. My dick has been aching all night."

She gasps when I set my mouth to work beneath her ear. Nibbling, sucking. Fuck, she tastes like mint candy and I can't get enough. "Even though they made it necessary for you to carry me around?"

"Especially because I got to carry you around." My mouth finds hers and delivers a nasty kiss. The kind that's going to make her think about me eating her pussy. And yeah, I know it works like a charm when her thighs shimmy up higher around my hips, little whimpers leaving her throat and traveling into my mouth. "I loved carrying you on my back. Quickest way to let everyone know you're all mine." I rasp against her lips. "You are all mine, aren't you, honey?"

"Yes." She breathes against my lips for few beats, then leans back just enough to whip the green dress off over her head. "Maybe I should have left the boots on. Rookie move."

Christ, it's like a surgeon slaps me with electric paddles the way my pulse slams into hyper drive. There's her tits, two plump little temptations, swelling over the edges of purple silk. In my periphery, I can see her panties match and I'm fucked. I'm so fucking fucked. My cock is way too stiff to be confined in my jeans. When she leans forwards for another kiss, pressing down on the erection from hell and I groan like a dying man through my teeth, understanding dawns in her beautiful, flushed face.

"Oh, we should get your jeans off."

"I knew I liked you, Snaps," I manage, my voice sounding like smashed glass. "Just . . . just the belt and zipper so he can breathe, huh?"

Her eyes widen, as if it just occurred that I'm hoping she'll perform the job. I'm already crazy for Katie—let's just face it—and I sink a whole lot deeper when she takes a bracing breath and squares her shoulders. Her blue eyes flick up to mine, once, twice, as she unfastens my belt. We both stare down at the trunk of flesh battling my zipper for freedom, our heavy breaths colliding in the space between us. She makes a sound of sympathy and hurries to slide my button through the denim hole and lower my zipper. My dick bobs out and rebounds off my bare stomach, the sudden lack of pressure wrenching a hoarse sigh from my chest.

"You . . . you don't wear underwear?"

Unbelievable. I want to nail this girl until she's a sticky, sobbing mess and she can't even look at my cock without blushing. Everything she does ties my organs up in knots. "Might have to start wearing some around you. I've never had to worry so much about being hard in public."

Her upper lip curls. "Don't pretend you care about offending people."

My heart squeezes. "Caught me." Keeping our eyes locked, I slip my hands around to her ass, cradling her cheeks in my palm, skimming up and down, listening to her inhales and exhales accelerate. "You want to play a game, Katie?"

She nods jerkily, her throat working with a swallow.

"Since I don't have any underwear on, why don't you share yours with me?" I knead her tight, rounded ass. "Try to get my cock inside your panties. No using your hands, though. That would be cheating. Just your thighs and hips, you understand? If you manage to get me inside that purple silk with your wet pussy, you win."

By the time I finish outlining the rules, her eyelids are at half-mast and I know, I know I could throw her down and give us what we both need right now. She's ready. But I don't just want Katie ready. I want her screaming for my cock and clawing me when I hold out. I want her to resent every second I'm not slamming into her. I want to own her.

Turns out, she's going to own me, though. She kisses me once—to gather courage?—then the slick material of her panties settles against my erection. The back of my skull meets the head-board and lights flash in front of my vision. And that's before she starts moving. That first slide of damp silk up and down my dick burns the inside of my throat, turns a molten hot wrench in my belly. She turns me into a desperate beggar and I want every inch of her against me. Want nothing between us. I release a broken growl on the next stroking writhe of her pussy, my hands flying to the front clasp of her bra, flicking it open with shaking hands.

"Ah, Jesus, Katie. You've got the sexiest tits." Keeping one hand on her sweet ass so I can feel her ride me, I use the other to mold her left breast. Lifting it for my starved mouth to feast on. I do, too. I start by opening wide and rubbing the center of my tongue over her pointed nipple, up and down, until the pace of her hips kicks up. Then I lick a circle around the rose-colored bud, before sucking it hard between my lips.

"Jack! Oh my God." Her breath shudders in and out. "D-do that again. Again, please."

Praise Jesus, the Virgin Mary and Santa Claus. My girl has sensitive nipples. Not everyone does and if I couldn't get my mouth on these little handfuls as often as possible, it would have been fucking blasphemy. "Move my head, honey. Put me anywhere you want. Make sure I give them both enough attention."

I'm going to have a sore neck in the morning, but it's going to be worth it. Katie drags me from right to left, demanding I suck her nipples with throaty whimpers that have precum beading on the head of my cock, dripping down the sides. "Please, Jack, please."

"Good girl. Fuck me through those sexy little underwear." I take a chance and slap her ass—a nice, firm swat—and I'm rewarded with a shocked moan of pleasure. "You haven't won the game yet. Your pussy is still all alone inside those panties, isn't it?"

CHAPTER 13

Katie

Yes," I reply through clenched teeth, a hot, uncontrollable shiver passing through my limbs, making them tighten around Jack. "I . . . It doesn't want to be alone, though."

Christ's sake. He actually has me referring to my vagina as an it. I don't care, though. I don't have the available worry space to loan out. All I want is Jack between my legs, filling me, moving. Just like back on the subway, I'm lost to the sparkly, echo chamber known as lust and Jack is the one who locked me in here. He's done what I thought was the unthinkable, getting me to a point beyond self-consciousness or thoughts of consequences. I'm lost to Jack's magic.

His mouth on my breasts has turned my panties sopping wet, but I shamelessly arch my back and beg in a shaking voice for more. More of the addictive sucking. Lusty eyes glitter up at me as he dives in, capturing my nipple between his lips, worrying it, pulling on the bud with a harsh groan, his forehead wrinkling. "Feels so good." I grip the sides of his face, holding him to my chest as my hips buck wildly. I'm mindless and hot and aching and exploding with need. Jack challenged me to a game and now, knowing he was serious about it, I wiggle right and left, trying to slide the head of his erection under the seam of my underwear. All I succeed in doing is rubbing my clit against his impossibly thick flesh and making myself throb all the harder. "B-but impossible. It's . . . I can't."

"Try again." His voice is a croak against my nipple, sending a rippling vibration through my core. I look down at him through hazy vision and catch the devilish wink he sends me. "If you need to cheat and use your hands, I won't tell anyone."

He levers up and catches my mouth in time to stifle my laugh. I really should slag him over using the ploy to get my hands on him, but I feel only appreciation. When we walked into the room, my nerves were hopping all over my skin and now I'm right here. Every ounce of my concentration centered on Jack and the insane way he makes me feel. My lips curve against his as I reach down and circle my hand around the base of his erection, holding tight. Stroking up to the tip and back down to the bottom.

"Fuck. Holy shit," he hisses, his words running together. "Really loving those callouses about now, Snaps. Feels like you're giving me a little teeth. God, don't stop."

Callouses. Who knew? Amazed that the simplest of touches can turn this experienced man into a shuddering mass of bunched muscles, I ease my grip up and down again. And again and again. Until Jack is pumping his hips into my grip, rasping my name between curse words. But he goes completely still when I tuck the head of his arousal into the wet swath of silk between my thighs, slipping him through my wetness, awe and need storming in my middle. "Did I win the game?"

I'm glad he recognizes my voice, because I don't. "Yes. You win all the games. Forever." Sweat starts to form on his upper lip, veins straining in his arms and neck. "Come on, Katie. Don't be afraid to rub me on that clit. She and I work very well together, remember?" A memory of Jack's head between my legs, his shoulders pressing my thighs apart, shimmers in my mind. The breath in my lungs run scarce, but I manage to slide his flesh closer to where it's needed. "Yeah, you remember," he says hoarsely, nipping at my mouth. "Remind her how much I love her."

His hips give an encouraging nudge, then he's

there. I am, too. Rubbing that smooth part of him over a place only Jack and I have touched. In a matter of seconds, there's a tightening in the dead center of my body. Like a spinning ball of feathers, tickling my bloodstream and nerve endings, making them clamour and race. "Jack . . . Jack, I'm going to . . ."

"No." His hips edge back, taking his erection out of my greedy fist. But I only have half a breath to experience disappointment, before Jack shoots forwards and my back lands on the mattress, sending a thrill racing down my spine. He looms above me in the near darkness, looking like a thirsty man who suspects I'm the final source of water. "All that's left is your panties, honey. But I want them off. And I want them off right fucking now. That work for you?"

"Yes," I whisper, twining my fingers in the ends of my hair. "Yes, Jack. To everything, okay?"

His eyes flare, warm fingers dipping and curling into the waistband of my underwear, wrenching them down my legs. Throwing them aside. I'm naked. I'm totally naked with Jack Garrett and I'm thrilled about it.

"Everything, huh?" He falls forwards onto his elbows, sucking a red mark onto the inside of my right thigh. Following suit with the left as his hands slowly scoop beneath my bottom, holding it at the ready. He's such an overwhelming sexual being in that moment, I feel a flutter of apprehension. Until what he says next. "Does everything include holding you all night? Kissing you back to sleep if you have a nightmare?"

An invisible hand slides between my ribcage and tweaks everything beneath. "Yes."

Jack finishes leaving the marks and focuses on my center, humming deep in his throat as he gives my flesh a long, deliberate lick. The pillows are kicked off the bed by his anxious feet as he surges closer, pressing his mouth as close as it can get. It's everything I can do not to scream as his tongue finds my clit, circling, circling until I begin to go mad. A fresh storm is building just south of my belly button and Jack is conducting it, whipping it into a frenzy. My thighs are draped over his wide shoulders, but I have no idea which one of us put them there.

"Oh God. Stay." I trap a scream behind my teeth. "Don't stop doing that."

"Easy, honey. We'll get there."

His tongue leaves me, though, and I lose myself completely, locking my heels and trying to keep his mouth in that perfect place where I need it. Need it so bad. When Jack lays a kiss on my stomach and whispers my name, I loosen my muscles. Just in time for him to ease a finger into my dampness. Pumping it. And again, the storm whips. I'm looking up at the ceiling, but I don't see it. His knuckle twists on top of my clit, his finger jiggling inside me. My pleasure is blinding me. I'm shaking. There are tears or sweat or both sliding down my temples and I don't care. My

body has a mind of its own, arching and clenching, my voice begging.

When he adds a second finger and flickers his
tongue against my clit, I scream. Loud. I actually
scream his name. I want him to fix the bone-
shattering ache inside me and he finally seems
inclined to do that. Although when he prowls up
my body, the idea that he might have been reluctant to ease my pain becomes ridiculous.

If possible, Jack is needier than me. His eyes are
so dripping with lust, he almost appears haunted
with it. Even in the darkness, I can see his pupils block out every bit of green. His erection is
parallel to his hard stomach, skimming up my
curves as he crawls up and devours my mouth.
Falls on it like I'm going to keep him alive. We
kiss like the sky is collapsing, a roar beginning
in my ears, but through the white sound, I hear
him opening a condom wrapper and the sound
of latex unrolling.

"Katie, I'm fucking dying," he grates against
my mouth. "Open your legs for me."

They're already open, but I don't bother telling
him. I'm too rolled up in his hunger, becoming
a servant to it. I nod, running my thumbs over
his cheekbones, lips, chin, and I hike my knees
up, letting Jack feel them at his hips. Our breath
races out of our mouths like two overheating en-
gines as Jack reaches down and guides himself
to my entrance, pushing in deep and collapsing
on top of me, grinding a vile curse into my ear.

"Goddammit. Katie, Katie, Katie. You're so motherfucking tight."

There's a slice of pain, but it's nothing compared to the pleasure of being filled. The pleasure of knowing the secrets of my body are enough to make Jack vibrate like a tuning fork. I'm pinned, like a sacrifice, to the bed . . . and I love it. It's as though I've drunk a potion that sensitizes my skin, makes every inch of me feel sexy, and I throw my head back and drink in the miracle, even as the urgency builds and builds in my loins.

Jack's lips drag across my collarbone, up my neck, over my cheek to finally settle against my mouth. His eyes burn into mine and an answering bell rings inside me. "Feel this?" He slides his inches out of me and punches back in with a growl. "It's yours for as long as you want it. You've got it locked down. The only reason I'll take it out is to piss a circle around you." His head dips, those sensual lips closing around my swollen right nipple and suckling, his cheeks hollowing until he sets my breast free of his torture. "Understand me, Katie?"

Satisfaction expands inside my chest. "I understand you, Jack."

His mouth is on mine again before I finish chattering the words, his tongue invading to set off a new, stronger detonation in my belly. "You hurting?" he asks between long, filthy, searching kisses. "Ah, honey. Tell me you're not hurting."

"I am."

"No. No."

A hot, rough melding of mouths. "I am because you're . . . pushing against all these places and making me crazy. I need you to move against them. Me. Please."

Apart from those two initial thrusts, he's been a hard, pulsing presence inside me. It was more of a shock in the beginning, but I must have gotten used to his size, because this time when he drives deep, I almost come off the bed, carried by a sizzling bolt of pleasure.

"Jack. Don't stop." I release a sound halfway between a gasp and a sob. "You feel amazing. Please, please."

His head falls into the crook of my neck, a guttural moan pelting my skin. "Jesus Christ. This is it, right? You're okay now?" His hands find my bent legs and push them wide, his own knees bracing, readying on the bed. "You feel too tight for a rough fuck, Katie, but I don't know if I can stop myself." He tightens his ass and grinds into me, circling, circling. "Fuck me. You've got such a hot little cunt."

"It's yours," I whimper without hesitating. The way he's speaking to me should be offensive. Or something. Too bad I adore it and want more. Want him to give me his worst, filthiest speech so long as he keeps looking at me as though I'm a prize he's won against all odds. So long as he keeps pumping that thick part of himself down

deep inside me. And ahhh . . . he does. Telling
Jack "it's yours" sets off something inside him.
He goes still a moment, his eyes boring into mine.
That's when he's fully set loose, driving into me
with such wildness, my bones jolt, my back teeth
clacking together.

"Going to make you come, honey. Don't worry.
Just . . ." His voice cracks on a moan, his incredible body moving like a raging ocean. "Shit, I've
just never felt anything like you. Not just between my legs, Katie. I feel you fucking everywhere, you know?"

My heart tugs in answer. "Yes."

"Keep looking at me. You're keeping me here."

In my head, his words make no sense, but my
heart speaks his language. "I've got you."

Jack's warm breath coasts across my face, harsh,
fast. "I've got you, too. I've always got you."

Strong fingers glide down my stomach, finding
my sensitive clit and rubbing vigorously. Head
to toe, my body quickens, like Jack has my reac-
tions on a string. He swallows my whimper with
his mouth, kissing me with increasing passion as
the slap of his hips, the movements of his fingers
pick up the pace. My body doesn't know where
to focus. Jack's mouth, his fingers, his thick, slippery flesh that rifles in and out of that previously
untouched part of me. Jack himself, who watches
me under hooded eyelids, emotion brimming
from every pore of his gorgeous face.

"My Katie." His voice is uneven. "Don't want

anyone else to have you. Wish no one else had ever had me, dammit. Wish, I wish . . ."

I pull him down on top of me, just as my body wins the battle, reeling in the orgasm that ironically, sends me out to sea. A current carries me, rippling over and through my body, my eyes full of nothing but exhilarating blue. Above me, Jack grits out my name and joins me, bringing the violence of the water, his muscles jerking, his throat gasping for oxygen. My arms and legs wrap around him tight, forcing him to share his spasms with me, forcing him to accept mine. Afterwards, we lay there, too spent to move for what feels like hours.

Finally, Jack lifts his head to study me, brows drawn. There's an air of expectation about him, as if he's waiting for something. What? The uncertainty makes me nervous. So nervous. But only for a fraction of a second, because whatever he's waiting for seems to arrive. Or doesn't? And his answering smile is heart-stopping, shining all over my face like the sun.

His laugh comes out in a long gust. "Holy shit."

"You read my mind."

Jack stands, but keeps returning to the bed to plant kisses on my cheeks and forehead, so clearly reluctant to leave me for even a second that I grin like a loser. Eventually he takes care of the latex still attached to his body, the muted city lights hugging his flexing backside as he walks to the bathroom. When he returns, he pulls back the covers, lifting me into the coziness of the warm, fluffy interior. Looking stunned to find himself in a position to be in bed with a girl—with the intention of sleeping—his jaw is nonetheless set with purpose. His eyes dance with . . . awe? Yes, I think so.

And that awe, staring down at me, tinged with bafflement, is the last thing I see before drifting off in the safety of Jack Garrett's arms.

CHAPTER 14

Jack

My head is so clear when I wake up, I must be living in someone else's body. I open my eyes and squint into the sunlight pouring in through the hotel room window, waiting for a headache or fuzzy memories from the night before to come trickling in . . . but it doesn't happen. Even more unbelievable, I never crashed last night after being with Katie. Never retreated to those dark corners of my mind to get lost in the past, swapping the current good for that past moment of weakness. No, I was right here with Katie, feeling her inside me, as well as out. Sensing she could feel me in her head and chest, too. We were in it together.

For a long time, lies have gone hand in hand with sex for me. Lies I tell myself about why I kept chasing the high, when what I secretly wanted was the crash afterwards. The honesty between me and Katie kept me elevated in this warm, inviting place, though. Made me feel like I belonged there.

Do I, though? I've shared more truth with Katie than anyone in my life, but I haven't been entirely honest, have I?

I ignore the troubling reminder and focus on her.

A rainbow variety of Katie versions that dance through my mind. Bright, moving, beautiful pictures that I captured last night. There's another one right in front of me that I quickly snap with my mind's eye. I'm spooning Katie and we're both facing the window, my face buried in her red, tumbled hair. My left eye is covered by the incredible-smelling strands, but my right travels over the messy length of it. Wavy ends gather in her neck, whorl around her ear, brush against her mouth. Sunlight sets the long mass of it off, making her hair look like dark red fire and my arms tighten around her, dragging her as close to my body as possible, tucking my knees into the backs of hers, warming her feet with the soles of mine.

She's a heavy sleeper and my chest aches with the secret. Something no one, save maybe her parents, knows about her. A fact her brother probably knew, once upon a time.

The smile I wasn't aware of fades at the reminder of Katie's pain. She's in New York to celebrate the memory of her brother. Would I fit into that if she knew about my problem?

Relax. It's not a problem right now. It won't be again. If I could survive talking about my past last night while drinking nothing but a Coke, I'm not going to fuck up. Not while Katie is in New York and not after, if I can damn well help it. The reminder she's leaving, however, lands me smack in the middle of the problem that kept me awake into the early hours of last night. This girl—the one I've begun referring to as mine—is leaving in a week.

And God, I don't want her to go.

Which is flat out, fucking selfish. She's the only girl I've ever slept with that made me feel . . . whole. Afterwards, there was no impending doom clogging my throat. No nausea. Hours later, I'm still floating on the relief. I'm not broken with Katie. When we're together, I'm grounded in the moment. I don't want to blink or look away. Since we met, she's been challenging me to be better and I've shocked myself by rising to the occasion, proving I'm not useless at the academy, spending time with her outside the bedroom.

I want to keep doing those things. For her. For myself.

But the way she repairs my damage with her touch, her presence, isn't a reason for *Katie* to stay. What am I doing for her? How am I making her happy? So I provided a decent date, made her moan and chaperoned her murder excursions.

Compared to what she's done for me? My contribution ain't shit.

I've never been a driven person. Do just enough to get by. Don't take anything seriously. Those sentiments were how I operated. Right now, though, I'm feeling suspiciously close to ambitious. Is that what this is? Ambition? Wanting to do whatever it takes to better myself? Right now, I would be selfish asking Katie to stay in New York.

But what if I had something to offer?

Katie murmurs in her sleep, shifting her ass against my lap. I press my lips together to keep from groaning as my balls tighten up, my dick thickening along the inside of her bare thigh. Yeah, knowing there isn't going to be a sickening fall after we have sex is making me a horny maniac. Not to mention, Katie herself, with her sunlit skin and warm curves. If last night hadn't been her first time, I'd wake her up the way the devil intended, but I want to make sure she's not sore. Which means talking to her first. Fuck, I can't wait to talk to her.

She's leaving. What the hell am I going to do?

Katie's sleepy voice cuts into my panic, all scratchy and muffled by the pillow. "It's silly to feel guilty waking up naked with a man on a Sunday, right?"

I laugh into the curve of her neck. "Is this the famous Catholic guilt I've heard so much about?"

"Its powers are not to be underestimated." Her ribcage expands on a long breath, as if she's gathering courage before rolling over. And I know I was right when she's finally facing me and her cheeks are painted pink. "Good morning. How long have you been awake?"

"Long enough to count the freckles on your back."

The pink turns to fuchsia. "What number did you reach?"

I rub my knuckles under her chin and she sighs. A warm, muffled sound that belongs to lazy mornings, but I've never heard it with my own ears. "I lost count around eighty-seven because I was distracted by that minty smell of yours. Where does it come from?"

"A combination of tea bags and my hair conditioner." She tucks a corner of the comforter under her chin, snuggling into it. "My parents think I'm from another planet for not liking traditional Irish tea. They drink loads of the stuff, but it was always too strong for me. My mother brought home the mint tea one day as a laugh, but it backfired since I loved it." Her lips curve into a smile. "It became a running joke after that. Mint flavored everything. Mint bath soaps for Christmas and so on. The smell makes me happy."

It makes me happy, too. "Tell me about your parents. They dragged you to church every Sunday?"

"Yes, ten o'clock mass, like clockwork. My brother and I called it Itchy Clothes Day and we'd stomp around making sure Mam knew we were miserable." We make eye contact over the mention of her brother, but Katie continues on without missing a beat. "My father is a perfectionist. He clips his nails every day, needs the newspaper folded a certain way. I'm sure he was in the sixth row at Sunday mass this morning."

"And your mother?"

"There beside him." Katie's voice grows softer. "She's messier and more spontaneous than my father. She loves to give presents, especially gag gifts and you never know when one is coming, but it makes people feel so special. That's why she does it. Her dream in life was to have a gift-wrapping room, so my father turned our garage into one." I'm so drawn into the soft warmth of Katie's voice, my pulse leaps unexpectedly when she reaches beneath the covers and rubs my chest, up and down in the center. It feels so incredible, I press into the touch. "It's the happiest room. Colorful paper everywhere. Ribbons and glitter. My father can't go inside without trying to tidy up, so he's been banned."

What would it be like to walk into that room with Katie and meet her mother? What would her parents think of me? Will I ever have the opportunity to find out? I barely manage to stop myself from asking Katie what their judgment would be, but I keep on wondering.

Katie's denim eyes are quiet and solemn as they watch me, probably guessing about what I'm thinking. "Tell me something happy about your mother, Jack."

There it is. This is why I'm losing my shit over Katie. Why I feel so fucking great when she's around. Because as soon as she asks to hear a happy story about my mother, I realize how badly I've wanted that. To say something positive out loud about her, instead of reading sympathy on the faces of others when they find out how I was raised. Katie not only sees what's going on inside me, she wants to go exploring. She actually cares that there's more to me. All I can do is show her what's there and hope she's happy with it.

Most of it, anyway. There are certain things I've got inside that are too ugly to bring them in the same vicinity as Katie. Yeah. My own private hell stays right where it is.

"She kept me home from school once when I was thirteen. Didn't warn me, just surprised me with packed lunches and bus tickets. We went to Atlantic City for the day." Katie's hand is still on my chest now and I circle her wrist, carrying her fingers to my mouth so I can kiss them. "Best part? We were standing on the shore and she felt sand crabs under her feet. Lifelong city girl didn't know what the hell they were. The scream she let out, Katie . . ." My laughter vibrates the bed. "Afterwards, she laughed about it, though. Sitting right there on the sand. I'd never seen her laugh like that." I press Katie's hand to my forehead, as if her touch has the power to keep my memory from fading. "It was a good day."

"It sounds like it." She passes me a serious look. "What are sand crabs?"

We're both laughing when I drag Katie up against me, turning so half of my body is on top of her. As soon as she feels my hard cock on her thigh, the laughter dissolves into a moan and we kiss. A long, searching kiss that I will gladly turn over my man card to admit makes my head spin. Damn. She's got a lot more confidence now, her tongue rubbing mine, hands copping a feel of my ass, and it's no wonder, right? Last night, I came so hard for her, I almost split the fuck in half.

The heel of my hand skates down her belly, massaging a circle against her pussy. But when she jerks, a wince crossing her beautiful face, I remove my hand like I've been burned. "Sore?"

She shakes her head, but seems uncertain. "It's fine."

Sorry, dick. This is going to hurt. "We wait."

"Jack—"

I stop her protest with a thorough kiss. One I hope is comforting so she realizes I'm not going to blame her for my blue balls. "We wait."

Katie tilts her head on the pillow. A red eyebrow goes up. "Or."

"Or?"

After biting her lip for a moment, she pushes me onto my back. I'm momentarily hypnotized by the bounce of her amazing tits as she kneels over me, tugging down the sheet. I snap right out of it, however, when she grips my cock in both hands. "It seems only fair after you've . . ."

"Say it and feel my dick get harder," I rasp. "Go on, honey."

"After you've gone down on me," Katie murmurs. "Twice."

My stomach fills with pressure, edged with a delicious twist of my abs.

"Wow."

My laugh turns into a groan, because she's giving me a nice, tight stroke, leaving no inch behind. "Definitely don't mind the word *wow* when you're holding my dick. Just thought I'd mention it."

"Noted," she whispers, leaning down, her breasts swaying, lids drooping. So fucking sexy I'm going to come the second she wraps her mouth around me. Her lips brush over the head, her tongue joining them in the barest of touches, but my balls feel like they're being squeezed in a fist. "They definitely frown on blow jobs on Sundays. No question."

"Think of it as a form of healing." Intense sexual frustration makes my voice raw. "Healing is a kind of miracle, right?"

Another too-light lick, right along the top ridge has my hips jerking off the bed. Through the blurred quality of my vision, I can see the teasing curve of her lips against the thick stalk of my erection and my blood goes up in flames. "I suppose if I'm your only chance to be healed, I'll be forgiven."

"You're my only chance, Katie. Please. Please," I ground out, gathering the comforter in my hands, twisting the material and moaning when her mouth takes in at least four of my swollen inches, her lips tightening as she drags back up to the tip. "Oh, that's good, honey." My voice is a shaking, slurring mess. "That's real fucking good."

Katie hums on her way back down, that red hair falling like curtains onto my thighs and I swear to God, I'm on the edge of blacking out. Nothing about sex is new to me, but everything about sex with Katie is bright, fresh and incredible. I didn't need liquid courage to be with Katie, liquid courage to brace myself for the fall afterwards, because deep down I had faith it wasn't coming. Not with her. I never want a drop of that shit in my system when I'm with her because it might obscure one single second, dim the perfection of this. Of her. Of how strong I am when I can overcome the need to blur my memories. She's woken up this belief that I can be more than a drunk lay, the next morning's regret. Hell, I don't want a drop in my system period. Not ever.

My nerve endings are exploding bombs going off beneath my flesh. I can feel every stroke of her tongue right in the pit of my belly, causing my climax to speed towards me. My feet are digging into the mattress, my hips upthrusting slow and nasty, like I'm a stripper working the stage on my back. Fuck, fuck, fuck.

When I realize Katie is looking up at me, that's when I begin to lose it. Her lips stretch as she sinks down to my root, keeping those blue eyes on me the whole time. She's excited. There's a light in her gaze, like she can't believe what we're doing. Can't believe how much I'm enjoying it. As if . . . it's her first suck-off. Jesus Christ. Am I a pervert for wanting to flip our positions and fuck her mouth hard now? Just like last night, when I hit this point of no return, all I want to do is claim her. Make her mine.

The one thing I want more than that, though, is to make her happy.

"Come here, Katie." Holding back my climax has me roaring the command, smacking my chest. Once, twice. "Sit on my chest . . . and for the love of God, don't stop what you're doing."

Blue eyes widen as she visualizes what I'm asking, but she hesitates only a couple of seconds before crawling up the bed alongside me and doing what I ask. She's still wearing underwear when her cute ass perches on my chest, body facing away, but as soon as she bends forwards and wraps her lips around my pulsing erection again, I waste no time shoving the silk to one side, revealing the pink flesh I had for the first time last night.

"Look at you, so fucking wet." I wrap one arm

around her waist, tugging her hips back just enough to greet her pussy with my tongue and begin stroking that tiny nub, up and back, up and back. Fast. "You're sore where I pounded, but not so sore you don't want your clit licked, huh, Katie? Good girl, giving me that pussy so I can lick it all better." I yank the panties more securely to the side. "Tilt your hips for me so I can tongue the whole thing clean."

"Oh my God . . ."

Speaking of holy Sundays, I'm pretty sure Katie's ass up in the air is what heaven looks like. Her trembling thighs are the pearly gates and I'm just a sinner, begging Saint Peter to get inside. I'll work on that metaphor later. Right now I'm a little busy sixty-nineing with the girl I never had the courage to dream about. She's going for broke now on my cock, whimpering as she sucks down, down to the base, thanks to the tongue whipping I'm giving her. My lungs are going to explode I'm breathing so heavy, my hips pumping like a desperate animal's. Fuck, I could have busted already, but I'm determined to taste Katie's pleasure before that happens and—

"Jack!" She grinds back against my mouth, thighs shaking out of control and come shoots up my cock so fast, I groan and flick my tongue along Katie's convulsing flesh, refusing to stop until she's wrung out. My stomach constricts so hard with the climax, I must be dying. My body moves without any kind of mental command, writhing and bucking, trying to get rid of the liquid lust that seems to be never-ending.

Across the room, I catch sight of Katie in the mirror. Bent over, her eyes are squeezed shut, but her hand pumps up and down my dick, white drops of moisture landing on her tits . . . and another round of spasms seizes me, turning me inside out. "Katie, Katie. Jesus, Katie."

As soon as I'm back down on earth, I sit up and wrap her in a bear hug from behind, truly not giving a rat's ass what fluids end up where. My universe slides into a sweet spot when she sags back against me, her head lolling against my shoulder. "Amen," she sighs.

Our winded round of laughter is interrupted a few seconds later when my phone rings, somewhere in the room. A quick check of the bedside clock has me frowning. Who the hell is calling me at ten o'clock on Sunday morning? The mystery is solved when I find my jeans and retrieve my cell from the pocket.

"Ma?" I answer, sitting on the edge of the bed. "What's up?"

"Jackie, you around?"

For some reason, my mother can't seem to grasp that I don't live in the neighborhood anymore. In her mind, I should still be downstairs playing video games with Danika. "I'm across town." Sensing Katie curling up on the bed behind me, I reach back and stroke her hair. "Everything okay?"

"There's no hot water again and the super is on vacation." I hear her roommates in the background, cursing the man to an early grave. "Can you come have a look at the boiler? You've still got that key to the basement, right?"

If by key, she means the jimmy I used a few times to beat the lock, then yes, I have it in my sock drawer, back at my apartment. Dammit, I was going to take Katie out for breakfast. I'm still new at having a girl, so eggs are as far as I've gotten, but a plan for the rest of the day would have formed once I got some coffee into me. No way I'm dragging her across town on Sunday morning, either. Not when she looks so peaceful, glowing from an orgasm in the messy white sheets. And asking her to meet my mother could freak her out when everything is so new. I can't chance it. "Yeah, Ma. I'll be over in about an hour. Hang tight."

I hang up the phone, stowing it in the pocket of my jeans as I pull them on. "Hey, my mother needs me over in the Kitchen—just for a while."

She nods, studying me. "You have to go."

"I don't want to, Snaps, but yeah." Finding my shirt and shoes on the floor, I make quick work of getting dressed. After I pull on my coat, I lean over Katie on the bed, taking a long inhale of mint. "I need to see you later."

She smiles up at me, stretching her arms up over her head like a lazy kitten. "You know how to find me."

My mouth works hers in a slow, promising kiss. "Damn right I do."

When I take one last look at her beautiful form on the bed and leave the room, I don't expect to be a different man the next time I see her.

CHAPTER 15

Katie

Is it a trait exclusive to women where the slightest thing can make you second-guess everything? Or it is just me who is now obsessively replaying the last twelve hours and wondering what went wrong? Each time I think I've landed on my potential misstep, however, I remember the way Jack looked at me while leaving my hotel room this morning. Like it was tearing him apart just to walk out the door. So where is he now?

I didn't start worrying until an hour ago, when Sunday afternoon turned to evening and the sky dipped from eternal blue to butterscotch gold. My phone is deadly silent on the bedside table. Not that I've been sitting here all day, waiting for Jack to call or anything. No, I showered and brought myself out for a bagel, ate it while wandering along the East River, dodging joggers and bike riders all the while. I'll never apologize for the frivolous shopping spree for knickers that followed, because purchasing silky underthings and having them wrapped in tissue paper is simply good for the soul. Calls to my parents were made to assure them I'm still breathing. My mam detected in my voice that I'm keeping a secret, but she didn't hassle me about it too much, since my da was standing within ear shot.

Remembering the conversation with my da causes my shoulders to sag. Before leaving Dublin, I was so sure we were past any talk of the Olympics, but he'd brought it up this morning, mentioning some new equipment he bought. Just in case I want to work on my competition technique when I come home. His attempt at casual had failed miserably, however, stretching a long silence between us. Am I being selfish? Refusing to give my father the outlet of training me again? My goal for this trip was to begin remembering Sean for his life, not his absence, but maybe it will take my father longer to get here. Like another four years.

Laughter in the hallway outside my room jolts me back to the present, making me realize I'm sitting in the dark. Night is creeping in, the sun having set. How long have I been sitting here thinking? I move to turn on a light, shifting the knots in my stomach. Was I a one-night stand for

Jack? I want to call him and make sure he's all right—at this point, I'm worried—but what if he ignores my call? Or worse. What if he answers and explains that his whole spiel about seeing me again later was nothing more than standard protocol?

I eyeball my phone, my fingers itching to dial. *Don't do it.* The unknown is better sometimes, isn't it? If Jack wanted to see me, he knows where I am.

Resolved to make the most of the night, I begin shoving items into my purse. Hotel room key, cell phone, credit card, ID—

There's a knock at the door.

My heart bottoms out at my feet like a plunging elevator. Jack. It has to be Jack. No one else in New York has my room number. I shouldn't have doubted him.

But when I open the door, my gaze drops several inches from where I expected to find Jack's reassuring green eyes, landing on appraising brown ones instead.

"Instructor," says Danika, sliding past me into the room, leaving a trail of orange blossom scent behind her. "Nice digs. You ready to go?"

"Go?" I try not to be obvious about my disappointment—or searching the hallway for Jack—before closing the door. "Go where?"

"Out." She spins the desk chair around with a single finger. "Jack got held up in the Kitchen with his mother's boiler. He's not sure if he'll make it out tonight, so he sent me to be your guide for the evening."

"Which part of that was a lie?" I say it without thinking, but I'm glad for having the question out there. Even if it hangs in the room like dirty laundry. She's made the mistake of telling an untruth to someone with more law enforcement experience and I can't let her get away with it. Honestly, I want to. I want to take her word for it and believe Jack is being thoughtful. Knowing I'm being duped would eat away at me all night, though.

Danika cocks her hip and laughs, obviously having decided to double down on the fib. But her eyes are troubled. "Jack didn't mention you were the suspicious type."

"I'm not. Not outside of work, anyway." I toss my purse onto the desk. "I appreciate you coming here and offering to take me out, but I'll be fine on my own."

Her lips thin, spine straightening. God, she really is gorgeous and . . . I like her. There's so much going on inside her head that she can't fully hide. Throw in her obvious backbone and she might as well be Irish, for all her stubborn qualities. Too bad she's met her match. And her match's confidence is being bolstered by frilly pink underpants. "I promised him I'd show you a good time," Danika says. "I don't break promises to my friends."

"Jack told me how good a friend you are. How you and your family . . . helped him when he was younger." Her mouth parts with surprise, but she seems more upset than touched. And all at once, this stand-off seems stupid and pointless. "Maybe I shouldn't have blurted that out, but my stomach is all gross and queasy. Could you just tell me if he's with another girl and get it over with?"

"Another—" Danika cuts herself off with a laugh. "No. I mean, shit, McCoy. Did you just hear yourself? Jack talked to you about how he grew up. He won't even talk to me about it. And I was there." She throws a hand in my direction and plops down on the bed. "You showed up and . . . look, it's corny, but I swear a light went on inside of him. Trust me, he's never been this way about anyone and . . ."

"And?" I manage.

She closes her eyes, shoulders sagging. "He's fucking it up. I don't know. Something happened today when he went to visit his mom."

Just like that, my worry from before multiplies and expands to fit every available inch of my insides. How many hours have I wasted waiting for him to call, when I should have been trying to get in contact? "Do you know where he is?"

Her laugh holds no humor. "I can probably narrow it down to a few places."

Something heavy thuds in my belly, like a dropped baton, but I ignore it and focus on the problem at hand. "Okay. Just take me to Jack. We'll find out what happened today when we see him."

Danika chews on her lip a moment, then shakes her head. "I can't." Her voice is agonized, but firm. "I'm sorry. If he wants to fuck this up, fine. But I won't do it for him."

"Don't you think it'll happen sooner or later?" I move to stand in front of her, waiting until she lifts her gaze from the floor. "Take me to him. Or I'll go to Hell's Kitchen and track him down myself. Alone. In the dark. Holding a big, touristy map and an I Love New York T-shirt."

"So no matter what, I end up on Jack's shit list." Defeat seems to weigh her down. "You drive a hard bargain, McCoy."

Seeing she's about to cave, relief cools the burning in my chest. "It's not a bargain unless we both get something out of it, right?"

Danika stands and gives me a long, level look, as if she's searching me for clues. "There's a possibility we could find my friend and bring him back. That's enough for me."

It's obvious she's not merely referring to the present. To finding Jack tonight and bringing him home. And I'm suddenly terrified about what I'm about to discover.

Danika and I don't talk much, except to agree that taking a cab crosstown will be quick this time of night on a Sunday. The bellman hails us one and we do nothing but exist in the heavy silence as the car flies through yellow lights and honks at pedestrians, all while punching buttons on the radio. Danika is the one who gives the driver our destination and obviously I don't recognize the streets or location.

Until we pull up outside.

I met Jack on the curb outside of this bar, when I was taking pictures of my mob hit sites. He asked me to come inside with him for a drink, but I declined. Told him I don't go into bars. I still don't, right? No. But if Jack is inside there, I have no choice. Until now, I haven't allowed myself to wonder how I'd find him. I'm starting to get an idea, though, and my heart is knocking against my ribcage, my fingers clutching my purse so tight, they're bloodless.

Danika raps on my window, having already exited the cab. The dread in her expression is almost enough to make me ask the driver to return to the hotel. Then I think of Jack. His face in the candlelight last night, eyes vulnerable.

I want you to understand me.

Everything is different with you, Snaps.

Forcing some steel into my spine, I climb out of the cab and slam the door behind me. The sidewalk feels funny beneath my feet as we walk through the bar's entrance. Danika links her elbow with mine as we enter. Jack is inside. I know it before we've taken two steps—and I'm ashamed of myself for almost chickening out. Now that he's nearby, all I can think of is fixing whatever is wrong. Finding out what kept him from me tonight. Pounding piano music, singing and laughter comes from the rear of the establishment. Danika and I trade a look and head that direction. The smell of beer and cologne and dust fight for attention. The male customers we pass do the same, elbowing each other and hooting, shouting offers of drinks. Honestly, I'd like to box their ears over some of the cruder offers. Shameful.

A crank turns in my middle as we progress towards the piano music, my skin crawling over the drunken state of so many people. Bleary eyes leer at me from the bar, bottles are raised to lips, a chair tips and crashes to the ground to my right. All I can think about is my brother. How one person having too good a time resulted in him losing his life. Resentment builds up inside me so tight, I can barely breathe.

But my lungs must have drawn in a fair amount of oxygen, because every last bit whooshes out when I spot Jack.

He's playing the piano with an almost desperate focus, an unlit cigar stuck in the corner of his mouth. His body lists to the right, eyelids drooping, before he jerks back upright and continues to play. Stubble decorates his jaw and chin. He's still wearing his shirt from last night, but black ashes crisscross on the front, directly over his heart, like he's been rubbing at it with soot-stained fingers. Around him, the decidedly older customers dance, slapping his back occasionally in encouragement. Amongst a scattered deck of cards, there's a bottle of vodka perched on the piano, almost empty, within Jack's reach . . . and every sound is blocked out, apart from the rapid breathing in my ears. Everything begins to connect. That feeling Jack was lying to me in the park, the night I danced in the fountain.

No. Not a regular thing. Meaning showing up to the academy drunk.

I won't drink around you again, Snaps.

There's been a niggling voice in the back of my head, telling me I was missing something important. And to me, this is as important as anything else in my world. Does Jack have a drinking problem? Is that what kept him away from me tonight?

"McCoy," Danika calls over the noise. "You all right? Katie."

The piano cuts off abruptly and Jack's head flies up, his gaze landing on mine like a plane crash. His face pales, mouth forming the word *no*. No. Everything around me stops, moving in slow motion, but my thoughts fly by at a million miles per hour. My leg muscles are screaming from the strain of not running. Of standing still. I should go. I should leave now. This is bad. Jack lied to me about something he knew was important. Alcohol took my brother away. I'm not rational about that. I never will be. I'm so mad and helpless and sad, all at once.

I'm leaving. I have to leave.

Jack stands slowly—cautiously—and staggers his way closer. I see the torment in his glazed eyes. My name is on his lips, but I can't hear anything over the pounding in my head

Run. Go.

He reaches out for me.

Jack

Eight hours earlier

M a," I call, letting myself into the apartment. "Check the water now. Let it run for a few minutes."

There's no answer, just a chorus of voices squawking in the living room. Sighing, I close the door behind me and lock it. I'm anxious to get back to Katie. Fixing the boiler has taken a lot longer than expected and I've been down in the basement for a good two hours. Breakfast is only a pipe dream now, but maybe it's not too late to bring Katie out for lunch. Or shit, a museum, more old crime scenes, the Empire State Building. Whatever touristy thing she wants to do.

Knowing Katie wants to spend actual time with me out of bed is, like, this crazy fucking rush and I'm standing right in the middle of it, letting it whip and twist around me. I'm trying not to think about the borrowed time we're on, but the ticking clock sits in my throat like a dried wad of glue, making itself known every time I swallow.

"Jackie," my mother shouts from the living room. "Come in here. There's a couple someones who haven't seen you in a while."

Curious, I set down my backpack containing the jimmy and some tools, then move down the unlit hallway towards the voices. As soon as I turn the corner, I see them.

Two women.

Faces from my past that have changed slightly with age, although it's only been about eight years since I was eighteen and they were in their late thirties. Since the last time I saw them. Which was the night before I secured a job unloading freighters down at the docks, moving my mother and me out of the brothel weeks later.

After what happened in the dark while my mother was out running errands, I couldn't stay there anymore, spending every single night on Danika's couch, even when my mother wasn't working. But they're here now, smiling at me and it's as though not even a single day has passed since—

"Jesus. Say hi, Jackie," my mother prompts me, coming over to pat my shoulder. Her expression is incredulous, probably over my uncustomary silence. And of course it would be, because she has no idea what happened with her so-called friends. She'll be finding out over my dead body, so I break through the ice surrounding me and croak a greeting.

"Hiya, ladies. Long time no see." I reach out for a handshake, preparing myself not to flinch when they touch me. They scoff at the formality, though, closing in on me at the same time and wrapping me in a bear hug. Nausea pumps wildly in my stomach and I breathe through my nose, in, out, in, out, focusing on not throwing up. The ice on my skin turns to sharp shards, puncturing the outer layer, making me bleed. At least, that's what it feels like.

They're still wearing the same perfume. It burns the insides of my nostrils and I resent the hell out of the smell, because it's marring the mint Katie left on me. Just having their bodies pressed to mine makes me want to rip my skin off and grow a fresh layer. My mother is looking at me strangely over their heads, so I force a smile onto my face and pat the women on the backs a few times, before extricating myself.

Sucking in a few deep breaths, I pray my voice sounds normal. "Listen, Ma, the water should be hot now." I back towards the hallway. "Call me if it goes cold again."

My mother takes a step in my direction. "Is everything okay, Jack?"

She didn't use my nickname, meaning she's genuinely worried. My gut grows even sicker knowing I can't stick around and reassure her. What the fuck would I say anyway? Eight years later, there's nothing she can do about what happened. She feels enough guilt for raising me in a cat house—I'm not adding to it. "Yeah, Ma. You're such a worrier. Call you later."

One of the women blatantly checks me out behind my mother's back, the other throwing me a secretive wink. I barely manage not to hurl as I escape into the hallway, snatching up my backpack and burning shoe rubber out of the apartment. I'm down the stairs in seconds, moving at breakneck speed, throwing myself out into the cool afternoon air. Dragging it into my lungs. A cab slows at the curb, the driver probably sensing I want to get the fuck out of Dodge. I do. I do. I want to get to Katie and wrap myself around her.

The smell of floral perfume reaches up and smacks me in the face. Christ, I can't go to Katie like this. Not only with this smell on me, but with the deceitful touch lingering on my skin, this bile clogging my throat. I'd take one look at her and confess everything, but I would regret it. Yes, I would. Because she would never see me the same way again. Katie already has too many reasons to be ashamed of me. My history with girls, the fact that I have nothing to offer her, professionally or economically. And those are just the things she's aware of.

I won't give her more.

Banishing the image of her laying naked in

the hotel bed, smiling at me, I wave off the still-waiting cab and start walking. There's a piercing howl in my ear, telling me to turn around or get an Uber back to the East Side, but I can see the familiar, fading sign up ahead and know. I know as soon as that liquid burn hits my throat, I'll be closer to forgetting.

Need to forget. Need to.

I'm so sorry, Katie.

Before I enter the bar, I dig my cell phone out of my pocket and call Danika. She answers on the second ring, her voice wary. "What's wrong, huh?" I croak. "You've been waiting for the god-damn shoe to drop?"

Silence. "It doesn't have to. You sound fine." She reverses directions and tries to be casual, but can't pull it off. "Where are you? I'll come hang out."

My snort probably has her bristling. I'm too desperate to get inside the bar to smooth her feathers, though. "I need you to do me a favor." The door handle bites into my palm. "I'm going to text you Katie's hotel and room number." Saying her name, knowing I'm disappointing her, makes me want to lie down on the curb. "Will you go over there tonight? I don't want her going out alone. Just . . . show her a good time. No guys. Don't let other guys talk to her. Don't let them look at her. Please, D. I'll fucking owe you for the rest of my life."

"You already owe me." She curses. "I didn't

mean that, all right? We're even. Just come home and we'll go see Katie together."

Yearning twist in my belly. "Can't see her like this."

"Like what?"

I punch the door, scaring the dog walker passing by on the sidewalk. The dryness in my throat is getting more intense by the second, my back muscles straining. Maybe I should have seen this coming after denying myself too much too quick. Keeping the difficulty of stopping my vice on a dime to myself, locked up. Now it's breaking out and thirsty for blood. "Look, I have to go. Are you going to help me out or not?"

"Jack." I don't answer, just wait, my jaw ticking. "Fine. I'll go."

"Thank you."

I hang up and walk into a perfect combination of heaven and hell.

CHAPTER 16

Katie

J ack reaches out for me.

But then his hand pauses in midair and drops to his side.

There's a sharp object lancing my ribs, twisting, pushing deeper as he searches my face. Does he see my indecision? Can he tell I want to run, but the gravity of him is holding me in thrall? Even intoxicated, he's magnetic and beautiful. God, he's so beautiful. There's sadness swirling in the green of his eyes, taking the place of his usual mischief. His tall, muscled frame is somewhat hunched in on itself, but there's no doubt of his strength, even in this moment of utter weakness. Or maybe I'm the only one seeing it as weakness, because Jack's sensual mouth suddenly lifts into a devastating smile. It doesn't banish the lurking sadness, but I can see he's made a decision. A decision to brazen out the situation, instead of talking to me. Instead of making me understand.

Danika droops a little to my left, her arm unhooking from mine, as if she was hoping for something different. So was I. But what? I have no idea what I expect from Jack anymore. Maybe I was naive to expect anything in the first place, when I had a feeling all along there was a monster swimming beneath the surface. Waiting to rear its head.

Here is what I'm sure about. I'm not leaving Jack tonight. Tomorrow will be a time for hard decisions and even more difficult execution of those decisions, but with him standing right in front of me, I remember last night. Remember the care he took with me, how he put me at ease. Before we part ways, I can try to do the same for him.

"I know you don't do bars, Snaps. But, look. Honey. It's going to be fine, right?" He realizes there's still a cigar clamped in the side of his mouth and tosses it away. Then he goes searching for two stools, giving some male customers a hard time about not giving up their seats for ladies. They grumble about having to stand, but eventually gain their feet and Jack drags the stools over. Danika hops onto her seat, arms crisscrossed over her middle, but before I can do the same, Jack lifts me onto the creaky wood, smoothing hands over my clothes and running his fingers over my face, like he's unsure if I'm really there. "I'll play you a song, huh? Anything you want to hear. It'll be fine."

"Jack—"

"Van Morrison. He's Irish, right?" I start to protest again, but his expression turns imploring and I'm convinced there isn't a person alive who can deny Jack when he's like this. All cajoling and sweet and apologizing with his hands, his eyes. He's not an angry drunk. Not a belligerent one. He's the sad, soulful kind. A single nod is all I can manage, otherwise I might begin sobbing, and his head bows with relief. His gaze falls to my mouth like he's thinking of kissing me, wanting it badly, but he swallows, turns away and returns to the piano.

"Thanks for staying." Danika voice is rusted smoke. "I know you wanted to bail."

"I won't. Not until tomorrow."

She sucks in a breath. "It was a mistake to bring you here."

There's no answer for that, so I stay silent. Danika doesn't know about my brother. If she did, maybe she would sympathize. But I'm too rubbed raw to explain how much it hurts to be around Jack like this. How much it reminds me of what I've lost. Nothing good comes from drinking to excess, only bad decisions and pain. I won't subject myself to a fresh, daily delivery of mine.

As soon as Jack plays the opening notes of the song, I recognize *Astral Weeks* and I'm transported back to my parents' living room in Dublin. Watching them slow dance in front of the fireplace on Christmas Eve. Sharing an eye roll with Sean, even though both of us were secretly loving watching them behave like two lovesick fools. For a beat of time, the memory comforts me, but I don't want to be comforted. Not in a place like this. And not by Jack who is watching me closely over the top of the piano, half of his face obscured by the vodka bottle. It's too tempting to forgive his faults. To excuse his lie.

Suddenly I'm restless with the need to prove a point, even if the reasons are murky. I'm sad, I'm hurt, I feel like I've been duped into betraying my brother's memory. The only method I had for so long to keep Sean alive was staying away from alcohol. Keeping away from bars and drinking and reminders of people losing control of themselves. That abstinence was meant to honor him. As was this trip. Maybe what I decide to do next is completely arse backwards, but I need someone to understand the hurt. Need Jack to understand.

Taking a deep breath for courage, I turn to face the bar, happening to catch the bartender as he passes. "Excuse me. I'd like . . . a shot. Whiskey, please."

"She doesn't mean that," Danika says, having spun around at record speed. "We'll both have a Sprite."

"No," I say patiently. Sort of. "I'll have whiskey."

Danika pinches the bridge of her nose as the

bartender whistles under his breath and trundles a few feet away to fetch a glass. "Look, I get that I'm missing something here, but I know damn well that two drunk people are never better than one."

"What's going on?" Jack appears between us, his face turning the color of ash when the bartender sets down the shot of golden liquid in front of me. "Who is that for?"

"Me."

"Katie," he breathes, gripping the edges of the bar for balance. "Please, don't."

He makes a tortured noise as I drain the shot.

It's horrible. My eyes tear up and my throat screams like its scorched. There's also a gong of victory in the back of my mind that I hate. The hate doesn't stop me from wanting to hear it again. This is the ripple effect of bad decisions, isn't it? Jack lied to me, I went along with it like a besotted idiot, ignoring the warning signs. Am I drinking to punish myself for being stupid? That's part of it, yeah. I'm also punishing him for lying by making him watch the consequences with his own two eyes. I need him to understand pain. My pain.

It's more than Jack's lying that has me angry, though. His good time isn't always a good time for the people that care about him. Danika, me, his friends, his potential. Jesus, his potential is through the stupid roof and he's throwing it away. For what?

"Another one, please," I call to the amused barman.

"No. No more. Katie." Jack wraps his arms around my waist, burrowing his face into the crook of my neck and sawing his forehead back and forth. "I get it. I get it. Please, stop."

"Why? Why should I stop?"

"Because you're killing me."

A hole is punched in my defense, but I plug it with determination. "No, you're killing yourself. This is what it looks like from the other side."

Needing to distract myself from the colossal urge to hug him back, I dig American money out of my purse and lay it on the bar, exchanging it for the shot in front of me, plus the one I drank before. As soon as the man leaves with my bills in his hand, I toss back the second shot, my entire body vibrating with Jack's agonized shout. It echoes in my skull, making me wish I'd stopped after one. Even though he lied, even though he kept his problem from me, my whole body aches with his pain and I know. I know tomorrow is going to be excruciating.

I can't see Jack's face because it's turned into my neck, but my gaze catches Danika's and her leveled expression tells me I've done enough. Unshed tears shine in her eyes and it looks as if she wants to vanish through the floor.

"Let's go home," I say softly.

Jack yanks me off the stool into his arms, staggering some before getting his feet planted. I remain there limp, like a rag doll, being squeezed and admonished and apologized to, over and over, his hoarse voice making my throat hurt. There's a slight buzz moving along my blood, but I'm still stone-cold sober and I'm grateful for that. I'm even more grateful when we walk out of the bar, Jack's arm still keeping me plastered to his side, and hail the first cab we see.

Over. It's over, I think.

But the night is far from finished.

Jack

I can't go to sleep. Can't.

If I go to sleep with this much vodka in my system, I'll be passed out. Not sleeping.

Which means I won't wake up when Katie tries to leave.

She's going to leave, too. Even now, she's thinking about it. There's not a fucking doubt in my mind. And I'm not too drunk to be scared about waking up alone.

Danika escaped into her room the second we entered the apartment, leaving me to follow Katie through my kitchen like a scolded puppy. Ever since she took those shots of whiskey in the bar, I've been walking around with electrocuted bones. My brain hurts. Don't even get me started on the organ in my chest. It's beating like it already gave up on me, too.

Katie doesn't drink because of her brother. The way he died. But I drove her to break that personal code tonight. I reached into her life, her beautiful, noble convictions and turned the switches until they pointed at something negative. Destructive.

This incredible girl subjecting herself to the same vulnerability I have was unacceptable. I *know* alcohol abuse is an ugly thing. It blurs something ugly inside me, but watching it potentially blur the *beauty* in Katie? It was like being slapped by a wave of ice. I'm blurring my ugly, but I'm erasing anything that could grow in its place, too. I'm robbing myself of a life.

Too late, though. I'm seeing this all too goddamn late.

The lack of communication between me and Katie has my pulse ebbing out like low tide, until she hands me Advil and a glass of water. Then it goes wild like the crowd at a Yankees game after a grand slam.

I savor the action of taking the pills, knowing Katie gave them to me. "Thank you."

It's a feat, keeping my voice steady. Not running my words together. Focusing and answering when I'm addressed. Not repeating myself or rambling. But I have a lot of experience being drunk around sober people, so I've grown adept at appearing normal. I don't think Katie is buying it, though. She's looking right through me with those eyes, those eyes, those fucking gorgeous eyes I just want to keep on me. Keep them on me.

"Okay, Jack. I'll keep them on you," she murmurs, telling me I'd spoken out loud. "Come on. Let's get you to bed."

"Nope." God, why do I do this to myself? I can hear myself sounding like an absolute moron and there's no way to stop. "Nope, as soon as I'm asleep, you're going to climb down the fire escape or join the circus and I won't be able to find you."

Panic crashes in when she doesn't make a joke or even answer me.

We walk into my room and I attempt to see it through her eyes. Clothes draped over a single chair, full-sized IKEA bed with a red comforter, my Rat Pack bobbleheads. Nothing hanging up, apart from a picture of my mother, a couple of old street signs from Hell's Kitchen, a cracked mirror I can't remember breaking. An image of her perfectly packed suitcase of purses jumps to mind and I shake my head. "This isn't how I pictured my room looking when I imagined you here." I don't realize I've been attempting to unzip my jacket without success until Katie stops in front of me and completes the job in one efficient movement, easing the leather off my shoulders. "Sometimes I imagine you in a field of flowers, which . . . I don't even know what that looks like.

I think my brain hijacked it from a Ralph Lauren commercial."

She flashes me a somber look from beneath that crowd of eyelashes. "Whenever I picture you, I think of the day we met. You're walking away, telling me it's going to take a long time to forget my eyes."

My heart wrenches sideways. "It would have taken a long time after five minutes, Katie," I rasp. "Now it would take forever. Maybe longer."

"Can you sleep in this?" Katie says quickly, her attention on the ground. "In your jeans and shirt . . . ?"

The way she ignores me throwing my soul at her feet makes the small talk pointless. A waste of time when I need to be figuring out how to fix what I broke. If she'll let me. She shouldn't let me. I'm praying she does. "I'm so sorry about tonight." I reach for her, but she steps away, wrecking me. "How bad have I fucked up?"

"It's not about fucking up, Jack." She stops to glance at the picture of my mother, before swinging her quiet focus back to me. "It's just that our broken parts only make the damage in one another worse."

"No." I shake my head, kicking up a round of resented dizziness. "Jesus, Katie. You couldn't damage me any more than I am. Not even if you tried."

"I tried to tonight." Regret lines her pretty face. "I drank that whiskey to hurt you."

"Because I hurt you first." Throbbing begins down the center of my skull, like it has cracked down the middle. "I lied to you. I broke my promise and no amount of shit in my head is an excuse for that."

"What shit?"

My ears ring from shouting. I press my lips together tight to keep everything from spilling out. I breathe through my nose to calm myself down so we can have a conversation that doesn't end in me making things worse, but it doesn't work. How can I be calm when I'm losing this girl? My girl. A direct result of my actions. How long did I really think I could get away with lying to her? Lying to myself had been easy for so long, but with the ultimate failure staring me in the face, the full magnitude of what I could lose is pounding down on me like a violent storm.

I can feel rationality slipping from my hands. The vodka's heat is still kissing my insides, too, trying to give me the false sense that I'm dreaming. That this can't be real. Blackness is starting to creep along my edges, like a siren's song, luring me to close my eyes and forget everything until tomorrow. I've done it so many nights. It won't work this time, though. As soon as I'm conscious, my reality will be without her. Hang on. Hang in there.

Sex. Can I fix this with sex? God knows something inside me was healed when I woke up this morning, before I was ripped wide open again.

What if I just remind her? Maybe clearing one another's minds will hit a reset button and tomorrow I can work on making sure tonight never happens again. Even with alcohol fueling me, I'm aware this is a desperate move. An ironic one. I got tanked tonight because of something physical that happened when I was eighteen, now I'm trying to fix things between me and Katie with more sex. Those memories have no place in the same room with my girl, but Christ, I'll try anything.

Almost too ashamed to meet her eyes, I pull off my shirt and start to work on my belt. The same belt she unfastened last night with her perfect fingers. This. Right here. This is everything about sex that never applied to us. To Katie. It's false, it's using my looks to distract from everything else underneath. She asked me about the shit I've got stored in my head, but I'm asking her to fuck instead. To forget about what's real. The polar opposite of what we've been doing since we met. Here I am, though. Willing to dance with the devil to keep her.

"Jack, stop."

Too bad her voice ripples with heat and I keep going. Easing my zipper down an inch and letting her see I'm hard. Gripping the flesh that tents my jeans. "Still yours. Always yours."

She backs up a step, tripping over a shoe and I lunge, grabbing her elbow to make sure she doesn't fall. I'm so fucked up, though, I stumble sideways and hit the wall. Thank God I manage to turn and accept the impact with my shoulder, leaving Katie unhurt. She looks hurt, though, breathing heavily and staring up at me from in the cradle of my arms.

"You'll let me kiss you, Snaps." I trace my knuckles down her cheek. "Won't you?"

My brain mistakes her silent stillness for an opening. I dip my mouth, but she shakes her head before I can claim her lips. "I . . . no." She's out of my arms like a shot. "I can smell it. I'll be able to taste it. I don't want to remember kissing you like this."

Remember me. She's going to need to remember me, because I'll never get another chance to kiss her. The end. It's curtains. Before I can fall, I stagger forwards and drop onto the bed, holding on to my knees to stay upright. "Oh God, Katie. What if you need me while I'm passed out and I can't fucking wake up?" I cradle my head in my hands, gripping my temples hard enough to feel pain. "I never . . . I hadn't thought of that. I don't think I would have drank tonight if I'd thought of it like that."

She lays a hand on my shoulder and calm tries to sweep through my body. "I'll be fine, Jack. I won't need you."

I mentally bat the comfort away. "I want you to need me."

Even though I can't see her face, I can feel her

eyelids crash down. "I'll stay until you wake up, okay?"

"If I could think of one damn reason why you would do that, I might believe you."

Katie sighs and I sense her moving about the room behind me. I turn slightly to find her digging in my training bag, removing my pair of handcuffs. She slaps one end onto her wrist and hooks the opposite metal brace to my headboard. Relief is a fluffy cloud wrapping around me as I fall forwards, our heads lying side by side on the pillow. I'm too grateful and intoxicated to be horrified by the irony of keeping someone in my bed, probably against her will. Tomorrow it will hit me, though. It'll hit me in the gut like a sledgehammer.

"I'm sorry, Katie."

"I know. Me, too." She glides a hand down my face, closing my eyes with her fingertips on the descent. When I can no longer see her, I have a stabbing flash of panic, but the blackness swallows it, along with her golden voice. "Goodnight, Jack."

CHAPTER 17
Katie

I stare down at the hotel phone where it sits, the receiver still warm from being pressed between my ear and shoulder.

"Holy shite."

Perhaps those shots of whiskey two days ago were reckless and stupid, but being totally impulsive—even for just a brief speck of time—may have inspired an epiphany. After my training session at the academy this morning, I made a phone call to a ladies' fashion boutique in the East Village and made an appointment to stop by with some purse samples. Surely I'm going mad, cold-calling some fancy New York shop without a proper introduction or electronic communication beforehand, but it would appear, however, my accent is something of a commodity in the States. Brilliant. I'm not going to split hairs.

Not now when I'm gagging for something good to happen. I need *something*. My morning was filled with tortured glances from Jack across the firing range and I can't sit down, stand up or focus in the wake of them.

I woke up an hour before Jack yesterday morning—Monday—my bladder screaming at me, my head pounding from the whiskey and tears I'd finally let fall after he passed out. When he jackknifed on the bed beside me, shouting my name—*KATIE!*—they threatened to begin coursing down my cheeks all over again, but I managed to lay there quietly while Jack retrieved the handcuff key and set me free. He sat on the edge of the bed, his head buried in his hands as I left, neither one of us able to find an appropriate goodbye.

That's what I reckoned it was, anyway. Goodbye.

His shadowed eyes said anything *but* goodbye this morning, though. The apology in them was blatant, but I already lost two days to wallowing over what happened in the bar. I can't spare any more time wondering if I acted harshly. If he misses me in the fierce, rather dramatic way I can't seem to stop missing him.

Or if he's all right.

He didn't seem all right after all those drinks.

It was as though the Jack I'd come to know had gone into hiding. Stopped trying. Or he'd been catapulted back to day one when we met and sex was all he could offer me. In lieu of words. Honesty. But . . . when he left me Sunday morning, that wasn't the case. Did something happen? Whatever the opposite of closure is, that's what I've got. I can't help but think I missed something important.

Pushing up from the desk, I cross with a purposeful step to my suitcase of handbags and unzip it to reveal the rainbow contents. My trip is fast approaching its end and I have yet to cross a major item off my adventure list. Selling a bag. Will that actually change today?

This afternoon is about something very important I need to prove to myself. I have free will. I have dreams. They don't coincide with my father's—not anymore—but they're important nonetheless. Allowing something I love as much as crafting bags to be inconsequential would mean letting myself down and I won't do that. Jack sidetracked me for a while, but he's no longer absorbing all my focus. Or he *shouldn't* be, rather. Maybe getting out and doing something positive for myself will distract me from thoughts of him.

Where will I find a distraction from thinking of Jack back in Dublin? The sights and sounds of the Olympic arena infiltrate, the feel of the rifle bag on my shoulder, but I shake them off. That's not a decision for today.

Refocusing on my bags, Jack's voice drifts from the ether into my ears, pausing my reach for a blue clutch in midair. *I'll buy all of them right now. Just give me a couple hours to sing on the subway.*

"Dammit, Jack," I whisper, forcing measured breaths. Choosing carefully as possible with the specter of Jack in the room, I withdraw a navy blue handbag, white-and-cream, plus a clutch with some creative gold stitching on the front. I place them carefully in the small tote bag I saved from knickers shopping the other day and leave the room. Hoping it will temporarily clear my head of an unrelenting pirate smile, I quiz the front desk clerk about how to catch the new Second Avenue subway downtown and twenty minutes later, find myself climbing aboveground at the Houston stop.

"Now for the hard part," I murmur, checking my written directions. The current of brisk-paced New Yorkers tangles around me, but I finally get moving in the direction of the shop. It's up ahead with a smart, subtle red awning and with mere, tension-riddled moments to go, I review my goals. Do I want them to make a large order for bags? No, of course not. I don't have near enough inventory to fulfill a massive order. Even *thinking* about such an outcome is getting well ahead of myself. What I'm hoping for is the following: some sort of confirmation that I'm not chasing some silly dream of being a part-time handbag designer when I'm not up to par. If I could only convince the owner to test them with her clients, I would be happy. A baby step.

I'm reaching for the door handle when a loud collection of notes goes off in my bag. It takes me a few breaths to realize my phone is ringing, since I've only been turning it on to make calls home to Dublin. But when I check the screen and see it's my father, I answer right away, hoping nothing is the matter. My father is the one that called to tell me Sean had died, and I still haven't quite beaten the cold, polarizing trickle that hits me whenever he rings.

"How are you keeping, Da?"

"Fine and yourself?"

His jovial response makes me relax. "Grand." I look down at the bag dangling from my fingers, cream, navy and white winking up at me. "Just out for a walk."

I hear my mother fussing in the background, spoons clinking like they're having an evening cup of tea. "Was something the matter?" I keep my tone light. "We only spoke this morning."

"Are you sick of us from three thousand miles away?" My mom's giggle is muffled, but I hear it and can't help but smile. They've always been one another's biggest fans when they're not having a bickering session. "Sure, that must be some kind of record."

"No, of course not." I back up against the building to let a group of people pass. "I was only making sure nothing was the matter."

"Fine enough." There's a long pause and I imagine him taking a long sip of his tea. "After we hung up this morning, I called over to the facility."

"Why?" The sharp question is out of my mouth and snatched up by the wind before I realize I've spoken. The "facility" is a shorthand way of referring to the Irish Institute of Sport in Dublin, where I—along with dozens of Olympians—trained prior to Rio. "I mean, was there something going on or—"

"Nothing specific." We've spent so much time together, I know when he's testing me, deciding how much to say. Maybe the distance separating us is the reason he goes for broke. "They've announced the date for the Olympic trials. It's a fair bit away, but you know how those years go by in a blink."

Not for me. They dragged like sloths crossing the road. While stuck to glue traps. Silence passes while the foot traffic around me blurs into a carousel of colors. "Please, Da. Why are you telling me this?"

"They're opening the facility to hopefuls in the coming months. You've upped the standard, Katie. Resting on our laurels isn't an option if we want to be contenders come Tokyo. They're going to throw everything they've got at us." He rushes on before I can respond. "I know you were having misgivings about training again, but we don't have to pack the schedule as tight this time around. You've got the job now. But we could work around it."

That's how it starts. Just a weekend at the range, here and there. Until cracks in my technique require more time, more fine-tuning. Before long, it's a seven-day-a-week obsession with being the best. Neglecting everything else, particularly the outside world. And never once, not once, talking about why my father's drive is at full volume. Sean. "I don't want to work around it," I say, louder than intended. "I'm done. We . . . we talked about it and I'm *done*."

"At least take some time to have a think about it." His hurt is tangible through the phone. "I didn't realize training with me was such a hardship."

"It's not. I never said that."

"It was implied." His laughter is flat, a little desperate. "You know it means the world to me, Katie. I'll go mad stuck in the house."

My scream is internal but loud. Fingers tightening into a painful fist around my bag, I do a quick mental count to ten, visions of my father's devastation after his son's death passing by like a funeral procession behind my eyes. "I'm sorry." I swallow hard. "I will. I'll think about it."

When we hang up a moment later, my hand lifts to open the dress shop door, but drops before it can close around the black metal. The future doesn't seem as open as it did on the ride downtown. It doesn't feel like mine. Maybe my future doesn't belong solely to me. Am I being selfish wishing it did? Does it make me a bad daughter?

Looking down at my phone, I have a dizzying urge to call Jack, but I manage to push it aside, worried that in my state of mind I would use him for comfort and regret leading him on afterwards. Still, I imagine him walking beside me, keeping me tucked into his side, and it manages to be just enough to keep me moving.

Nonetheless, I walk back to the train with the bags clutched to my chest, the weight on my shoulders growing heavier with each step.

Jack

How did I go from the master of random hookups to a stalker in less than two weeks?

I'm sitting in the lobby of Katie's hotel trying to pinpoint the exact moment my DNA was swapped for someone else's, but it's not helping. Fuck no, it's only making things worse. Because a revolving door of scenes from the last two weeks are having a goddamn party behind my eyelids, which are swollen from lack of sleep. Katie telling me about her brother, glowing in the morning sunlight, taking a picture of the recruits for her Instagram, peeling off her dress, beaming up at the waiter, swaying across from me on the subway.

I'm wrecked. Since I took up my post on a bench in the hotel lobby an hour ago, two people have asked me if I'm okay. I can't even remember if I answered them or just stared into space like some lobotomized creature from a horror film. The fact that my hands are shaking doesn't help, I'm sure. They won't stop and I'm too exhausted to push them into my pockets, so screw it. Here they are, everyone. Proof I have a sickness.

Somehow I've managed to stay off the bottle since Katie bailed yesterday morning. No, sorry, since Katie was *released* yesterday morning. Knowing I would see her at the academy helped me cross the mile marker to this morning, but it turns out, seeing Katie and not speaking to her or touching her was almost worse than staying away. I'm craving a drink so bad, the pressure in my chest is growing unbearable. As soon as I take a sip, that tightening knot in my chest will loosen, so the temptation is huge. Every city block in Manhattan seems to have a bar. I passed a good dozen on the way here. They're *everywhere*.

Where is Katie? Logically, I know she's not upstairs with someone else, but the lack of sleep and alcohol is doing funny things to my common sense. Like telling it to go fuck itself. If she's met someone or agreed to a date, I'm going to rip this place to shreds. I know it like I know my own name.

I suck in a long breath and push it out, forcing myself to calm down. Causing a scene is not why I'm here, but in order to accomplish what I came for, I need to see Katie. God, I just want to see her so bad without the academy walls surrounding us.

When she finally walks into the lobby, I swear my mind is playing tricks on me. But, no . . . no, the closer she gets, I can smell mint and need rains down on me like a waterfall. Not need for sex, although it's right there under the surface. This need is for contact, though. Being close. Absorbing her truth and honesty. Reminding myself at one time she thought I could be more than the academy's resident slacker with vodka on his breath.

"Jack," Katie breathes, slowing to a stop five feet from where I'm standing. "What are you doing here?"

Trying to be near you any way I can. "I, uh . . ." I stand and finally manage to bury my hands in my pockets, but I can't tell anymore if they're shaking from alcohol or Katie withdrawals. Around me, the lobby seems to animate after moving in slow motion for an hour. Like she brought it to life. My fingernails dig into my palms to stop from reaching out to brush her hair back. "I haven't had a chance to talk to you. There's something I need to say."

She doesn't come any closer, but I sense she's wishing for escape. "Whatever it is . . . maybe you could let it go for now?"

There's a hint of a plea in her voice and for the first time since she walked in, I notice her eyes are red, her lips patterned with teeth marks. "What's wrong?" I move forwards without thinking. "You've been upset. Did something happen to you?"

"No."

"Katie."

"I promise," she whispers, holding my gaze. "I'm fine."

My feet move all by themselves, carrying me closer like she's a force of gravity. "That makes one of us."

"I can't do this now." Misery ripples across her expression. "I'm trying really hard to ignore how rotten I feel and I can't do that when you're *looming.*"

And shit, I am looming. I'm right up in her space, trying to inhale her, with no memory of coming so close. I start to back up a pace, but blue leather peeks out at me from the bag she's holding, grabbing my attention. Right away, I recognize the purses and a rock sinks in my stomach. Oh Jesus Christ. This is what torture feels like. Not being able to scoop her up into my arms, carry upstairs and let her cry into my neck. Being stripped of that right. "Ah, honey. What happened with your purses?" She gathers the bag to her chest, but doesn't answer. I can tell she's reluctant about sharing what happened with me, but those denim eyes track up to mine like she can't help but seek comfort and fuck, my heart kick starts with a sense of purpose. "Strike one doesn't mean you're out, Katie. They're amazing. You can see . . ." I tamp down the impulse to kiss her forehead. "You can look at those purses and see how much thought went into them. Someone is going to bite or I'll walk down Broadway in a fucking dress."

Laughter tilts her eyes at the corners, but doesn't leave her mouth. "I appreciate your confidence, but I didn't even go far enough to get rejected." Her shoulders bunch. "I guess you could say I chickened out."

"You won't next time. I won't let you. Same way you didn't let me chicken out of doing that demonstration."

Warmth flares in her expression a split second before she shuts it down. And I curse myself for making the implication that I'll have the privilege of helping her get through anything. My words put an invisible distance between us, impenetrable enough to make me panic. Panic about what, though? She's not available to me anymore. It's in the way she steps back, rolling her lips inwards, the picture of someone searching for a way out of an awkward encounter. "If there was something you wanted to say . . ."

"Yeah," I say, pushing through the rust in my throat. "Yeah, I've already apologized for what happened at the bar Sunday night. There's really nothing I can say that's good enough. But I was too fucked up over you leaving in the morning to say I'm sorry for . . . the handcuffing, Katie. I should *not* have let you do that. I shouldn't have been relieved when you did it." My hands slide out of my pockets and I barely stop myself from reaching for her. "I'm sorry, honey. I'm sorry I kept you somewhere you didn't want to be."

"I forgive you." I swear she's staring at me without breathing, like a mathematician trying to work out long division. "I'm sorry I drank that whiskey in front of you."

"Don't be," I say louder than planned, stepping back into her space. Christ, I can't help it. My heart misses being pressed up against hers. But she'll run if I grab hold, so I stop short of embracing her. She needs to hear this. I need her to understand what I'm starting to realize myself. A reality check that has been a long time in coming. "I never thought about anyone but myself and my own bullshit before when I drank. You helped changed that. I see what my friends see now. What *you* see. And it's . . . shit, Katie. I need to change."

For a second, I think she's going to cave. Her features are soft, her gravity inviting. She wants to give me another chance. But the elevator dinging behind me—or maybe a memory from Sunday night—seems to break her of the trance, jerking her back. "That's good, Jack." Like a whisper moving through the air, she goes past me. "I wish you the best of luck. You know I do."

Needing to give her the same reassurance, even in the face of my disappointment, I hold the elevator open with a hand. "Next time. You'll find someone who loves those purses."

"Or you'll wear a dress," she murmurs. "Don't forget that bit."

Claws sink into my heart. "I won't."

"Bye, Jack."

"Bye, Snaps."

When the elevator door closes, I *feel* her moving farther and farther away. The lobby starts to move in slow motion around me again and the absence of Katie makes the cravings noticeable once again, my neck and chest tightening, my tongue dry. She's right. She's right to run away from this. Not only because I'm a reminder of her brother's life being taken, but . . . it's possible I need her too much. Katie was the one to show me my own reflection, but now that I know the image I project back to the world, my recovery has to be up to *me*.

Clarity hurts like a bitch right now, but it's a cop-out to deep drowning memories at the bottom of a bottle. I don't want to make excuses for myself anymore. I definitely don't want to be seen as a liability to the people who care about me. Now that I'm conscious of what I've been doing, continuing the same way would be inexcusable.

Where the fuck do I start, though?

My sense memory kicks in and I recall the feeling of being in the firing range. The calm, collected process of aiming, focusing, feeling in control. If I could feel that sensation right now, if I could be assured of my own capabilities, it could get me through this one day. I'd worry about tomorrow when the sun came up again.

I snag my cell out of my pocket and dial Charlie.

"Hey, man." Taking one last look at the elevator, I back towards the street. "You want to kill a couple hours at the range?"

CHAPTER 18

Katie

Tuesday afternoon is not the final time Jack shows up in the hotel lobby, but it's the last time we exchange words, apart from basic instructions during firearms training. He's usually there around dinnertime when I pop out to find food. Sitting on the same bench with hands clasped between his knees, he waits until I'm safely inside the elevator, his eyes gobbling me up like his own evening meal, before getting up to leave.

He always maintains his distance, never approaching me or following me to my room. Sometimes I manage to have tunnel vision, staring straight ahead at the elevator, but I slip every so often. I slip because I miss him. Because I want to tell him pressure to commit to the Olympics mounts every time my father calls. Even when he doesn't mention it, the issue sits between us like a thousand-pound gorilla, creating awkward silences and stilted goodbyes. Jack would say just the right thing to make me laugh, wouldn't he? Whenever I get weak and consider ringing him, though, I think of Sean. I rekindle my pain on purpose. And I end the call.

During my three training sessions at the academy this week, Jack's rapt attention rode over my skin like little trolleys, making me lose concentration midsentence, throwing me off my game. If he would just be bossy and resentful, I could start moving on. But he's being Jack and respecting my space, letting me know that he's there if I need him.

It's hard for him to maintain his distance—that's quite easy to tell. More than once, I've noticed his white-knuckled fists when I pass him in the gymnasium or during a session. There's a massive part of me that wants to forget he has a problem that directly clashes with the way I've chosen to live. I'm afraid I'm upsetting him to the point he'll drink even more than usual and get hurt. Or hurt someone else. That possibility keeps me wide-awake at night.

Fact is, though, I'm leaving anyway. Today is Thursday and I'm leaving on Sunday.

This moving on process was always inevitable. But even though I haven't talked to Jack since Tuesday afternoon, the idea of never seeing him again has my stomach scraped hollow. Aching. How long will it remain like this? I miss him. I miss his hands on me, his piggyback rides, his winks. His heart. He was just starting to expose it to me. Now I'll never know what's written there and I loathe it. I loathe missing out on Jack.

Furthermore, I loathe others not being aware of his potential. My mind is blown by how much he continues to improve during my training. His technique is natural and bordering on flawless, in a way that took me years to achieve. And while I know I can't recommend him for ESU—being aware of his issue—there is no way I'm walking out of here without someone being aware that they've got potential greatness in their midst.

My chest aches with responsibility as I sit down across from Lieutenant Burns. He nods to let me know he's aware of my presence, but his pencil continues to scratch across the papers in front of him. Good. It gives me time to gather my bearings after passing Jack in the hallway, walking in between Danika and Charlie. He'd stopped and turned to watch me go by and I couldn't help glancing back. Thank God today is my last day at the academy. It's getting too hard to stay away.

"Ms. McCoy." Burns drops his pencil, stopping it from rolling with a single finger. "It has been a pleasure having you aboard. I trust your final session went well."

"Yes." I flip open the file folder on my lap, keeping the flaps in place with my elbows. "I'm sure it will come as no surprise that I've decided to recommend your brother, Charlie Burns, for consideration as an ESU candidate. Although I feel obligated to point out, he's receiving my vote based on his own merit. Not his name."

"Of course. Noted." Pride makes the lieutenant momentarily gorgeous—highlighting looks I hadn't noticed before. But I can only compare them to green eyes and a pirate smile. "ESU isn't part of his career trajectory, but I'm sure he'll be thrilled to know he has options."

I nod, well aware that Charlie Burns is being groomed for greatness. It's impossible to miss the hero worship in his fellow recruits' eyes whenever he's in the vicinity. But lately I've noticed that admiration directed at Jack, too. He doesn't seem to notice it, which makes the silence between us all the more difficult, because I want to point it out. Want to watch him become aware of the changes he's inspired with his own hard work. He's *earned* those changes.

Swallowing hard, I pass my report across the desk into the lieutenant's waiting hands. When he stands and extends his hand for a shake, however, I remain seated. "There's another recruit I wanted to speak with you about."

Burns returns to his chair, steepling his fingers in front of his mouth. "Really."

Something about the way he drops the single word makes me wonder if the attention Jack pays me hasn't gone unnoticed. "Yes. Really." I lift my chin. "If my recommendation were based solely on firearm proficiency, I would be giving you Jack Garrett's name."

The derisive curl of his lips prods like metal spikes. "You'll excuse me if I have a hard time believing that."

"Believe it." I refuse to look away, no matter how intimidating the lieutenant is becoming, second by second. "If his . . . temperament were better suited for ESU, I would encourage him to begin training with their department as soon as he graduates."

"His temperament?" Burns laughs without humor. "Let's not dance around the truth, McCoy. He's not fit to wear a uniform. At the earliest opportunity, he's going to throw it all away in grand fucking fashion. All we can do is sit back and watch him flame out."

My body is shaking as I come to my feet. "Shame on you, then." He has the grace to lose the smirk. "Shame on you for letting a talent like that slip past because he didn't have the same advantages you or your brother were afforded."

"You don't know a damn thing about us," he returns coldly, leaning forwards.

"Fair enough." We trade glares for a few beats. His is impressive, I'll give him that. If I were a perpetrator, I'd be babbling about calling a lawyer right about now. But I've been to the bloody Olympics and won a medal, so he can shove that stony glare right up his hole. "Jack Garrett is good. Do you hear me? Yes, he has some personal problems. But if someone took an interest in him and actually encouraged him—which is *your* job, I might add—I think he could be heroic."

"My job isn't to single out bright shiny stars, McCoy. My job is to conform these men into team players. Groom them for something larger than themselves. Lone wolves get their fellow officers killed, the way *my* partner was killed, and that's exactly what Jack Garrett is. A lone wolf with no respect. And I have no respect for him."

A sound to my left has me whirling around. Danika stands just inside the door, mouth dropped open, horror radiating from her tense frame. Her glittering eyes are trained squarely on Burns. I turn back just in time to watch defeat etch itself in his features. And yearning. Jesus. The yearning for Danika is so intense, she must feel it. If she does, however, what she overheard might have put her outside the lieutenant's reach, if she wasn't there already. Her loyalty is to Jack and I'm so grateful for that fact, I press my lips together to keep a sound from escaping.

"We're ready for sprints." Danika's voice is choked. "I wasn't sure if I should come get you. I didn't know you were in a meeting—" The door handle creaks in her grip. "Actually, you know something? Fuck you, Lieutenant."

The door rattles on its hinges with the force of her slam.

A deafening cheer goes wild inside me. Had

I really spent a single second being jealous of Danika? Thank God Jack has her in his life. That he'll have her as a friend when I'm gone. But . . . it wasn't enough before, was it? Friendship wasn't enough to shake him up or change his path before. Could I have been enough if I'd stuck it out?

If I'd stuck it out. I'd done the opposite, hadn't I? Ran out the door like a coward as soon as the key turned in the handcuffs. Had Jack predicted I would react that way? Is that why he kept his problem a secret? Well, I proved him right. I quit. He needs help right now and I'm sitting here with my neatly typed report, nothing but self-righteousness to keep me company.

What would Sean say? Knowing I pushed away a flawed, but wonderful man in his name? Would he be proud of me or . . . disappointed?

With Greer's disparaging words about Jack still ringing in the room, I realize I'm no better than the lieutenant. I might have let Jack down easier than Greer ever would, but I let him—and myself—down. I gave up on someone I like. A lot.

Someone I damn well know wouldn't have given up on me, if our roles were reversed.

At that moment, the screensaver pops up on the lieutenant's computer screen, a panoramic view of the New York City skyline, which fades into a picture of Grand Central Station. A moving image of Jack carrying me on his back, smiling over his shoulder and pointing out the landmark station on our way to the train catches me off guard and I know. I know it's another sign. How many have I ignored over the last four days?

"Excuse me," I murmur, following Danika's path out the door. She's nowhere to be seen as I jog down the hallway towards the gymnasium. When I round the corner into the bright, artificial lights, every head swivels in my direction, but there's only one recruit I'm interested in speaking with. And of course, I find him in the crowd with no effort, because I can feel him, watching me with his heart in his eyes.

"Jack Garrett." I clear the rust from my tone. "Can I speak with you a moment?"

This morning, I would not have been so brazen as to ask to see Jack alone in front of everyone. But I've just turned in my final report, meaning I'm no longer his instructor. Also, my head of steam is so strong, my indignation over Burns's assessment of Jack so mighty, I don't think I'd give a right fuck either way. Without waiting for a response, I sail out the back entrance of the gymnasium, which leads to a sliver of space between the academy building and the tenement next door.

I'm pacing for only a split second before Jack exits the gymnasium, concern lining his insanely handsome face. Concern. For me. Even though I counted him out and acted so typically.

There's something special inside this man. I feel it all over. He needs to feel it, too.

There's no second-guessing my actions as I take two giant steps and leap into Jack's arms, crossing my ankles at his back. I catch the flash of shocked joy on his face . . . and then there's just the long slow melt that follows. Jack's kiss. How did I survive without his mouth on mine for so long? It's total and complete magic, his masculine lips pushing mine open on an awed groan, his feet carrying us back, back, until I'm pressed against the brick wall. Without trying, he's the most sexual being on planet Earth, but there's more now. There's the reality that being apart from one another was like being inflicted daily by painful wounds.

Supporting me with his hips, Jack's forearms settle against the wall, on either side of my head. His mouth slants across mine, eager and . . . cautious. Yes, cautious. I can tell he's afraid to hope. I can taste it on his tongue.

He pulls away, eyes squeezed shut, his breath laboring against my forehead. "What made you want me again?"

My thumbs smooth along the curves of his ears. "I didn't stop."

A hoarse sound leaves him. Our lips meet with increased desperation, Jack's lower body pressing tight into the notch of my thighs, his tongue exploring deeper, more thoroughly. There's a low, rumbling growl building inside him, all for me. His big chest is heaving so hard, so fast, it's hampering my ability to breathe. I don't care, though. Not with his stubble scoring my chin, his fingers tracing the edge of my face. Gentle mixed with rough.

I need to care, though. There's a reason I came out here. As much as I want to let the heated moment carry me away, there's a battle to win. A battle for Jack. And we need to be on the same side. We need to fight for him together.

With an incredible effort, I force our mouths apart, taking a moment to catch my breath as green eyes devour me. "Do you still want to be with me? Until I go back to Ireland?"

His disbelief could not be any clearer. "Jesus, you have to ask me that, Katie? I've been living in your hotel lobby since Tuesday just hoping you'll look at me." He strokes my hair with unsteady hands. "I want every second I can get. You know I do."

"Okay." I swallow my nerves. "Okay, then we're going to a meeting."

Stillness creeps over him. "A meeting."

I nod, searching his face for a readable reaction. "I would have recommended you to Burns, Jack. For ESU. I wanted to do it so badly, because you're the best I've trained. You've gotten even better practicing on your own, haven't you?" His Adam's apple lodges beneath his jaw, eyes flickering, but he doesn't respond. "You're going to do it the hard way. Graduate, push through the ranks, take the test when you're ready. And I know you can do it. You're going to get better first—and then you're going to prove yourself. I believe in you."

"Why?" he rasps, pressing a kiss to my mouth. Another. "Why, Katie?"

"Sometimes we're afraid to try, thinking we won't be enough." I hear the hypocrisy in that statement, remembering my failed attempt to sell my bags, but I stubbornly focus on Jack. "But you *are* enough. You're *more*. More than alcohol. More than sex." I think back to the night he slipped up. His reluctance to open up. *No amount of shit in my head is an excuse for that.* "Whatever is going on inside you . . . whatever brought on Sunday night . . ." His body tenses against mine, confirming my belief that I'd missed something important. "Let's take care of it. Get rid of it. It's blocking the best that's yet to come. Okay? I'm Irish and stubborn and I refuse to be wrong. I'm not wrong about you, Jack."

It seems to take forever for his gaze to circle back around to mine, but when it does, the combination of beauty and fear there is so breathtaking, my heart lifts and squeezes. "All right, Snaps. Let's go to a meeting."

CHAPTER 19

— Jack —

Concentrating on drills for the remainder of the day is impossible.

By some stroke of blind luck, I have Katie back. Until Sunday, anyway. I'll cross that bridge when I come to it, though. Right now, I'm floating around like a hot air balloon, waving at bluebirds as we all sail through an endless row of clouds. I've never changed faster than I am right now, standing in front of my locker. Water soaks into my fresh clothes because I barely took the time to towel off after my warp-speed shower. Charlie stands a few feet away in a towel, shaking his head. He's happy for me, but it's a cautious happiness.

Danika looked at me the same way when I returned to the gym after kissing the stuffing out of

Katie. God. God, I don't think I'd taken a satisfying breath until her lips touched mine. Not since the last time we spoke. Hell, maybe even before that. The last time I *held* her without alcohol fogging my brain. Not only does Katie forgive me for fucking up . . . she *believes* in my ability to not do it again. To take this ability of mine and do something positive. Her words, her confidence are still echoing in my head on a loop.

My own confidence has been building slowly, like a stoked fire, since I took back control of my actions. Instead of numbing myself out in a bar, I spent the last couple of days honing my skill in the range, even helping out some of the recruits who wanted to put in extra hours. It felt great, not only proving to myself that I could remain sober on my own, but witnessing improvements in my technique, seeing the fruits of both labors paying off.

Am I shitting my pants over admitting to a room full of strangers that I have a problem? You're goddamn right I am. There's even a small, insistent part of me that still doesn't want to admit alcohol is my own personal devil. Doesn't want to roll over. But something happened down deep inside me when Katie told me I had something to offer the world. A pebble-sized object began a slow roll in my mind, my heart, my stomach and it snowballed into something I think might be hope. God knows I never thought I'd make it this far in the academy. Yet here I am, a few weeks from graduating. I'm going to be an NYPD police officer. When Katie tells me I'm talented, that I have a skill not many people can claim, I trust her.

Trusting myself is going to be the difficult part. But hey. A year ago, it would have been impossible. Steps. It's going to be a series of steps. The ground is shaking under my feet right now, but I'm going to try to be what Katie sees. What I want to see myself become. Moving forwards at the department without Katie beside me isn't something I want to consider at the moment, so I'm focusing only on tonight. On getting out of this locker room and wrapping my girl in these arms. They ache for her.

"So." Charlie steps into his jeans. "Big plans for tonight?"

I'm not ready to tell anyone I'm going to a meeting. Probably won't be for a while. Mentally, I realize it's nothing to be ashamed of, but I want to make sure attending on the regular is something I can follow through on before getting anyone's hopes up. "Uh. Big plans? You could say that."

"You're slipping, man. That was a perfect opening for a dick joke."

"Shit, you're right. Rain check?"

"Yeah."

I drop onto the bench and shove my feet into boots. My mind is set on getting out of there fast as possible, spending every available moment with Katie, but something else has been prickling at my neck for hours. "Hey, do me a solid, Charlie boy?" I glance towards the locker room door, continuing to lace my boots. "Check on Danika for me. Something was off with her today."

"Why don't you check on her?"

"We're not talking right now."

"I sensed a disturbance in the Force. She's been hiding out in her room all week." He shoots me a curious look. "What's up?"

"Good fucking question." My best friend and I are complicated people. Putting into words what makes us tick is next to impossible. It probably has something to do with her being a woman and me being a man, but I'll leave that conclusion to the experts. "She brought Katie to find me Sunday night. And she knew the condition I would be in."

Charlie whistles between his teeth, falling onto the bench beside me.

"Here's my stab at an explanation." With a sigh, I kick my locker door shut. "I'm not upset at Danika. I put her in a shitty spot, right? But she thinks I should be upset. Or that I am. So she's playing offense and getting pissed at me first, for being pissed off at her. Should I continue or do you want to stab yourself in the eye yet?"

"Stab. Eye."

"That's what I thought." Chuckling over the far-off expression on Charlie's face, I zip up my gym bag and check the clock. Katie is meeting me down the block in five minutes and a combination of nerves and anticipation tumble in my gut. "When you're raised in a four-bedroom apartment by a constant rotation of women, certain things begin to make sense, even when they damn well shouldn't."

My friend considers me a moment. "When Ever and I were going through our breakup . . ." He stops to cross himself, shivering as he completes the action. "Your advice was terrible. You told me to go out and find another girl. Now you're the fucking love guru?"

"Maybe I was just trying to help you realize there was no other girl." I tap my temple. "Ever think of that?"

"Apparently living with women schooled you on mind games, too." He sounds disgusted with me. "Good thing I realized Ever was it for me or I'd still be moping around on the locker room's shower floor."

It's my turn to shiver. "That reminds me, have you gotten tested for tuberculosis yet?"

"Ha." Charlie looks suddenly grim. "Yeah, I'll check on Danika for you. Right after I figure out what's wrong with my brother."

I check the surrounding area to make sure no one is around listening. "Unfortunately, those two things are probably related."

"Fuck." Charlie drops his face into his hands. "I thought I was the only one who noticed Greer checking Danika out. All the damn time. I was hoping I imagined it."

"Nope." I stand up, throwing my duffel bag over my shoulder. "Your brother has it bad."

"This is not going to end well."

"Make sure it never starts." I give Charlie a rare, serious look. "She might come across like she'll eat a dude alive, but she's actually a wimp."

"I heard that," Danika says from the locker room entrance. Clearly not giving a shit about walking into the male domain, she saunters into our row and crosses her arms. She's a foot shorter than both of us, but we'd like to live to see our next birthdays, so we back the fuck up. "Did you just call me a wimp, Jack Garrett?"

"I meant it in the most loving way." I clock the exits. "How much did you hear?"

"Wouldn't you like to know?" She throws a tight smile at Charlie. "Mind if I talk to this silver-tongued jerk alone for a sec?"

Charlie moves faster than a preacher's daughter trying to make curfew, saluting me as he blows out the exit. "See you guys at home. Ever is—"

"Spending the night," Danika and I say at the same time. "We know."

Then it's just me and Danika. And a few naked guys who we ignore.

Danika shoves me back a step. "I've got something to say to you."

"Only took you four days," I drawl. "Let's hear it."

She scowls at me. I smile back. "You actually

tried to stay sober for Katie," she says quietly, so no one will overhear. My smile vanishes. "She's the first person you actually cared enough to try for. And maybe it was a mistake, but I thought . . . I thought if I brought her to the bar Sunday night, you'd have to admit there's a problem. You'd look at her and remember why you were trying. And you'd start again."

"I'm going to a meeting tonight." So much for not telling anyone. "Katie is taking me."

If I hadn't already been kicked in the ass Sunday night, being confronted with the effect of my actions, watching my best friend's face crumple would have done it. "Really?" I've never seen Danika cry before and it's . . . awful. Jesus, did I really spend so long floating around without any awareness of how badly I was hurting the people who care about me?

Knowing she would rather gargle lighter fluid than be babied—especially in the dude's locker room—I snort. "Christ, D, you really are a wimp."

Her laugh is grateful and watery as she punches me in the arm. "I like her so much. Katie." She swipes at her eyes. "I wish she was staying."

My chest threatens to cave in. "Me, too." The clock overhead reminds me where I need to be—with my girl—but I know Katie will forgive me when I tell her what kept me.

"Sorry! You have to go." Danika takes my elbow and propels me towards the door. "It goes without saying that I'll go with your ass to a meeting anytime, right?"

"Yeah." I ruffle her hair, laughing when she smacks my hand away. "Thanks, Danika."

"And . . ." Her cheeks darken. "You don't have to worry about the lieutenant. I wouldn't get with that asshole on my worst day. Even in a Garden of Eden type situation where we were tasked with populating the earth. Or if we were stranded on an island—"

"Message received."

That's what I say out loud, anyway, so I don't ruin the moment. What I actually see on Danika's face inflates my concern, though. She's . . . angry. Has something happened between her and the lieutenant while I've been sidetracked? Before, when I needled her about having the hots for Burns, she would give me a signature eye roll. And she sure as shit never brought him up herself. This is new.

Danika seems to realize I'm on to her, because she pushes me out the door. "Go."

Right. One problem at a time.

My boots hit the shiny hallway floor at a fast clip and by the time I exit the academy, I'm jogging in the direction of Katie. As I draw closer, I recognize the outline of her in the window of the coffee shop, a white paper cup lifted to her mouth. The mouth I want to kiss until she's ripping my clothes off. But when she walks out to meet me, she hugs me instead, spreading warmth to my bones. Reassuring me.

"Ready?" she asks.

A quaking begins in my stomach, but I don't let her see it. Don't let her glimpse my worry that this will be the final time she looks at me like I'm whole. Like I'm worthy of her. Instead, I swallow hard and brush my lips across her forehead. "Lead the way, Snaps."

CHAPTER 20

— Katie —

When I follow Jack into the church basement, every head turns in his direction. Not because he's the youngest one in the room—along with me—and new to the group. No, it's more.

He's like a treasure chest with blinding light shooting out from the lock. It's easy to see there's something substantial inside. The wood splintering and revealing its contents in your presence would be a miracle. Who wouldn't want to witness it?

The day we met, I found Jack's charisma and looks entirely too overwhelming, but glimpses of the man he's been hiding pulled me in, revealing more by the day. Making me feel at home. Jack . . . feels like home. My hand is tucked inside his, the smell of his leather jacket and soap keeping me cocooned in tight. I look up at him and know what everyone else sees. A pirate, a rom-com movie actor, a womanizer. A beautiful man who couldn't possibly want for anything. But I'm more compelled by the man whose grip increases the farther we wade into the crowded room. The man who smiles trying to cover his nerves. I want to climb into his arms and worship him for being so brave. When he glances down at me, I can tell he senses that. Already he can read me, same as I read him.

Case in point, Jack asking me on the walk over what I'm upset about. Not wanting to remove focus from the upcoming meeting, I'd answered, "Nothing." How would I explain the guilt I've been weighed down with since another phone call from my da this evening? He brought up the Olympic trials again, this time with far less subtlety. Since I won the gold medal, he's been livelier, but that spirit is beginning to fade from his voice, and in turn, so is my hope for being free.

"We should have dessert for dinner tonight," I blurt.

The strained lines around his eyes grow soft. "Been hiding a sweet tooth from me, Snaps?" He bends down and brushes a kiss across my forehead. "Damn, I had flowers hiding in my jacket the last couple days. But maybe I could have tempted you with chocolates."

All that time he spent sitting in the lobby, he'd

been hiding flowers? An anchor sinks in my stomach. "What kind were they? So I can imagine them, at least."

"Roses, honey."

I whimper. "What color?"

He laughs, probably because I sound so pathetic. I don't care, though, because that's how I feel, knowing I'd walked past a gift-bearing Jack. But if my wistfulness has succeeded in making Jack less nervous—and it appears it has—I don't mind morphing into mush for a while. "This is where is gets complicated," he says. "Did you know different-colored roses mean different things? Yellow is friendship, but it also means sorry. I was sorry as hell, but I didn't want to give you some goddamn friendship flowers, right? So I added red." Quicker than I can react, he snatches a kiss from my lips, letting his smiling mouth hover close. "Red means passion. Which is a fancy way of saying I spend a sick amount of time picturing you naked and moaning."

"Right," I breathe. "Red and yellow."

His voice falls to a whisper near my ear. "Don't forget white for the innocence you gave me. Pink for admiration." A hand ghosts over my hip, rasping the material of my shirt against skin that's grown flushed. "Blue for the impossible, because I never thought I'd get you back."

"That's a lot of colors." I have no clue how I manage to respond or function like a normal human being, my heart is hammering so hard in my throat. "If I'd seen the roses, I never would have been able to walk past without stopping, you know."

"Yeah. I know you're sweet like that." His sigh brushes back some flyaway strands of hair. "I think . . . I wanted you to come for just me."

"I'm here now."

He nods slowly, like he still can't believe it. "What's the reason behind dessert for dinner?"

I twine my arms around his waist, inhaling deeply of his scent. "It's something to look forward to. No matter what happens in the next hour, there's chocolate on the horizon."

He's quiet a moment. "Promise?"

"Promise."

"If you'd all like to take a seat?"

The firm, but friendly female voice from the opposite side of the room sends threads of tension back through Jack, but he comes along when I lead him to the rows of chairs. We take our seats halfway back, sharing our row with an older gentleman. There's a short introduction from the group moderator, a lady in glasses and a heavy sweater, before she begins a presentation about the program. More specifically, she talks about the first step out of twelve, which is admitting a person's life has become unmanageable, because of alcohol.

Silence falls, heavy and expectant, when she asks if there are newcomers in the room. Jack doesn't raise his hand and I don't expect him to, even though a handful of others indicate it's their first time. Over the next twenty minutes, people leave their chairs and approach the podium, sharing challenges from the week, telling the room how many consecutive days they've been sober. Without looking over at Jack, his stillness and almost breathless attention makes me hopeful the meeting, finding out he isn't alone, is having an effect on him.

There doesn't appear to be anyone else interested in sharing, so the moderator returns to the podium. "Thank you all so much for your honesty today. If there's no one else—"

Jack stands up. He's still holding my hand as he tries to exit the row, but I realize it's me clutching his fingers in a death grip, probably out of pure shock. He leans down and kisses my knuckles, giving me a reassuring nod as he lets go. I watch in disbelief as he strides around the grouping of chairs to the room's front, running a finger around the back of his collar, boots thudding on the floor. Just like when we entered the room, Jack's very presence has the attendees in thrall. No one moves an inch, their curiosity spiking around me.

"Uh, hi. I'm Jack. And I wasn't planning on coming up here." He slides a glance at the moderator who has taken her seat once again in the front row, then his gaze finds mine and holds.

Holds tight. "But I'm not sure when I'll have my girl here with me again. I need to get this out now, when I know . . . when I hope . . . she'll be around afterwards to help make it better."

I have fallen flat on my arse for Jack. It's crazy, isn't it? Yes. Mental. It's like he's dragged my heart up to the podium behind him, though, bumping and stuttering along. I would be positive he'd accomplished that feat of physics if I couldn't feel the organ slamming sideways in my chest, the impact reverberating through my entire body like an earthquake. I'm so proud and scared I might pop.

"This isn't pretty, Katie, I'm sorry," Jack says, yanking back my focus, slaying me with those green eyes from yards away. I shake my head to let him know I don't care how ugly, that I won't leave no matter what, but he's already begun. "I drink because I don't want to think. Like a lot of you said." He pauses so long, I'm afraid he's lost his nerve. "I'd tried beer before, but the first time I actually got drunk was my eighteenth birthday. My mother wasn't home—" His words cut off abruptly, his throat muscles sliding up and down. "My mother wasn't home, but some of her friends were there. And they got it in their head that I deserved a celebration." Green eyes flash to mine. "They poured me some whiskey and it was fine at first. For hours. I felt . . . great, actually. Like nothing could touch me. I knew these women well, right? I wasn't acting like myself—I was wasted—but, hey, at least I was being safe about it.

"Later on, though, we ended up in one of the bedrooms. I don't even know how we got there, but suddenly they have me on the bed."

It takes Jack some time to continue and I'm grateful. Grateful as the full minute ticks by, so I can force my breathing to stay normal. My bones are shaking, but I'll be damned before I let Jack see the righteous anger beginning to trickle in, my intuition beginning to hum in anticipation of the oncoming blow.

"They tied my hands." He clears his throat. Loudly. Like he can't control it. "I didn't like what was happening and I wanted to express that, but I kept my mouth shut instead. Men were supposed to want sex—*I* was supposed to— so saying no would mean something was wrong with me, right? I don't know. It felt wrong . . . but my body reacted, so they kept going. Felt like it went on forever. Why didn't I say no?" His eyes are apologetic, focused on me and it's everything I can do not to cry. "In my head, I was screaming it, but I just bit down and let it happen. Let them use me. And through it all, the only thing that made what was happening bearable was being drunk. I . . . hid inside the buzz. Let it blank my mind. Same way I do now every time I think about what happened. Or shit, any time I—" He throws back his shoulders, jaw clenching. "Anyway, that's all I got. Thanks for listening."

Jack

Katie hasn't said a word since we left the meeting. Did I go too far?

Her fingers are threaded through mine as we walk towards her hotel. That physical contact and the fact that she hasn't split yet is the only thing keeping me sane. Swear to God, I didn't plan on dropping my baggage on a room full of strangers. I also wasn't expecting to listen to their stories and feel like I belonged there. I'm not the only one that plans their day around drinking or not drinking. How about that?

So I'd taken a shot and shed about nine layers of skin, right there for Katie to see. And Jesus Christ, I'm not sure it helped yet. There was an expectation in my gut that finally saying the words I'd kept inside for eight years would be a relief. Or I'd experience some magical lightness. Honestly, though? I still feel dirty. Still feel like Jack.

It seems like forever I've been punishing myself for not saying no that night. For closing my eyes and vanishing into my buzz while control was taken from me. Maybe it would have been more productive or therapeutic to be mad at the women who tied me up, but that anger and guilt has always been directed squarely at myself. I should have *done* something. *Said* something. If

I'd tried hard enough to stop what was happening, my mind and body wouldn't have retreated to two different camps afterwards, my body continuing to seek satisfaction while my mind told me fulfilling those needs was a weakness. Just like it had been that night.

Nothing I do with Katie makes me feel weak, though. Only strong. Capable. I choose to be clearheaded when I'm with her. I don't have to make bad decisions to justify my guilt, because for the first time, someone believes I'm capable of making good ones. I'm slowly starting to trust that belief as well, but I'm still standing on shifting sand after exposing myself at the meeting. Not knowing what's on Katie's mind is tearing me up.

We ride the elevator to her hotel room in silence, although her head is lying on my shoulder, so I'm calm. For now. When we step inside her room, though, the tension inside me ratchets up, watching Katie rock on the balls of her feet, standing just out of my reach.

"If you can't look at me the same now, honey, just tell me." My blood is either a thousand degrees or twenty below zero. I can't tell. "Put me out of my misery."

Katie goes still. "Can't look at you the same?"

"Yeah." I rip off my jacket and fumble it, sighing when it falls to a heap on the floor. Part of me wants to do the same, the honesty of the last couple of hours making me exhausted. "Look, you wanted to help. But if this problem of mine is too much for you, I understand, huh? I'm sure as hell going to argue and try to change your mind, but give me a starting point. Something, Katie."

"I do look at you differently," she whispers through stiff lips.

Her words hit my stomach like a semitruck. "Okay. All right—"

"You're even more amazing to me now." Her exhale is so heavy, she sags a little. "You're brave, Jack. And yes, you're stubborn to carry that awful memory around without telling anyone, because what happened to you was awful. It was wrong. But to walk up in front of those people a-and bare yourself like that? I'm so proud of you. That's how I'm looking at you."

"So what is it?" Relief is finally drifting in, lightening the metal I swallowed eight years ago. Knowing Katie doesn't think worse of me—is even proud of what I did—has allowed it to happen, and fuck, it's like running at top speed without moving my legs. Almost. "Why aren't you over here in front of me, where I need you to be?"

She presses both hands to her cheeks without responding.

"Katie." I breathe in. Out. "Please."

"You told me once that looking at yourself in the mirror after sex is difficult. Now that I know why, now that I know you drink to numb yourself, I'm worried you have that same problem with me. After we—"

"No." A laugh tumbles out of my throat, because this worry of hers is one I can lay to rest. Finally, something I can actually control. "When I told you everything is different with you, I meant it." My voice is sliced raw and I don't care. "I've never held someone through the night until you. Never needed someone's skin against mine so badly I can't eat or think. Not ever." Her body relaxes and she's about to come to me, but I'm not done. I didn't share everything in that meeting because some of the explanation belongs only to Katie. "Before what happened, women always looked at me a certain way. And I understood that interest between men and women because I lived with it, right there in my home. But after that night, it became less about fun and more about . . . doing what I was meant for. If I couldn't open my mouth and say no that night, why shouldn't the answer always be yes? Wasn't I *supposed* to enjoy it?" I tuck my thumbs through my belt loops. "By then, I was drinking more and more often. So I stopped caring about being anything more than . . . serviceable. That's what I was good for. This whole time, until you, that's how I've been living." I pause for a breath. "It's more than that, though. I've hated myself for not saying no and . . . fuck, until you, I was saying yes to punish myself."

A whimpering sound slips out of Katie's mouth and my body moves on instinct, closing the distance between us, cupping her face in my hands.

"Until me?" She covers my hands with hers. "You promise it always feels right afterwards now?"

"Right is an understatement, Katie," I say, my tone rough. "You looked for more in me so I went to go find it. There's no guilt in saying yes to you when you look at me . . . and I feel like more. Like I might have something to give."

"You *are* more." She studies me a beat, then nods, her gaze shining. "But I'd like to shank those bitches."

A laugh puffs out of me, making her frown. This girl. She's in my goddamn bones and she's going to stay there. Whether she leaves or not. "If you'd come to my mother's the morning I fixed the boiler, you'd have gotten your chance."

Flames light in her eyes. "They were there. That's why you—"

"Yeah." My thumb brushes her cheek. "I'm sorry. It caught me by surprise."

Just remembering the way they'd hugged me, leered at me, is multiplying the hot clench in my stomach. Does the urge to drink accompany it? Yes. Hell yes, it does. Shooting at the range helped calm the cravings over the last couple of days, but I have no weapon in my hand at the moment. So I focus on counting the freckles strewn across Katie's nose until I come out the other side of the need. This demon is one I'm going to fight forever, but I'm not going to give up. When I decided to stop hurting the people who took the risk of caring about me, I didn't take that vow lightly.

"I'm sorry you had to face that alone," Katie murmurs, watching me with concern. "Sorry for every time you have to face it in the future."

"It's okay," I say, to make her feel better. Even though it's growing more obvious with every passing minute that I'm going to be pretty goddamn far from okay when she leaves. The worst of the craving has passed, but there's still a layer of grime on me, leftover from spilling my guts. Laying a kiss on Katie's nose, I back towards the bathroom. "Listen, I'm just going to rinse off. Be right out."

Her right shoulder lifts slowly, tucking up near her ear. "You didn't shower after training today?"

"Yeah, I did." Katie is seeing right through me again, so I turn on a heel and enter the bathroom, already stripping off my shirt. After flipping on the hot water tap, I meet my own eyes in the mirror, which is like a slap in the face. A reminder to be truthful and stop hiding. "All those things I said . . ." Her small form appears in the doorway. "They're just sitting on my skin, you know? Making me feel filthy. I don't want to feel anything but clean when I touch you, Snaps." Because her expression is so heartbroken, staring back at me in the mirror, I toss her a wink over my shoulder. "You are going to let me touch you, right?"

"Yes," she says without hesitation, before closing the bathroom door and peeling off her shirt. Damn, she looks pissed. Pissed and topless. My cock presses against the zipper of my jeans, begging to be let out. "But you're clean for me right this minute. Just as you are. So I'm not letting you wash an inch."

My heartbeat drowns out the drumming shower spray.

CHAPTER 21
Katie

I've never fancied myself a natural-born seductress, but maybe I was wrong. Jack looks ready to fall on his knees as I saunter close, then change directions, climbing into the shower. Pulling the heavy curtain closed behind me, cocooning myself in the steamy darkness, I wait, letting the hot water glide over my back, down my face. Only about three seconds pass before Jack follows, slowly closing in behind me, his energy wrapping around me and squeezing like a python. His big hands settle on either side of me, braced on the marble wall, and we simply exist in the lack of light, gaining strength from one another.

When he releases a long, ragged breath against the back of my neck, I'm filled with purpose.

There's no logic here or right answers, there's only the blueprint my heart is demanding I follow.

The impact of his confessions has left me aching, but as I turn around to face him, I bolster myself. Because Jack's head is hanging forwards, his eyes are closed, muscles bunched. And I'm going to heal him. For now, at least. Just an increment along the scale of recovery he'll need to face. I'm not so confident that I believe my touch can turn his tide, but right now, when we're the only two people in the world, my pulse, that steady, insistent thrumming, does believe it.

Soothe, fix, heal, love.

My body has been blocking the shower spray, so Jack is mostly dry. Until I trail my wet hands down his ridged torso, leaving dampness in my wake. Immediately, his body begins to shudder, his stomach muscles clenching and releasing. His breath runs short when I conform my thumbs to the grooves of his hips, pressing, stroking. Between my legs, I'm warm and slippery already, just having him close. Every inch of me yearning for what he can give me.

But this is about me giving to him.

"Kiss me, Jack?"

His mouth is on mine before I'm prepared, sending me stumbling back a step in the shower. No matter, though, because he gathers me back by my elbows, making a hoarse sound as our lips part, tongues meeting on a starved lick. His erection is thick against my belly, tempting my palms, making them spark and tingle. So I don't deny them. I can't when his mouth is making me frantic, when he presses his forehead to mine between kisses and whispers my name. As soon as I enclose him in my fist, he breaks the kiss and makes a choked noise, his gaze glassy and unfocused. "Christ, I'm never going to get used to how good it feels when you touch me. Nothing ever felt right until you, Katie. You know?"

"I know," I manage, even though my mind is blown. Even though it settles responsibility more firmly on my heart, my mind. "Look at me."

His breath rasps against my mouth, green eyes a mere inch from mine. "Always."

I fail to swallow. "You're not dirty, Jack. You never were. You never will be."

"You can't know that," he whispers, lines creasing his forehead.

My hand slides down his heavy column of flesh, then strokes back up as he moans through clenched teeth. "Yes, I can know. Tell me and I'll believe you."

Wariness steals through his big frame. "What do you mean?"

"I mean . . ." I go up on my tiptoes, laying kisses on his lips while my hand stays busy, pumping up and down on his stiffness. "I know you had a physical before the academy, which means you're all clear. Have you used protection every time since then?"

"Yes. I've never, Katie. Never without."

Our foreheads bump when I nod. "So tell me you're clean, like I know you are."

His breath races in and out. "I can't let us do this. You're—"

"I'm on the pill." With lust lacing in my blood like lightning, I bring his erection between my legs, dragging it through my wet heat. "Yes or no, Jack?"

There's no earthly description for the sensation of a man's muscles shaking, the heat of his hands hovering above my ass, his flesh thickening in my hand. It's the epitome of anticipation. An aphrodisiac. "Yes, I'm clean for you, but—"

He breaks off with a growl when I tuck the head of him inside me. A plump, pulsing inch that stretches me and zaps eagerness to my nerve endings. "Have me." I raise my knee, resting it on Jack's hip. The movement allows him to slip deeper, just a touch, but I might as well have pushed him in all the way, his reaction is so intense. I'm pinned to the wall by his eyes. They're digging past layers of tissue and burrowing their way into my soul, making a permanent home. He's unsure, but hungry. Desperate and hopeful.

"Katie, honey." He shakes his head. "I'm only clean on the outside."

"No. That's nonsense. Look at me and trust me. Do you trust me?"

He sounds almost tortured when he answers, closing his eyes. "Yes."

His concern for me is going to win. I can see it

blanketing everything else. So I burn down his resistance. "Fuck me, Jack." I guide him deeper, rolling my hips, exulting as his mouth drops open, his chest heaves. "Show me how much you want me. Prove it."

Jack

Prove how much I want her?

My hips are moving before the command fully forms in my brain. Pushing forwards and up like a well-oiled machine. I'm too rough, way too aggressive as I surge forwards, filling Katie with my cock. Lights and shadows flicker and dance in front of my eyes when that tightness surrounds me. When her ragged gasp greets my ears.

I'm cutting off her oxygen and I need to move back, need to stop pressing against her so hard— she's flattened between me and the wall—but I'm reeling from the sensation of her warm pussy. It's clenched around my dick without a barrier of latex and it's not just the insane feeling. No, no . . . it's the fact that it's Katie. She trusts me this much? I don't deserve it. God fucking knows I don't, but I'm pulsing head to toe, my heart screaming at me, laboring under the weight of the responsibility she's giving me. Having her without protection, being trusted at my word by this girl . . . it's a responsibility I didn't even know I needed so much. Katie knew. She sees me. She's inside me, under me, around me. And it's still not enough.

I want inside of her, too. So deep she can't dig me out.

"Jack," she half gasps, half whimpers. "Please."

My hands tighten on her ass, trying to heft her higher, but I'm crowding her so closely against the wall, it's a long, torturous drag of petite curves over muscle. Every single wet inch of her body slides between me and the wall, until her pussy is positioned at the exact height where I need it. So I can pound her. So I can own her for life.

Her mouth is just above mine now, her thighs clamped around my hips. And something about those lips, the ripe berry color, how they part to accommodate her breaths, burns me with a fevered need to worship them. "Thank you," I groan, swooping in to feast on her with a tongue kiss so nasty, I should be delivering it to her cunt. "Thank you, mouth."

"You're thanking my mouth?" She breathes, her eyes glazed over, head falling back.

I hum low in my throat, leaning forwards to lick a path up the side of her neck. "Your lips open so you can breathe, right? I'm thanking them for helping my girl breathe." Keeping her propped with my lower body, I take one hand off her sweet ass, dragging it down between her tits. "Thank you heart for beating. Lungs for staying filled. All the things I can't do for you, but wish I could."

Tremors pass through her body, her hands lifting, dragging me in for a kiss. A kiss so raw and full of everything—lust, torture, happiness, sun, mountains, sky—my breaths rasp in and out by the time we break away, joined by the pelting of the shower spray that lands on my skin. "It feels so different than the first time," Katie whispers at my mouth. "There's nothing but good. I-I need you to move. You have to move."

Yes. The second she challenged me to prove how much I want her, I was lost. Nothing can bring me back now. I'm so mesmerized by her open, beautiful face, the heat of her pussy wrapped around my dick, all I can do is work myself to the point of agony for her pleasure.

Unfortunately, I could come right now.

With a condom on, sex with Katie obliterated me, but this? My balls are hard as stones and tucked up against the base of my cock, expecting me to relieve them inside the tightest space I've ever known. Sorry, boys. I haven't even moved yet and I already know I'm never, ever going to recover from this. We might be fucking—and make no mistake, I'm going to bang her brains out—but my balls aren't the only part of me in danger of imploding. She's got my heart in a chokehold, too.

"Jack, please."

"Almost there, honey," I say through clenched

teeth. "Feels a little too good without a rubber. Be patient while I talk my dick down."

"I don't want him to go down."

My laugh releases in a burst. "Figure of speech. Trust me, it's up for the duration."

Katie smiles at me and my pulse triples. "I like the idea of you going crazy. Like you can't control yourself."

My abs seize, the blood flow to my dick raging hotter. "Oh shit. Stop talking like that."

Her breath grows choppy and I sense my doom approaching. Maybe I'm a masochist because my cock swells, lengthens and my hunger speeds towards the danger. "I want to watch you use me," Katie whispers. "Want to watch you hurt. Watch the relief hit."

A groan wrenches from my throat. "No, you . . . fuck, Katie, you gave me this . . . privilege. Being inside you like this. I'm not going to screw it up."

"You'd be giving me what I want." The hands she's been resting on my shoulders drop down between us, slipping up to cup her tits, basically setting the world on fire around me. "For me?"

There's no stopping myself now. I'm a man who has gone four days without his girl. A girl who has given me more selfless gifts than I can stand. A girl I was the first to claim. The possessiveness roars through me, a brutal flood of urgency. With one hand on her ass, I flatten the other on the wall above her head. Then I rear my hips back, dragging my aching flesh out of its home, then ramming it back into the hot perfection. My vision doubles as Katie is driven up against the wall, her hands clutching her tits like they can save her. Like anything can. "Fuck, I'm . . . I'm not sure how to hold on." My voice is made of burnt coal. "I've been too depressed to jerk off since you left me."

Katie is past hearing me. She's writhing between me and the wall, tempting and gobbled up by lust. "Harder, Jack. Harder."

"Jesus. Jesus Christ. I'll eat your pussy afterwards, honey." A mental curtain drops down, blocking my resistance or coherent thought, leaving nothing but a driving hunger to fuck. Tether. Snapped. Both of my hands find Katie's bottom, holding it in place as I plow into her, my hips scooping, slamming, scooping, slamming. "Can't get it any deeper. Found where you end, didn't I?" Her knees lift and I press them into the wall with my shoulders, pinning them there. "Does it hurt? I can't stop pumping. Fuck, Katie. Goddammit. You're wet as a motherfucker." My mouth is crammed against her ear, my vision winking to black, my stomach shuddering, clenching with the oncoming release. "I can't wait to fuck your little clit with my tongue. Rubbing against it with my cock right now. Making it nice and swollen for myself, so I can wrap my lips around it. Tell me you want that."

"I want that."

"Good. You're going to get it." A growl shivers

up my spine, spearing me in the throat. I'm hovering right on the brink of a mind-numbing climax. But now I sense Katie is close and my mind is pulling back the reins, responsibility and affection making it impossible to be selfish. "Drop your legs," I order in a desperate voice. "I've got you."

Confusion wrinkles her brow, but she follows my order, leaving her feet dangling down near my straining calves. A split second later, when I thrust up between her thighs, a scream leaves her mouth, the advantages of the position clearly hitting her. "Oh my God, Jack. M-more. Please, more."

Easier said than done, shout my balls, but my mind, my heart is obsessed with the pleasure on her face. My experience isn't something to be ashamed of in that moment, but something to be celebrated. And no one on the planet but Katie could make that a reality. I just want to repay her, any way I can. Over and over forever. "Feels better for your clit, doesn't it, honey? Tilt your hips forwards—good, Katie, fuck, that's so good—and let me make you come."

As I drive into her in slow, measured thrusts, gravity grinds her sweet spot down on my cock. Dazed blue eyes look at me, but she's blind, her mouth opened in an O. The points of her nipples drag up and down my chest, the top of my abdomen. Her nails dig into my shoulders, breaking the skin and knowing how good I'm making her feel sails me even closer to the edge of the world, leaving me teetering right over the drop.

"Mine," I groan into the top of her head. "Mine?"

"Yes."

"Mine to come inside?"

"Y-yes." The single, incredible word splinters into husky cries, her pussy clamping around my dick. And I lose it. I bend my knees and fuck up into her in a rough push, smacking her ass against the wet wall and circling my hips, grinding into her spasming flesh, marking it as mine. The battle ends when she screams *Jack*, her fingernails raking down my back and burying in the flesh of my ass. My orgasm is painful in its intensity, rocking me from the soles of my feet to the top of my head. I press my mouth against the damp marble wall and shout through the ringing of my insides, the emptying of my lust.

And for the first time, there's no guilt or shame or doubt chomping on the heels of my release. The first time with Katie ruined me for any other experience, but we hadn't laid ourselves bare yet. There's been a tiny piece missing. Now? As I stand in the shower, my world rocked on its axis, holding her against me? The whole fucking picture is right in front of me and it's bright and colorful. Beautiful. Everything I never knew existed.

There's a tinny refrain in the back of my head, though.

She's leaving. She's leaving.

That unwanted reminder shoots me full of holes, denials springing to my lips, but instead of voicing them, I set Katie on her feet and drop to my knees. "Said I would eat you. Let me. Need to taste it."

Still dizzy, I manage to push Katie's legs open, parting her pussy with a long lick. I seesaw my tongue right where she needs it, unable to play games or tease after I've just had my mind and heart rearranged. She's smooth and salty, my come just beginning to leave her. When she cries out, her cunt vibrating against my mouth, I've barely gotten my fill, but she's tugging my face away, words and protests barely coherent, so I tuck away the rest of my appetite for later, knowing she needs something else now.

Gaining my feet, I turn off the shower, leaving our racing breaths to echo in the sudden silence. Then I scoop her up and climb out of the tub, collecting a towel on the way out of the bathroom. I set her down beside the bed, memorizing the sight of her half-damp, tumbled red hair, the teeth marks on her mouth, the swell of her naked tits, the curve of her hips. Towel in hand, I keep our eyes locked as I soak up the moisture I left between her thighs. Her sucked-in breath tells me she's sensitive.

My dick reacts. Because, of course.

But now isn't the time for another round, even though my mind is suddenly filled with the notion of pushing her back onto the bed and riding her tight body until she comes again. I could do it. I want to cram in as many experiences as possible before she leaves. Those experiences have to be more than sex, but I'm so fucking new at having a girl, coming up with new, better ways to make her happy is like throwing darts in a pitch-black room. After all she's done for me, though, I'll throw darts until my arms falls off.

With a clogged throat and one eye trained on the fast approaching weekend, I finish drying us both off, peel back the covers and hold my girl through the night, the sound of her breath lulling me into the deepest sleep of my life. But not deep enough to stave off dreams of airplanes taking off and landing somewhere out of my reach.

CHAPTER 22

Katie

Waking up to a heart attack isn't something I recommend.

Just like the last time we slept beside one another—although, this time I'm not handcuffed—Jack shoots into a sitting position and shouts my name, sending a scream ripping up my throat, my hands reaching towards the lamp to use it as a weapon. My mind registers the lack of threat at the same time his big, warm, naked body lands on mine, tackling me gently into the pillows. Giving new meaning to the word *euphoria.*

"Sorry." His voice is scratchy, a lot like the stubble nuzzling into my neck. A heavy forearm drags my hips back, fitting me against a decidedly awake male lap, but just as the moisture begins to gather between my thighs, Jack's body tenses. "Don't tell me that's the actual time."

I don't realize my eyes are closed until I have to squint one in the direction of the bedside clock. Eight twenty-nine. "Maybe there was a power outage," I surmise in a hopeful tone. "It could happen, right?"

"Fuck this." He rolls me onto my stomach, his mouth hot and hungry against my nape, his erection heavy against the crease of my backside. "I'm playing hooky."

"You can't," I gasp, the brakes of my mind screeching. "Jack, I won't let you."

His miserable groan makes me laugh until he drops his weight, forcing the oxygen straight out of my lungs. "It's Friday. We only have until Sunday morning. I can't spend one of those days cooped up in a gymnasium, when I could spend it making you moan." He turns cajoling, rolling his hips and rumbling my name in my ear. "Don't make me go, honey."

Oh, I'm so bloody tempted to throw my mission aside and spend the day beneath Jack. Trust me, I am. But my leaving in two days can't be the reason he stays, it has to be the reason he goes to the academy. I haven't forgotten the meeting with Lieutenant Burns. The man's words are still ringing in my ears and I won't give him one more reason to overlook Jack's talent. I refuse to be the cause of him falling behind, then leaving him to deal with the consequences.

For the first time, the reality that I'm leaving punches me hard in the midsection. My leaving has been a given since day one. Something that will happen. With Jack breathing in my hair, however, boarding a plane to Ireland and watching New York grow smaller in a tiny window seems like a fast approaching tragedy. Do I miss my parents? Of course I do. Do I miss my job? Somewhat. I miss the fulfillment of laying my head down at day's end, assured that my instruction helps keep people safe. That my skills aren't going to waste.

They definitely won't go to waste if I agree to begin training with my father again, will they? The unmade decision is clinging to my organs like a leech, sapping me of the will to do anything for myself. Anything that could shape the future when it suddenly seems out of my control.

My father needs me. Jack needs me. What do I need?

"You've gone quiet on me, Snaps. Something tells me it's not because you've changed your mind about me ditching training."

"No," I whisper, shaken from my troubling train of thought. "No, I . . ."

A beat passes wherein I get the feeling we're both holding our breath. That is, until Jack flips me over onto my back, searching my face with worried green eyes. "You changed your mind."

"About what?"

"This. Us. Until Sunday."

"No." I scoot back and sit up, throwing my arms around his neck. His hands remain at his sides, like they've lost the ability to function. "No, I didn't change my mind, Jack. I'm only quiet because . . ." Despite the niggling fear that I'm falling into the same pattern of being needed, the truth is still crystal clear. "I didn't realize it was going to be so hard. To leave, you know?"

Slowly his arms weave around me, holding me tighter and tighter until I'm crushed to his chest. "Yeah, I know. I've known. This isn't new for me."

"It seemed so far away."

Silence thrums around us. "Are you worried about what I'll do when you leave? Is that what this is about?"

A tank crashes in my stomach, because I hadn't considered the obvious. But there's no pretending when our heartbeats are pressed together. "Yes."

"Me, too." He tilts my chin up. "You're the one who held up a mirror. You're the one who brought me to the meeting." Regret mixes with determination on his face. "But I'd be worried about slipping even if you weren't leaving. Fixing this problem of mine? That's on me. You're not responsible, Katie, understand?"

I want to believe him. God, I really do. Yanking the rug out from beneath his feet when he's only just gotten his balance, though? It's going to make getting on that plane brutal. What option do I have but to leave? I'm here on a short trip. I have no work visa, didn't apply for one because finding a reason to stay never entered my mind. Is staying an option now?

No, of course not. That would be impulsive. Totally mental. My entire family is back home. My job. Childhood friends, if not professionally connected ones. I've built a life in Dublin since the Olympics concluded and I haven't even given myself a chance to flourish. Whether or not I agree to train for Tokyo, my life is three thousand miles away.

Not to mention, Jack hasn't asked me to stay. Major detail. And a sign that I'm getting way ahead of the game and setting myself up for a disappointment when he inevitably doesn't ask. I'd have to decline anyway so this whole line of thought is total bollocks.

Bollocks, Katie.

"What is going on in that head?" Jack asks slowly, swaying us side to side. "It looks serious."

"I'm only just remembering we decided to have dessert for dinner. We didn't even eat."

"Order it for breakfast instead and save me something?" That pirate smile makes an appearance. His hand drops from my chin, down to my stomach, his knuckles trailing over my belly button. Lower. "I'll eat it later."

My libido dances in a circle. "This is a classic have your cake and eat it, too, situation."

He swoops in and captures my mouth in a

thorough kiss, before pulling away with a groan. "You think being so damn cute will help convince me to leave?"

When his erection nudges me in the belly, I know we're reaching the point of no return, so I force myself to back up. "I have a meeting today, anyway." I swing my legs off the bed and stand, only brazening out my nakedness for two seconds before snatching up a pillow and hiding behind the fluffy barrier. "I'll save you something sweet."

Jack has no such modesty and he's . . . dear God. He's stunning on a normal basis, but wrapped in morning light, the beginnings of a beard and no clothes? He looks as though heaven spat him out onto my hotel bed. "You'll just save me some, Katie, huh?" A wink in my direction has me sighing. "Come out with us tonight. Me, you. Charlie, Ever, D. We'll go grab Mexican food." His eyes are level. "Just dinner."

I nod right away, relieved there's a definitive point in the future when I'll see him again. Maybe I'll even be able to pretend Sunday isn't speeding towards me like a train with the brakes cut. "Okay."

My agreement has his shoulders relaxing. "After training lets out, I'll go to a meeting, then come get you."

"You're good to go alone?"

"Yes." Jack holds my gaze for a heavy beat of time. "Yes." He moves past me into the bathroom, emerging a moment later clad in boxer briefs, pulling his T-shirt down to cover his chest. Pity, that. "We'll head over to the restaurant together, yeah?" After stooping down to pull on his jeans, he leans in and kisses me, the tempo increasing, my blood firing hotter and hotter until he pulls away with clear reluctance. "Tonight."

"Tonight," I echo.

Jack takes a long look at me, then heads for the door, stuffing his feet into boots and picking up his jacket on the way. Before he can walk out, however, he returns on swift feet, stealing the pillow out of my hands and tossing it on the bed. "You're too beautiful to hide."

I stand, glued in place, and stare at the door for long minutes after he's gone, wondering how in the world I fell in love in just two short weeks.

TURNS OUT, IT'S not as much fun having dessert for breakfast while alone. That didn't stop me from devouring a basket of beignets with raspberry sauce from room service while still in my robe. Shameful behavior, really, but I was feeling self-righteous with my sore shower sex muscles. I'd earned a few extra calories and trashy television, no? Well, that attitude lasted all of seven seconds before my regimented training kicked in and I dragged my ass down to the hotel gym for a run. Someday I will learn to indulge without guilt, but for now I'm happy with baby steps.

A shower and change of clothes later, I'm walking into 1 Police Plaza for the meeting I told Jack about. What I hadn't mentioned was this: It was unscheduled. And the chance I'll pull off a face-to-face with the ESU commanding officer is about as good as a lampshade being elected mayor. That doesn't mean I'm not going to try. The CO and I had a cursory meet and greet last week, one of the brass big boys welcoming me to New York on behalf of the exchange program, but he doesn't strike me as a desk jockey. This could be a wasted trip, but I've made it downtown so I'm damn well going to attempt a sit-down.

When the officer stationed at the front desk looks up at me and does a double take, I tamp down the urge to check if my zipper is down. Oh God, what if I'm not even wearing pants? But no, he smooths his hair and adjusts his collar, as if he's interested. In me.

The sparkly feminine pleasure that slips around in my belly is new. There's no hesitation or surprise behind it. Before this trip, I avoided men in any capacity but professional because I was so sure I would make a bollocks of any encounter with so little experience in my arsenal. Not so far-fetched, considering the closest I'd come to a date was exchanging pleasantries with the cute checkout man at Tesco while buying cereal.

It's Jack having this effect on me. The way he looks at me lingers, even when he's not around. Like a sweater fresh from a clothesline warmed by the sun, it hugs me close, surrounding every inch of me with security. Earlier while getting dressed, I caught my own reflection in the mirror and saw a new glow on my cheeks. Less tension around my eyes. A languidness to my movements. Has this feminine confidence always been there waiting to shine? I think so. It feels so natural sustaining eye contact with the officer as I approach the desk.

"Can I help you?"

I nod and produce my ERU badge, looking past the officer down the busy corridor. "Yes. I'm Garda McCoy, here to meet with Commanding Officer Kirkpatrick."

The man ceases his interested perusal of my badge, giving me a skeptical head tilt. "Is he expecting you?"

"No, but we met last week. His exact words were, 'don't hesitate to get in touch if you need anything while in New York, McCoy.' And I'll wager he's not the type to make empty gestures. Don't you think?" I give him my best smile, a smidgen amazed when his cheeks go pink. "So I need a personal helicopter tour around Manhattan. With Jay-Z as my guide. Think he can arrange it?"

He backs up a pace. "Uh, yeah. Listen—"

"Ah sure look, I'm only messing with you, love.

Your face is classic." I give the hallway behind him a loose-wristed wave. "Five minutes of his time would be grand. That's it."

Officer Blushkins has no idea what to make of me. I wish Jack were here. He would be busting his sides laughing. Or better yet, Jack would play along without missing a beat. A tiny ripple fans out in my stomach at how easily I paint Jack into the scene now. In a short space of time, he's become the person I want standing beside me in all situations.

"Let me go check if he's available," says Blushkins, adjusting his belt and ambling off down the chaotic hallway, moving through a sea of blue uniforms. Two minutes later, he returns, giving me a chin jerk I've come to associate with New Yorkers since arriving in town. It means, *getcha ass over here.* Well, he doesn't have to tell me twice. Apparently this newfound confidence is working for me, because I've just gotten an audience with the CO.

He's on the phone when I enter his office, earning me another chin jerk. The leather seat creaks in welcome as I sit down, my eyes scanning the wall full of accolades as Kirkpatrick wraps up his call. Dust motes swirl in the air, slices of sunlight pouring in through wooden blinds. Then the phone smacks into its cradle and I'm being scrutinized by one of the sharpest minds in the NYPD. Not intimidating whatsoever.

"What can I do for you, McCoy?"

"Thank you for meeting with me, sir." Something tells me my helicopter joke wouldn't get a laugh, so I cut straight to the point. "Part of my assignment was to recommend a recruit for ESU."

The computer sitting on his desk gets a chin jerk. "Burns e-mailed me with your pick."

"Yes, the lieutenant is very efficient." The animosity in my tone seems to amuse him, twin sparks twinkling in his eyes. "I'm here because there's another recruit with a high proficiency for firearms, sir. I'd like him brought to your attention."

"Why didn't you recommend him?"

Heat prickles my face. Discussing Jack when he's not around makes me feel disloyal, but I remind myself doing nothing, never saying his name, would be worse. "He didn't have the best home life growing up. As a result, he has some issues. Issues he's sorting through. Actively." He starts to speak, but I interrupt. "All due respect, sir, if you tell me your job is to conform men into team players . . . or groom them for something larger than themselves, I'm going to be very disappointed."

His right eyebrow lifts in increments, as if operated by a crank. "That is my job." I open my mouth to issue the rejoinder on my tongue, but he holds up a hand. "But it's only half my job. Teamwork is certainly a value we ingrain in our men at ESU, but most of them were loners before I got a hold of them."

Something that feels like hope climbs my arms like ivy. "Maybe the best men and women learn to be strong alone, before they merge that strength with others."

"That's catchy."

My chin lifts. "It's the truth."

Kirkpatrick leans forwards, resting his large frame on his forearms. "I like you, McCoy. You seemed like a timid mouse when we shook hands last week."

"I was focusing on not breaking my neck in those high heels."

A laugh rumbles out of him, whipping the dust motes into a frenzy. Several beats pass as the CO settles back into his chair. "Is Jack Garrett really as good as you say?"

My forehead wrinkles. "I never . . . I don't think I told you his name."

"Lieutenant Burns included Garrett's name in the e-mail."

I whistle low and slow under my breath. "Well, that was unexpected. I might have to amend my judgment of the lieutenant."

Kirkpatrick shrugs. "He's a prickly bastard. Don't take away your resentment—it's what fuels him."

"Why?"

The humor dances out of the older man's eyes.

"It was a bad scene when he lost his partner. Well before he made lieutenant." He taps a finger on the desk. "I've seen it before. Officers react one of two ways. They get numb and slowly burn out. Or they work triple time and grow obsessed with procedure. Guess which option Burns took?"

"The latter." Guilt slithers through my ribs. "I see."

"What do you propose I do about Garrett?"

"Meet him," I say without thinking. "Watch him shoot. The rest will take care of itself."

I've given myself away. My affection for Jack weighs down every word out of my mouth. But I don't flinch under the knowledge in Kirkpatrick's eyes. There's a point in a woman's life when she has to trust that her accomplishments, the way she's lived, can speak for itself and earn enough respect to redirect any and all bullshit. And I do believe I've just reached that point. My relationship with Jack is not why I'm here and I dare him to accuse me otherwise. "I'm here because I refuse to let someone with that much talent get lost in the shuffle."

Kirkpatrick studies me a moment. "I'll meet with Garrett. If I think he can be an asset to this unit, I'll offer my support while he figures his shit out."

"Thank you." I'm not so brave that I can't admit I'm about to begin sobbing, so I stand abruptly and put out my hand. "I appreciate your time, sir. The boys back in Dublin will be delighted to know you're as fair and tough as your reputation."

"That's it, huh?" The CO takes my hand in a firm shake. "Back to Ireland."

"Yes, sir."

He presses his tongue against the inside of his cheek. "If you ever decide New York is more your scene, I'll have you on my squad as an instructor." His mouth tilts at one end. "I told you, McCoy. I like you. And I hate pretty much everyone."

Sobbing shall commence in three . . . two . . . one . . .

"Thank you, sir. That means a lot to me."

As I jog down the corridor with burning eyes, hearty laughter trails after me.

CHAPTER 23

Jack

S hit is starting to get real.

Two more nights with Katie. Then it's wheels up.

I'm surrounded by my best friends, new and old, going to town on some guacamole. There was a tense moment when the waitress accidentally set down a margarita in front of me, meant for the next table, but I survived. Even laughed. I've got an arm around this amazing girl, holding her up against my side so tight, they couldn't pry her away with the Jaws of Life. When she opened her hotel room door, though, looking so sexy in a loose red dress, I almost dragged her down onto the floor then and there. It hit me square in the face—definitely not for the first time—that we're temporary. Impossible when I swear she has always been here.

All my life, I've turned every problem into no big deal. Batted them away like flies, while they got worse under my surface. Pretending is my goddamn stock-in-trade, but I can't fake normalcy right now. The conversations are moving around me like marbles swirling downwards in a funnel. I can't seem to hold on to any of them, or catch their meaning.

Ask her to stay.

Right. Ask this beautiful gold medalist with the shining law enforcement career to gamble it all on someone who only attended their second AA meeting this afternoon? I'm trying my best to be proud of myself for walking into that basement alone today. For sitting in that hard seat and listening to harder truths. I've only begun to recover, but I haven't had a flashback to that night in days. I'm lighter for having gotten that memory off my chest, setting it free and unshackling myself in the process. I've started on this path that could lead to a better future for me if I don't fuck it up. But I'm nowhere near being in a position yet to keep Katie here in New York.

God, I can't stand the thought of her leaving. Missing her would be an understatement. Thinking of her missing *me* is almost worse. She didn't have an easy time staying away from me, either, when we spent those four days apart. That first kiss in the alley after being separated is still seared into my memory like a brand. Going indefinitely without her mouth and arms around me, her encouragement and sense of humor, just her . . . I'm beginning to panic imagining what it'll be like. And while I'm trying to remain true to my word, that Katie isn't responsible for my recovery, I'm not too proud to admit I'm on shaky ground. When she goes back to Ireland, I'm worried those tremors could develop into a full-blown earthquake.

"I'm celebrating tonight," Ever says, holding up a Coke, which I know she ordered on my behalf. They're all drinking soda, actually. At some point I hope they won't have to do that, but not going to lie, knowing my friends care that much kind of blows me away. "Guess who just scored the catering contract for your graduation ceremony next month?"

Ever and her roommate own Hot Damn Caterers, a small start-up that operates out of an old Brooklyn donut factory and their two-bedroom apartment.

"I'm guessing it wasn't the competition," Danika responds, clinking glasses with Ever. "That's big-time. Congrats."

"Thanks." Ever jabs Charlie in the side with her elbow, but the poor sap just smiles like a heart eyes emoji. "Some people might not take kindly to their boyfriend's bureau chief father earning them preferential treatment. Turns out, I am not one of those people."

"Hey. The only time my father has ever asked for seconds in his life is when you made him dinner. He knows a good thing when he eats it." *Wait for it.* "So do I, as it happens."

Ever slaps a hand over her face and Danika groans. "How am I supposed to eat tacos after that?"

Katie snorts into her cloth napkin at that, which makes the whole table erupt in laughter. She's been somewhat quiet since we sat down, but I've learned how she operates by now. She might start out shy, but a little encouragement and she'll do that adorable rambling thing, charming every-one within a hundred yards. I'm split between wanting everyone to witness that side of her and needing to keep it all to myself awhile longer. In the end, being proud of her wins. "Speaking of your pops, Charlie, does he ever tell stories about the mob?"

As predicted, Katie straightens in my hold.

"Oh my God, yeah," says Charlie. "I remem-ber when I was a kid, before my mother split, she talked him into a dinner party at our house. About halfway through, one of her friends begged my father for a story about his police work. Let's just say she regretted it, we never had another dinner party and my dad slept on the couch that night."

"You don't happen to remember the details?"

Katie asks, trying to be subtle, but her grip keeps tightening on my knee. Not that I'm complaining. She can grip me anywhere.

Charlie squints, probably flipping through the million and a half details catalogued in his police brain. "Something about a barbershop—"

"Oh." Katie's spine snaps straight. "I know this one. Early nineties. It was an assassination of the family boss, perpetrated by the new one who stepped into power. Was your father involved?" She doesn't wait for an answer. "Dinner and a chat are probably impossible after spending all day working that type of case. Did your scandalized woman at least get dessert and tea out of it? Is it terrible to wish I was there?"

"Not sure if there was dessert," Charlie answers, clearly enjoying Katie. "But I remember everyone needing refills of their drinks halfway through the story."

"Yeah. A refill and a tranquilizer," Danika says, her smile hesitant and she looks at Katie. "Charlie's father will be at our graduation. It's only a few weeks away—maybe you could extend your trip a little and hear some stories in person?"

My heart starts to hammer and Katie must feel it, plastered up against me as she is. At first, I'm grateful to my best friend for making the suggestion. For looking so hopeful, along with Charlie and Ever. But as soon as two seconds of silence pass, as soon as tension creeps into Katie's frame, I wish the subject hadn't been brought up at all.

Because her physical reaction is as good as an answer.

"I-I . . . well, I'm due back at work on Monday," Katie says quietly. "My bills are crammed inside my mailbox by now and my da, he's . . . he's looking for an answer from me about the next Olympics. Whether or not we're going to train again."

"What?" I barely register the fact that I've spoken too loud, because all my focus is centered on Katie. "I thought you were done. Thought you didn't want to do it again."

She takes a fast sip of her drink, her cheeks going pink. "Yes, but he's not having an easy time." Subtext: because of her brother. No one at the table knows about his passing except me, though. Or how much weight she's carrying on her shoulders over his death. Over her father's reaction to it. "The training would give him something to focus on and . . ."

"*Something* to focus on? You mean *you*, Katie." The idea of her being unhappy and alone again makes my stomach go sour. "Four years of your life."

"Yes," she says with some heat. "*My* life. Maybe I've changed my mind. I'm allowed."

The waiter chooses that moment to arrive with our food. But I might as well be watching the scene play out from a different planet. Ten minutes ago, I was considering the idea of asking Katie to stay in New York. For me. All this time, though, she's been considering another run at the

Olympics without even confiding in me about it. Was I an idiot to think her future could include me? Or that I could somehow make life with a recovering drunk seem appealing? Back in Ireland, she has another shot at Olympic glory, if she wants it. Here? A boyfriend with two roommates who hasn't even made it through graduation at the academy yet.

No one speaks as the waiter takes off, the sudden distance between me and Katie clear. Finally, Ever shifts beneath the arm Charlie has draped across her shoulder. "Ooh, Katie. I love your purse." She points at the emerald green clutch wedged between Katie and Danika on the leather booth. "Where did you get it?"

"She made it," I rasp, before clearing the rust from my throat. No way am I letting tonight be ruined over something I should have already realized. Katie is better off without me, as I am right now. This man who hasn't even begun to steer his life in a good direction. But this unexpected time with her is a gift and I'm going to live in it as long as possible. "By hand, she makes them. They're incredible."

Katie grants me a flash of worried blue eyes. "Thanks."

I draw Katie closer, determined to eat the full meal with my left hand, even though my appetite is gone. "How can I buy one?" Ever wants to know, making funny grabby motions. "Are there more colors?"

"Black or gray?" Danika asks hopefully. "I don't do cheerful."

The women launch into a discussion about handbags, giving Charlie the opportunity to give me a snap-out-of-it look across the table. He's right, and I'm fucking trying, but I still shoot him the finger because that's how we roll. There's no more talk of Katie's imminent departure throughout the rest of dinner, but it's no use.

My blood refuses to relax. I'm restless. The more I think about Katie leaving, the harder it becomes to remember what I was going to offer her in the first place. To make her stay. My honesty, my protection, shit, my heart. I would have spent every day growing into who I want and need to be. The man she deserves. Now Sunday is firing at me like a bullet and my fingertips are clinging to the edge of a cliff. I'm desperate to commit to memory the way only Katie makes me feel, lucid and present. Grounded. Healthy.

Every time Katie's hand slides over my knee, the desperation flares brighter. Every time she crosses her legs and the red hem of her dress skims over smooth thighs, I curl my fingers into fists. Those tiny buttons keeping her tits hidden seem to strain, begging my fingers to rip them open. Need her. Need, need, need.

There's a ticktock in my mind that drowns out the conversation. Only two more nights to spend with Katie. Two more nights to commit myself to her memory. Katie crying out my name echoes in my head. I was her first and I'm desperate, determined to mark her as mine so thoroughly, she thinks about me for the rest of her life. God knows I'll spend mine missing her.

By the time the dishes are cleared, my cock is tunneled down inside the leg of my pants, my abdomen permanently flexed, my throat dry. We are part of the late crowd, so the lights have been dimmed, candlelight and loud music turning the busy establishment into more of a boisterous lounge. Drinks are clanking all over the place, ringing in my ears, but I'm only thirsty for the girl beside me.

Charlie and Ever excuse themselves and head to the dance floor, located in a separate room beyond the service bar, salsa music now in full swing. Danika gets a phone call—either fake or real—and heads off to take it, leaving us alone at the table. My fingers brush down Katie's bare arm and she shivers. I think the tension between us from earlier has melted away during the ease of the meal, but when she glances up at me through her lashes, doubt creeps in.

"Just heading to the ladies'," she murmurs in my ear. "I'll be right back."

Unease coiling in my gut, I watch Katie weave though the tables towards the back of the restaurant. Only about two minutes pass before I follow.

CHAPTER 24

Katie

Every inch of my body is covered in gooseflesh. I'm one of three women in the restroom, but I don't let an audience stop me from patting cold water on my cheeks and attempting to restore my equilibrium. I don't even think Jack realizes how much sexual energy he gives off, but my hormones sure do. They've been riding roller coasters for the last hour, screaming their stupid little heads off, while Jack brushed his fingertips along every exposed portion of my skin. Sending me shameful promises with his green eyes. Groaning each time I crossed my legs.

As if I didn't have enough to think about during dinner, there was the added conundrum of hard nipples, flushed skin and my pulse jumping at the base of my neck.

Two young women appear in the mirror behind me, one smiling shyly, the other giving an
exaggerated sigh. They're tittering in one another's ear, just above a whisper, so I catch some of
their conversation and can't help but chuckle under my breath.

*She's the one sitting with the freakin' Armani model-
looking dude.*

We should ask if he has brothers.

Or if she has any tips for those less fortunate.

"Sorry, girls. He only likes natural redheads." I
give them a warm smile in the mirror. "Maybe in
your next lives."

"Shit," I hear the shy one say on their way out.
"I need to develop an accent."

"There's probably a YouTube tutorial," the other
one mutters back.

Left alone in the candlelit restroom, I try to
focus on anything except my damp underwear,
my fired-up pulse. Despite my heightened state
of arousal making it hard to eat without chok-
ing, tonight has been . . . fun. So fun. I love Charlie, Ever and Danika. They're smart, complicated
and warm, a combination I never realized would
appeal to me so much. All the while we were ban-
tering about everything under the sun, though,
my mind kept circling back to Jack's reaction to
me considering the Olympics again.

Four years of your life.

Before this trip to New York, I put the games in

my rearview mirror, but the increasing pressure from my father has me traveling backwards. It's possible I've just become so accustomed to being what keeps my father happy, I don't know how to shake loose of that responsibility.

Or it could be something else entirely that has me contemplating competition once more. This bone-deep intuition that once I leave Jack, I'll need to occupy myself 24–7 to keep from missing him. To keep from worrying about him.

But . . . if by some crazy twist, I stayed in New York, would it be the worry for Jack that keeps me here? My tendency to be relied on, no matter the cost to myself? Or would it simply be because the idea of living without him sends a shiver up my spine?

As soon as the thought touches down, the bathroom door opens. My breath catches in my throat, my thigh muscles contracting when I find Jack filling the frame. There's no question as to why he's here. Is his inevitable pursuit why I escaped the table? Did I know he'd come find me, put me out of this misery?

My knees begin to tremble as he saunters towards where I stand at the sink, the thud thud thud of his boots increasing the pace of my heartbeat. "You can't be in here," I murmur, uselessly, glancing to my right at the three private stalls that proclaim this isn't a private restroom. "Jack, just take me home."

His low laugh reminds me of someone twisting their heel in sand. "Ahh, honey. You know this can't wait."

Heat coats my stomach, spreading in every direction. My fingers, my nipples, my spine are all tingling with sparks. Every breath scrapes up my lungs and shudders out past my lips. I'm dying for movement, for friction, but at the same time I'm paralyzed. I can't move as Jack comes up behind me, drawing me back against him with an inescapable forearm. Then he walks me into the stall closest to the wall—a handicap one, may God forgive us—slamming and locking it in our wake.

There's a half-open window in the tiled wall, old, the glass clouded. Jack urges me towards the wide sill, which is painted by flickering light, courtesy of the candle sitting on one side. I drop my purse on the floor, uncaring how it lands or if it gets dirty. My hands need somewhere to brace and they do, curving around the windowsill's edge.

Jack's hands grip my hips, yanking them back to press my bottom against his lap, and I almost black out from the rush of urgent, red-hot lust. He's right—we never would have made it home with his sex so thick, prominent, refusing to be hidden by his clothing. The only way to fix him is by putting that flesh inside me and the thrill of being desired, needed, to that degree makes my neck lose power, as my forehead meets the glass.

Music plays loudly through a speaker overhead, fast-paced and dizzying, but it's not enough to cover Jack's curses as he grinds his lap against my ass. Pressing his open mouth to the pulse of my neck while he rolls forwards, me teasing back. Both of us groaning. If we were in a quiet room, I would hear the rasp of chiffon now while his greedy hands lift my dress.

"There's that sweet, sexy ass, Katie. All prettied up in a thong for me." His teeth abrade the back of my sensitive neck, his hot breath ghosting through my hair. "I haven't forgotten I wanted to take you from behind this morning. Hell no, I haven't. I've been wondering all day if you'd have sobbed from the pressure, same as you did when I fucked you on your back."

My feet slide out from beneath me, but Jack holds me upright, that steady, unyielding forearm keeping my hips angled back. "Oh. My God."

His expert mouth traces along my neck, shoulders, into my hair, leaving kisses. "Should I find out, honey?"

"Yes."

"About the sobbing, I mean."

"Yes."

My dress is rucked up around my waist, so I can feel the back of Jack's hand, his knuckles grazing the separation of my backside while he unfastens his belt, button, lowering his zipper with a metallic zing. "Reach back and tug down these sopping wet panties for me, Katie. Tilt your hips until I can see pink. All of it's mine. Hand it over."

I'm pretty sure I'm going to pass out, because blood has fled from my head. My thighs are wobbling so bad, they're chafing along the front of Jack's jeans, but despite the sudden loss of control of my motor skills, I manage to complete the task of leaning all my weight on the windowsill and reaching back to slide down my underwear. It slips to my knees and remains there a split second, falling to my ankles when I widen my stance, push up my bottom and present myself to Jack as he asked. "Like this?"

"Just like that. Jesus, honey. You're so fucking perfect." His calloused hands conform to each side of my bottom, tightening and releasing. Tightening again. Lifting me onto my toes. Dropping me down. I'm a whimpering disaster, attached to the puppet strings of his will, accepting every touch with gratitude and hungering for more. One hand falls away and I hear the crinkle and rip of foil. "Want to be inside you bareback again, honey. You know I do so goddamn bad. But I need to use a rubber this time, or my come will drip down your legs all night, okay?"

My mouth falls open, my core constricting, at the familiarity of his speech. The crudeness of it shouldn't make me this insane with want, but it does. I love that Jack is so well acquainted with me, my body, that he filters nothing out.

"You like me talking like that, don't you, Katie?"

The answer whooshes out of me. "Yes."

That's when the bathroom door opens and footsteps join our chorus of heavy breathing and salsa music. Irritation claws up my back—that's how far gone I am. Someone walking into the public space where I'm getting ready to engage in something illegal annoys me instead of causing me the normal reaction of panic. I'm only panicked that Jack will stop.

"Shh. There's no one here but us." I needn't have worried because his incredible hands grow even more determined. I've never been touched this intimately by anyone else, but instinct tells me Jack's touch is singular. Utterly unique. No man would rake his fingers up my scalp, mashing the tips into my nerve endings, tugging lightly on the strands and setting off explosions in erogenous zones I didn't know existed. Not when my panties are already down, my most private places exposed to his eyes. No other man would slowly, deliberately unbutton my dress, uncovering my breasts while high heels scuffle in the neighboring stall.

His breath races in my ear, his erection resting on my backside, sliding up to the small of my back when he works his hips. "These buttons have been making me crazy all damn night," he rasps. One hand slides into the parted material of my dress to cup and squeeze my breast, searing my skin through the lace of my bra. "They're the same size as your hard little nipples." His index and middle fingers coast into my bra, clamping around the bud in question and a shiver racks my body. "You're lucky we're in a dark restaurant or everyone would have seen how badly you need to get railed."

"Can you just . . ." I'm gasping for air, shocked by his blunt words, but thrilled by them down to my toes. "Do it. Please."

Jack's laugh tugs my stomach south, the uneven quality of it making me brave. My knuckles turn white on the windowsill as I sway side to side, circling my bottom on his lap, trapping his erection between my cheeks, lifting on my toes and lowering in as sensual a movement as I can manage when my self-control has withered and I'm going to die. His hands become punishing on my breasts, his low, rumbling growl sizzling my blood.

Water begins running out in the main area of the bathroom, but Jack pays it no attention, skating his right hand down my belly, his long middle finger finding my clit and teasing it. "Tiny little buttons everywhere, wanting to be pinched and stroked." The pace of his rubbing picks up until I'm biting my lip hard enough to draw blood, to stop myself from screaming. "Can't believe I'm the lucky bastard that gets to do it for you, Katie. You just give me those big eyes and flash me your hard nipples and I'll know it's stroking time, won't I? You trust me to know when it's time, don't you?"

"Yes," I gasp, my focus wavering. No longer do I care about where we are, who is listening or how deeply I've fallen for Jack. How scary and irreversible these feelings seem to be, gathering like storm clouds, preparing to pour down on my head. Getting him inside me is the pot of gold at the end of my life's rainbow and I'm so, so ready that moisture is trailing down the insides of my legs. "Please. Please. Please."

A kiss on my nape, followed by a rough bite. "It's coming, honey."

No sooner does that bathroom door slam shut, leaving us alone once again in the restroom, than Jack drives himself inside me so hard I'm elevated several inches off the ground. I scream. I scream without attempting to subdue the wild sound, but it's swallowed in the loud, fast-paced music and the sharp slap of Jack's thighs against my bottom. My orgasm is blinding, tightening and loosening bolts beneath my belly button, shaking my limbs and filling my eyes with startled tears.

"I love you," I attempt to say, but it comes out strangled, too quiet to be heard and unintelligible to anyone but me. I mean it, though. Somehow I mean what I said with every fiber of my being. But even as Jack's heavy flesh pumping into my body drags me back towards the edge, a nagging intuition tells me to keep the words to myself. That I need to hang on to one final scrap of my emotions for safekeeping.

From what?

Jack

I'm disappearing into Katie. Or we're vanishing into one another. I'm too strangled with sensation and need for this girl to figure out a goddamn thing. There's only the barest outline of her in the foggy window, my thrusts propelling her up and down, so I close my eyes and picture that gorgeous flush that deepens on her cheeks when she climaxes.

Can't believe she's already coming. Or can't I? I could spill every drop inside of her right now, if I didn't want to spend a little longer high on the unbelievable feel of her. Katie does something to me. Does everything to me. Gets me so crowded full of possessiveness and starvation that I can barely focus on lasting. Knowing I do the same for her makes me proud. Not in an arrogant way. Hell no. I'm humble as fuck. I want to kneel at her feet and beg for the continued duty of giving her orgasms.

"You're wrapped around me so tight, Katie." I lift her onto her toes, bracing her hips against the windowsill, desperate to keep her still, so my cock can drive the deepest. As soon as I get her in the right position, my head falls back and I groan, my hips moving with a mind of their own. "I'm fucking myself right up against the curve of your ass, watching it get pinker every time it bounces off my stomach. Looks like you've been spanked. Jesus, I'm going to love tucking that thong back between those slapped-up cheeks."

When she goes off again, her pussy clenching around me and milking, milking, I almost laugh over the perfection of her. The pleasure that curls in my chest, my head, over being the man who is allowed this privilege. Even though I'm now suffering, because I've held back from coming so fiercely, my body is moving without any kind of precision or direction, trying to find its way back to the Promised Land. I'm fuck-stoned on Katie, every skill or trick in my arsenal utterly useless against the magic we make.

My ability to be rational or make sense is dead. There's only me and Katie. What else is there besides this? Us? This is only the start, though. I want to be better. She made me believe Jack the Good Man is not a hopeless pipe dream and I'm dying for the chance to prove her right. Prove it to both of us, starting now. Now. It can't wait.

Stay, Katie.

My middle finger slips down to where our bodies are joined, where my cock rides into the only place it ever wants to call home, gathering moisture. I get my finger nice and slick, then use it to worship her poor, swollen clit. Rubbing her there until she's a whimpering mess, dancing around on my fat dick like she can't stand another second of feeling good. "One more time, honey. Just one more time, I promise." I make a soothing sound in her ear. "I'm going to finish so hard, just give me another squeeze, right where I need it."

As if I'm not already sprung as fuck on everything this girl says and does, she flattens her palms on the window and constricts those little muscles around me, her thighs shaking with the effort of not collapsing, of giving me that final push. Shit, shit, shit. The promise of shattering is like a manacle around my throat. Wrapping both arms around Katie, I go wild, bucking into her cunt and reveling in the wet sounds that echo in my ears.

"Give yourself to me. I'll keep you safe. Keep what's mine safe," I growl into her ear, a vengeful beast who has been stripped of everything but his desire for one thing. The girl. Forever. "I *need* you, Katie. Stay with me. I need you so much."

We both go off, my lower body pulverized by the intensity of the release. Through the teeth-clenching ride of finally giving in, though, I swear I sense a thread of tension in Katie. Must be my imagination, right? Must be. We're meshed together in a boneless heap against the window-sill, my fingers still desperate for the smoothness of her inner thighs, tracing shapeless symbols there, my mouth laying kisses in her hair.

As the seconds tick by, though, it becomes more and more obvious that I didn't imagine Katie holding back at the very end. What is it? I don't know, but I've just dropped every bit of my armor, leaving it scattered across the floor. It no longer fits and I don't know how to put it back on. "Katie?"

She eases out from beneath me, correcting her dress while I stoop down, gliding the thong up her legs, settling it back in place as promised. I dispose of the condom and zip myself back into my pants, buckle my belt with stiff fingers. When she still hasn't turned around by the time I'm finished, panic is a blade inserted in my jugular.

"Hey, Snaps." Taking her shoulders, I turn her to face me, swallowing hard when I see her downcast eyes. "What's wrong?"

She licks her lips, face ashen. "What you said . . ."

"About you staying?" I don't hesitate. I can't. The desire to let her see what's written on my heart is fierce. "I meant it. Stay."

Electricity zips back and forth between us. "There was more."

"Tell me what I said that bothered you." I reach out, tucking a strand of hair behind her ear. "Tell me what you didn't like, so I can apologize."

"This isn't out of the blue, it's something I've thought about." She shakes her head. "I'm not sure it's something you should apologize for."

"Let me decide that." My voice is growing hard with fear. What the hell is happening? "Was I too rough, or—"

"No. No, it's nothing like that."

Raking my hands over my head, I curse my stupid crew cut. I'd love to pull out some hair by the fucking roots right now. Especially when the bathroom door opens and two female voices ratchet up the thick atmosphere between Katie and me. As soon as I hear the girls lock themselves into stalls, chatting away happily, I take her hand and lead her out of the bathroom quickly. I stop in the dark hallway just outside the door, pressing her shoulders back against the red wall, dropping myself to eye level, searching her distress for an answer. "Talk to me."

She takes several deep breaths while my impatience and dread multiplies. "I'm sure you didn't mean to freak me out like this. I *know* you didn't. But saying you need me—"

A plate smashes in the kitchen down the hallway, seeming to divert Katie's attention. Like it's a sign or something. I take her chin and draw her back, trying desperately to maintain focus through the crashing waves in my head. "Keep talking."

Her expression remains clouded. "You're doing so amazing already with your recovery. You're going to try so hard to stay on track—I *know* it. But I've been needed by someone before. I still am." She shakes her head in quick jerks. "Even if you won't mean to, I'm . . . I'm just afraid of being relied on. More than I already am."

My breaths are deafening in my ears. Jesus, I've been worried about Katie's father using her as a distraction from his pain, a crutch. Am I in the same category? No. No, I need her because she's welded herself to my heart and she's going to rip the side off of it by leaving. I haven't even begun to try to make her happy and if she goes, I'll miss out on . . . *her*. What's next for Katie? What's next for us? I understand why she's worried about me leaning too heavily on her, but I'm at a loss how to ease her mind. What if I can't? "I told you, Katie." My voice creaks like a moored boat. "Me getting my act together is not your responsibility."

"Even if I stayed . . ." We both go still, the elusive possibility hovering in the air like a glowing halo. "Even if I stayed, I couldn't be the only reason you fight. Every time we argue or one of us gets busy with work, I'd worry I wasn't doing enough. I-I can't. It has to be about you."

"I'm not going to lie. Wanting to be a better man for you is a huge part of what's motivating me, but I know it's not your fight, Katie. I know." I shake her by the shoulders. "How do I convince you?"

"I don't know if you can."

Her mouth snaps shut, like she didn't mean to say it, but in degrees her resolve hardens and she can no longer meet my gaze, unleashing a legion of denial in my gut.

How does a man go from king of the universe to flat on his ass in the space of five minutes? Katie is the reason I started going to meetings, the person who made me realize I want more out of my future. All of that is true. But I have too much awareness now to rest all my fears and hopes on Katie's shoulders. I won't do that. Not after her father pinned his journey from grief to recovery on Katie, too. Put her through four years of training to occupy his mind.

No. I won't.

"Honey, look at me." I capture the sides of her face in my hands, devastated right to the core of my being when tears form in her eyes. "You can't fix the world. I'll never forget what you've done for me, because no one else could have gotten to me like this, made me realize I'm capable of better. But you alone can't fix me, either."

She blows out a breath and nods, but doubt lingers in her expression. There's a good chance I could hold her for a while in this hallway, take her home and get past this. At least until she gets on the plane, we could have fun, fuck until our bodies give out, discover a million ways to miss each other. But that's no longer enough for me. This girl has given me hope. I'm not going to rest until I give her the same. Until she, too, knows her needs are just as important as everyone else's. Mine, her father's. Even her brother's.

She came here with a plan for *herself*. And I got in the way. But I won't be selfish anymore. Even if making sure Katie realizes her own hopes and dreams means sacrificing mine.

And the one thing I have worth sacrificing is my final days with her.

Invisible teeth sink into my throat, making it impossible to swallow as I kiss Katie's forehead and back away. One step. Two. She looks confused by the distance between us, making what I'm about to do infinitely worse. "I'll be there before you go to the airport, Katie. Don't doubt me, okay?"

"Jack." Her hand lifts, curling around her throat. "Where are you going?"

"I'll be fine." I can't help myself, I crowd her against the wall one more time, pressing our foreheads together, looking her in the eye. "I will be fine. Nod if you trust me."

It takes her too long to nod, which makes what I'm going to do even more necessary. My heart is shouting at me from its position in my chest, trying to escape my ribcage. So I give in. Give in to what it's insisting I set loose. Who knows if I'll get a better chance?

"I love you, Katie." My mouth settles over hers and devours, impressing my vow on her with a hot glide of my tongue. A thorough tasting. Thumbs tracing her cheekbones. She sways forwards into me, and it costs me an effort, levering her back against the wall, leaving her there, supported by something other than me. "I'll make sure Charlie and the girls get you home safe."

Talking to Charlie, Ever and Danika on the busy dance floor is a blur, but I gain their promise to get Katie back to her room, locked inside for the night. No exceptions.

And then I go to work on my plan, hoping like hell my sacrifice makes a difference, missing Katie more with every step down the dark sidewalk.

CHAPTER 25

Katie

What have I done?

I'm sitting on the edge of my bed and my suitcases are packed at my feet and the sun is close to setting. There's a voice mail from Danika on my cell *and* my hotel phone asking me out to a late lunch, but I couldn't bring myself to call her back. Couldn't bring myself to do much of anything today but pack. I haven't seen Jack since he left me reeling in the hallway of the restaurant, his words ringing in my ears, lighting up my heart.

I love you, Katie.

I didn't say it back. I didn't say it back.

I feel the same way. But didn't return the words. If I'd said them, he would have stayed, I think. Maybe? Could he have left me if I'd looked him in the eye and told him? He definitely wouldn't have given me one, final tortured look and vanished into the mass of moving people, right? No, not Jack. He would have swept me up and celebrated.

Instead of being honest and admitting I've taken some wild leap into love, starting the moment we met, I fell into my usual pattern weighing the good and bad. Pro: It will make him happy. Con: I'm still leaving. Pro: It's the truth and I've vowed to be honest with Jack. Con: Telling Jack I love him back won't solve our problem.

Stay with me. I need you so much.

Boom. X marks the spot. I've been steeling myself against an unknown worry and words spoken in passion had uncovered it neatly enough. Knowing that a relationship between Jack and me could lead to him being reliant on me doesn't make me care for him any less, though. Doesn't make my heart beat any differently. God, no.

After coming home last night and showering, I've been sitting in the same spot in a T-shirt and underwear, petrified. Petrified that driving a wedge between us means Jack is out there somewhere right now, using alcohol to mask the pain.

But that only validates my worry that I'll funnel all my energy into keeping him healthy, doesn't it? I want to believe in him, the way he begged me to. I'm dying to have faith. The clock is mocking me, though. Calling me foolish for sitting here and waiting for Jack to show up. Why would he have left last night . . . if it wasn't to alleviate the stress I created the only way he knows how? He won't call me for help, either, if he needs it. Because I've severed the very hope I created.

Is this how life would be if I stayed? Sitting in the near-dark, waiting for my boyfriend to show up? Staring at my phone, hoping for and dreading a call from him or Danika, asking me to get in a cab and bring him home? Or worse, a call from the police saying he's accidentally taken someone else's brother away. Does my love outweigh the fear?

One thing is for certain. My flight leaves early in the morning. I scheduled the wake-up call for lack of anything better to do and it's coming at half-four. What is my plan? To sit here and wait through the night for some miracle to occur?

I can't do it. I can't sit here waiting for disappointment.

I've been stationary so long, my knees protest when I stand, moving in a cyclone of activity around the room. I pull on the jeans and sweater laid out over the desk, shoving my nightshirt into the front pocket of my suitcase. When I'm forced to search for a tissue to wipe my running nose, I realize I'm crying. So I stop, take a deep breath and steel myself, before shoving my feet into my runners and leaving the room, dragging my suitcases behind me.

I'd rather sit at the airport and wait until morning arrives than spend another second in uncertainty. This way, at least the decision will be made for me. I'm leaving New York, there's nothing more to it, and if I'm not sitting on my hotel bed like a sap, Jack can't arrive to either deliver a painful goodbye or apologize for slipping up.

As I step into the lobby downstairs, my heart is being wrenched from my body. I'm not returning to Ireland as my whole self. There are pieces of me scattered all over the island. In Hell's Kitchen where Jack kissed me in the park, on the subway where Jack sang while holding out his hat for donations, upstairs in my room where we made love, a few blocks away in a church basement, where Jack bared his soul.

My steps stutter beneath the giant chandelier, but I force myself to keep moving, my focus narrowed down to the string of taxis waiting at the curb. It's Saturday night. People are all dressed up for dinner, piano music swells in the lobby with a lively tune, luggage carts wheel past. There's something very ungratifying about the world continuing on as usual when your insides are collapsing, isn't there? Shouldn't someone ask me if I'm all right?

I'm not. I'm not okay.

Then again, I wouldn't be okay even if Jack spent the night, held me until my wake-up call and kissed me goodbye at the curb. I would have crumbled then, too, right? I'm only speeding up the inevitable, while holding on to that final image of him an inch from my face. *I love you, Katie.*

That's how I'll remember him. Not some other way both of us will regret.

Stepping out into the crisp evening, horns, whistles, wind kick up around me. The valet takes one look at my suitcases and gestures for the closest yellow cab to pull up. It takes him two attempts to pry the suitcase handle from my hands, which would be embarrassing if my blood wasn't freezing, ceasing to flow, my legs turning to concrete—

"Katie!"

The return of my blood flow is so immediate and unexpected, I sway left and almost fall into a potted tree. The world around me blooms back into color, starting with Jack. He's halfway down the block, stopped in his tracks and his expression will remain with me until I'm a grandmother, knitting beside a fire. He's dying. Oh my God, is he dying?

All at once, things start moving again. The valet taps my shoulder and grunts, indicating that my suitcases have been loaded into the boot of the cab, Jack starts running towards me and I realize I've made a stupid, impulsive decision by leaving for the airport without saying goodbye. My bones brace for Jack to reach me, to grab me, but instead he veers towards the cab, dragging my suitcases from the back, tossing them onto the sidewalk like they weigh nothing. The valet and cab driver aim a litany of curses at Jack, which shakes me out of my stupor. "It's okay." My tone is pitiful and tearstained. "It's okay. I-I . . . he's with me and I must have gotten the time wrong . . ."

Having finished removing my luggage from the cab, Jack wheels around with an incredulous look. "Must have gotten the time wrong?" He whips out his cell and checks the time. "It's six goddamn thirty. Your flight doesn't leave until tomorrow."

"I was only trying to make it sound plausible," I whisper, like a feckin' idiot. Without glancing around, I'm aware of everyone on the sidewalk staring. And my stubborn Irish roots gnarl around my throat, heat searing the backs of my eyes. "You've been gone a full day," I shout at Jack. "You scared me and I couldn't wait around anymore."

The worst of his irritation fades. "Okay, honey. I'm sorry, okay? I'm sorry you were scared." He slumps back against the cab, closing his eyes. "Jesus. You were leaving."

"Where have you been?" Someone give me a housecoat, because I sound like a scorned wife. And so be it. "Where did you go?"

Green eyes hold mine steadily, but some wildness still floats in their background. "Come with me and I'll show you."

"You going to need a cab for that?" asks the perturbed valet. "Otherwise I'm going to need this lovers' quarrel—entertaining though it is— to take place elsewhere."

Jack pushes off the cab, stooping down to pull

one of my suitcases out of the pile he made. "We only need this one. Can you give her a claim ticket for the rest?" He replaces it in the boot and slams it shut. "She's not leaving yet."

I should be indignant over decisions being made on my behalf, but the relief is like a cool blanket of snow, covering everything. Not only is Jack here, but he's fine. Clear-eyed, agile and determined to take me somewhere. I'll happily go anyplace with him on the entire planet, but I don't pass on the sentiment, because he doesn't appear receptive at the moment, his brows drawn, jaw tight.

Finally, Jack approaches, hovering a foot away with enough presence for ten men, scrutinizing me as the valet scribbles on a pink tag, handing it to Jack. "Done and done." The man opens the cab door and waves us in, knocking on the roof when Jack and I are seated on opposite ends of the vehicle. "Best of luck to you."

Something tells me I'm going to need it.

Jack

Surely there are things I'm supposed to be saying right now.

Well, I can't think of a fucking one.

I apologized for scaring Katie, so at least that's

out of the way. Now I'm working on recovering from the heart attack that seized my body when I saw her loading luggage into a cab. My limbs are numb, but somehow at the same time, my muscles are tight enough to snap. Lava pitches around in my stomach like I drank straight from a volcano. If I'd been thirty seconds later, she'd be gone right now. Flying through the Midtown Tunnel on her way to JFK, already putting me in her rearview. Is that where she wants me? Has everything I've done over the last twenty-four hours been for nothing?

"Where are you headed?"

It takes me a good five seconds to figure out the driver is speaking to me. Instead of Saint Peter welcoming me to heaven because I'm actually lying dead back on the curb. "Uh, Canal and Church. Thanks."

Katie shifts in her seat, her voice softer than a whisper. "What's happening there?"

"Nothing," I rasp, dragging both hands down my face. "Probably nothing."

"You're angry with me."

"I . . . fuck, I don't even know." Honesty is my default with Katie. Lying or softening isn't even a consideration. "I can't feel anything right now."

She blows out a breath. "Imagine a full day of the exact opposite."

I reach over to take her hand, because I hate hearing her leftover worry, but they're bundled in her lap, leeching her knuckles of color. "The only thing on my mind for the last twenty-four hours has been you. It has been all Katie. Nothing else." My swallow is heavy. "Just like you gave up four years for your father, gave up most of your trip for me . . . I gave up the thing I want most today. Time with you." Worried she's going to cut off her circulation—and dammit, needing contact—I pry her hands apart and warm them between mine. "I should have called. I'm sorry. I knew if I heard your voice, I would stop what I was doing to go be with you. And I'm done being selfish."

Her back straightens in a way that's become familiar. "You were never selfish. The drinking wasn't about you being selfish."

"In a lot of ways, it was." I bring her hand to my mouth, laying kisses on her knuckles. "I was so focused on blocking out my own pain, I stopped seeing how much it hurt everyone else. Then I met this feisty redhead who taught me all about selflessness. So I can't hide and be selfish, anymore, without being aware. Without caring about the effect it has." I smile against the back of her hand. "It's kind of a pain in the ass."

She lets out this adorable half-sob, half-laugh that crams my throat full of pressure. I'm already reaching for her when she launches across the seat into my arms. Her face buries in the crook of my neck, soothing the center of my chest, spreading to reach every corner of my body. "I'm sorry," she says. "I wouldn't have made it to the airport."

"If you had, I'd have come and gotten you."

"I just couldn't sit there anymore."

"I know. I'm sorry." I squeeze her tight as I can without breaking bones. "I think I got ahead of myself, wanting you to trust that I wouldn't fuck up. I'm an idiot."

"No, you're not."

The nerves I've been swimming in all day return with the ebbing of my numbness. "I guess we'll find out when we get where we're going."

CHAPTER 26

— Katie —

During my trip, I haven't ventured to this part of the city, but as Jack helps me out of the cab, I know I'm in Chinatown. Chinese writing adorns the store awnings, the banks, food carts. Traffic whizzes past on the wide street behind me, cars already blaring their horns for our cab to get out of their way, so I'm distracted when Jack leads me down the sidewalk, rolling my suitcase in his free hand. Jesus, I would be distracted no matter what, after spending most of the fifteen-minute cab ride in Jack's arms, listening to his heart riot out of control against my ear.

His hand is a touch sweaty intertwined with mine, a muscle twitching in his cheek.

Nervous. He's nervous. Why?

Night has swooped in, covering the city in glittering lights and cooler temperatures. Garbage whips past in the gutters, the brisk wind forcing men to raise their collars. I'm in too much of a trance to feel much, though. My gaze keeps returning to Jack's incredible face, my mind wandering through the last two weeks.

I'm still the girl who scouted mob hit sites in a backpack, but I've changed, too. Two weeks ago, there were no gray areas when it came to my convictions, but those very convictions almost alienated the man beside me, when he needed help. I've learned a lot about how I respond when I'm scared—like fleeing to the airport. I've also learned I can give propriety and rules the finger when a situation calls for it. Jesus, I'm complicated. But that's okay. Life is complicated. It's also ongoing. *I'm* ongoing.

I came to New York to have enough of an adventure for my brother and me both. Instead I've become involved with a man afflicted with a need for alcohol, the very thing that took Sean. How would my brother react to me spending every spare minute with Jack? Would he be disappointed or hurt?

No, Sean would take one look at me and know that Jack was always meant to be my adventure. He wouldn't hold Jack's issues against me—or him—he would understand. That's the kind of man Sean was. Generous of spirit. Capable of seeing the best in people. And while I want to help Jack, I think in an unseen way, I'm healing the part of myself that lost my brother, too. I'm correcting something in the fabric of my world that was ripped down the middle when Sean passed away. God knows my brother always had a peculiar sense of humor, maybe he sent Jack my way on purpose. His way of telling me to let go and love. Just love.

Maybe it wasn't the universe sending me all those signs. Maybe it was Sean all along.

Now I'm walking down an unfamiliar street, trusting this man to guide me somewhere . . . and feeling totally at peace with that decision. Suddenly, my world is huge and complex. I'm here because I choose to be. Because my life is my own. My decisions—*correct* ones—are what brought me to this moment in time, no one else's.

Knowing my own mind is responsible for this firm ground beneath my feet makes me feel strong. I might have had a crisis of faith back at the hotel. It's totally possible I'll have another one in the future. But I'll find my own way through it. Through anything.

I want to find my way with Jack. He wouldn't be on his own solid ground without me. And I wouldn't have discovered how tough I am without him. How unwilling I am to give up when I believe in something. Somebody. I'm independent.

I'm also with Jack.

And I don't want to leave. I don't want to leave him or this place behind.

I'm not going to go. I'm not leaving this man I love.

My steps falter and Jack—looking worried—catches my arm. "You okay?"

"Yeah."

Eyebrows drawn, he tips his head in the direction we're walking. "We're almost there."

"Grand," I murmur. "I have to tell you something—"

"Surprise," Jack interrupts, taking me by the shoulders and turning me sideways.

I don't process what's in front of me. Not right away. Probably because I can't believe what I'm seeing or that it's happening in real life. Danika, Charlie and Ever are standing a few yards away, smiling at me. Behind them is an empty stall, nestled among the other vendors selling wares. Handbags, mostly. And that's what tips me off. The second—bigger—hint is the sign hanging above the stall. *Katie McCoy Handbags. Imported from Ireland.*

"What is this?"

Jack blocks my view of the stall and his friends, hands sliding into his pockets. His voice sounds faraway because the thudding of my pulse is drowning it out. "You want to go home and spend four more years preparing for the Olympics, Katie, I won't stop you. But I wanted you to know you're important. More than what I want or your father wants. The things you love and want are important."

"Jack." My hands fly to my face. They're shaking violently. I can't even begin to process what this means, what he's saying. The magnitude is only occurring in increments. "How did you do this?"

"Pays to have friends in high places." Jack smiles over his shoulder at Charlie, who throws him a salute. "Turns out someone in the licensing division owed Charlie's dad a favor. But the permit is only good through tonight, so we better get selling."

"I don't know what to say." Comprehension dawns. Finally. "This is what you've been doing all day?"

He scratches the back of his neck. "Started last night, actually. Would have been done sooner, but the sign maker took his sweet-ass time."

My laugh is awkward and watery, but Jack only smiles. He actually has the bloody nerve to look relieved, as if this isn't the most amazing gift one human being could give another. "Oh my God. Thank you. What . . ." I look down at the suitcase of bags he's wheeling. "What if no one buys one?"

His confidence is back and it's blinding. "Come on, Snaps. Even if they weren't the best-looking purses in town, you've got four New Yorkers on the payroll."

I don't know exactly what he means until I see them in action. It takes ten minutes to hang the bags—all twenty of them—and everything after that is a blur. A happy, fantastic, life-altering blur. Danika and Jack pace the sidewalk, calling out to passersby, charming them until they relent and stop by the booth. Tourists, especially, don't stand a chance when faced with Jack and Danika's smooth wheeling and dealing. In one instance, a group of women actually cross the busy avenue and stop traffic to get a close up look at Jack, which Danika and Charlie eye roll so hard, they almost get stuck in that position.

A pattern forms, smooth and seamless. Once Jack and Danika hook the customer, Ever and Charlie close the deal by being flat out magnetic, all smiles and compliments, taking money out of the customers' hands before they even realize the transaction has begun. That doesn't stop me from being thrilled down to my fingertips every time someone walks away with one of my creations. Or mentally tap-dancing when women pause to compliment the style and colors.

Within half an hour, the bags are all gone. Except for one.

Jack reaches up and takes it off the hook, handing it to me. "Last one, Snaps. You want to do the honors?"

I start to say no, because after seeing these four in action, my career as a salesperson crashed and burned before it even started flying. I'm more confident with a rifle in my hand than sewn-together leather. Two truths stop me from passing up the chance, though. One, if I don't take advantage of this opportunity, I will always regret it. Two, after Jack went to this much trouble, I'm not going to let him down. "Watch and learn, Jack Garrett."

Heat slides into his eyes and I saunter past, walking with a lot more confidence than I'm currently feeling. My bravado deflates a little as I stutter through a greeting of the first man who walks past. He doesn't even glance up from his phone. But Jack gives me a reassuring nod, bringing back my poise.

Turning my attention back to the foot traffic, I'm brought up short by a young man coming towards me. His haircut, his clothes, even the way he walks reminds me of Sean. He catches me looking, so I don't even attempt to greet him, worried I might come off creepy.

He stops instead, glancing towards the stall, then back to the purse in my hands. "Are you selling that?"

"Yes." Shaking myself, I turn over the red bag, brushing a thumb over the silver buckle. "It's a lovely gift for your girlfriend or mother."

"I was thinking I'd use it for myself."

"Really." I clear my throat. "Sure, that's fine, too—"

He winks at me and I hear Jack growl. "I'm only joking. It's for a friend."

"Oh." We share a laugh. "I made this purse myself, you know. Walk up and down this street, you won't find another like it."

"Hey, I'm already sold." He digs a twenty out of his wallet, handing it over in exchange for the purse. "Someday when you're famous, I'll be smug knowing I have an original."

"You do that," I say to his departing back. And maybe it's the place and time, the magic of New York City at night, but I feel a tiny tick of closure as the stranger continues on his way. Like this stranger that reminded me so much of my brother was Sean's final sign that I'm on the right course. Doing the right thing by staying.

I have only a split second to reflect on the odd feeling, though, because Jack scoops me up, tossing me a foot into the air, catching me again. Charlie, Ever and Danika are attempting to perform a three-person wave in front of the stall. The blast of euphoria and gratitude that hits me is powerful, sending a laugh bubbling up from my throat.

Jack sets me back on my feet, taking my face in his hands and tiling my head back. "You did it. That was all you."

"No." I shake my head. "I had help. A lot of it."

"I love you, Katie." His green eyes seem to be memorizing my face. "Too much to ask you to stay." He breathes hard. A punctuation. And suddenly he can't look at me, clearly in physical agony. "Shit, I told you not being selfish is a pain in the ass."

My lungs expel every bit of oxygen, the world seeming to pause around us expectantly. "When you leave, Katie, the sun is going to keep coming up. But it's going to stay set inside of me, you know?" He brushes my hair back, picking up the strands and looking at each of them individually. "That's my cross to bear, though. Making you stay . . . it would be for me. And I refuse to make demands on your time. Not when I know that same thing has made you unhappy before."

I swear my heart is giving a death rattle, because what's the point of continuing living when you've already heard something so perfect and beautiful? "Remember when I told you about the handbags, Jack? I said if I could sell one, I would know what I love isn't a waste of time?" He nods slowly. "Do you remember what you said back to me?"

"That nothing you love could ever be a waste of time."

When I finally gather enough air to speak, my voice is thick with unshed tears. "Well, I love you, don't I? I love you, Jack, and you could never be a waste of my time. You're exactly where I want to spend it."

"Katie," Jack wheezes, pulling me against his chest. "Katie?"

"It's not going to be an easy conversation with my father, but I think it would be just as hard in four years. Or four years after that." I get the wobble in my voice under control. "I'm staying."

He pulls back, scans my face with disbelieving eyes, then yanks me close again. "Are you sure? Jesus, please be sure. I'll . . . we'll figure it out, honey. With your job. There has to be a way you can work here." His heart is pounding against my ear, wild and clear. "Just give me some time to get the right answers, but holy shit, you're not leaving."

"No. How could I when you're here? No." I hold him so tight my arm muscles strain. "We'll figure something out."

"Um . . . hate to interrupt." Charlie's voice drifts in. "But if I may?"

Jack eases back, but doesn't stop running his fingers through my hair, catching my tears with his thumbs. "Yeah?"

Not wanting to be rude, I glance over at Charlie, but I only catch a millisecond of how thrilled he is, before Jack turns my face back in his direction, proceeding to lay kisses on every square inch of my face. "You know how I like to work on a problem, right? Yeah. You guys know that about me." There's a smile in Charlie's voice. "I remembered my brother telling me about the NYPD supporting a certain amount of work visas each year, mostly for foreign cops in political positions, so they can come over and learn our procedures. But some of the time, they sponsor these ninety-day visas for officers with specialized skills. Which I think we can all agree, Katie has." Jack and I both turn our heads, finally giving Charlie our undivided attention. Hope flutters in my throat. Jack's hand tightens its grip on the back of my shirt. "Drumroll, please. It turns out, they haven't quite filled their maximum number of visas for this year."

Over Charlie's shoulder, a police vehicle cruises to a stop along the curb. Positive I'm mistaken and this whole evening is an elaborate dream, I watch Lieutenant Burns climb out with a handful of paperwork.

"I assume by your expressions, my brother showed up on time," Charlie says, dimples breaking out on his cheeks. "He's behind me, right?"

"Yeah." Jack's voice is raw. "He's there."

No one moves as Burns approaches, but I'd have to be blind to miss the longing rolling off him in waves when he locks eyes with Danika. It's only a fleeting look, though, before he's back to business, standing in front of us, the picture of stoicism. He hands the paperwork to Charlie and clears his throat. "McCoy. You need to appear tomorrow at the address on the form. Passport, badge, everything. Be prepared for a formal interview." He pauses. "If all goes well, the department is going to work out a temporary visa. Ninety days only."

He has to raise his voice to get out those final three words, because Ever lets out a squeal. And Danika smothers a happy sob behind her cupped hand.

Burns's cold eyes float over to Danika for a few beats, before he walks back to his car. He turns to face us again after a few steps, though. "One more thing. I stopped at ESU on the way over."

He's not looking at any of us, instead staring down the busy sidewalk. "When your visa goes through, McCoy, Kirkpatrick wants you to work with the squad." I'm turned thoroughly inside out at that news, but nothing compares to the joy that fills me at what Burns says next. "He wants to see you, too, Garrett. I wasn't surprised to find out McCoy had already stopped by and urged the CO to give you a look." He nods, cutting Jack a sideways glance. "I added my recommendation. Which means I'm going to be on your ass twice as hard now. You're not going to let me or yourself down. We clear?"

Jack appears nothing short of shell-shocked so I wrap my arms around his waist and hold tight, so tight. "Yes, sir," he rumbles. "Thank you."

When Burns drives off, Jack and I face each other. And we keep looking, and looking, telegraphing every thought in our heads—relief, astonishment, happiness—until we both dive for one another, holding tight. So tight it would take a hundred men to rip us apart.

"You talked to ESU about me, Katie?" His tone is low, urgent. "As if you haven't done enough?"

"All I did was talk. You're going to prove yourself all on your own."

A harsh sound leaves him. "Christ. What planet am I on that I get to keep you for myself?" His breath stirs my hair, ghosting over my forehead. "I'm going to bust my ass until I'm the kind of man who can give you everything. Love, Katie.

You have all of mine. And I know you still worry, but I'm going to get better every day."

"I know you will," I murmur, meaning it. "I know, Jack."

"When I say something, you believe it." He pulls back with a face full of optimism and it's as if the moon just got brighter. "You trust me."

It's not a question, but a statement. If I have my way, he won't question my trust in him ever again. "Yes."

"Well, trust this. They're going to write stories someday about us." His fingers tunnel through my hair. "About the man who didn't know he was worth a damn until he saw what he could be through a pair of blue eyes."

Jack's mouth finds mine, a hoarse sound leaving his throat and marrying my sob. Traffic bottlenecks around us on the sidewalk as he gives me the kiss of a lifetime.

One that promises the love of mine.

EPILOGUE

Jack

I 'm trying to put together this surprise before Katie gets home. Two days ago, not a single trace of the female gender existed inside the four walls of my bedroom. Forty-eight hours after Katie agreed to stay in New York? I've hung what are referred to as fairy lights around the perimeter of my ceiling. Pink ones. And if anyone thinks that makes me a pussy, they can come at me. Yesterday, I gave Katie a piggyback ride to Bed Bath & Beyond for decent sheets, a new mirror and oversized Scrabble pieces that spell L-O-V-E.

Again I say, come at me.

Making Katie feel at home in the apartment was the plan. Now? I'm just showing off.

Since we have to wait a couple of weeks for Katie's parents to ship her belongings from Ireland, she's out with Danika right now, shopping for clothes, which gives me another hour or so to finish the job. Both of those girls are important to me—for very different reasons—and them getting along so well is only adding to my almost freakish happiness. I'm awake, alert and fucking anxious for every moment. I never could have said that before, or even believed it was possible. Never before Katie.

With the toe of my boot, I nudge open the lid of lacquer, dipping in a paintbrush to give my project a second coat. Losing myself in the smooth back-and-forth strokes, I marvel how much has changed. Just like I knew she would, Katie knocked her interview with ESU out of the park and begins regular firearms training with the department in two weeks, as soon as the work visa is processed. As for myself, Kirkpatrick didn't pull any punches when we had our appointment. We met at the academy so he could watch me practice in the firing range, before using Burns's office to speak.

"Not bad," was all he said, before assuring me there would be no leeway for screwing up. We put weekly meetings in place starting after I graduate, during which the CO is going to check on my recovery. And, I quote, will put a boot up my ass if I don't show up on time, every time, with good news. He also warned me against hurting Katie—surprise, surprise, she charmed another one—on account of him taking a shine to her. As if I could. I've got this treasure and knowing what life was like before her? I'm incapable of taking Katie for granted. I won't.

Part of my recovery includes forgiving people, finding a healthy way to release the past, while remembering the lessons learned. The only person I had to forgive was myself, however. Letting go of what I deemed a mistake is taking time, but it gets easier every day. While it's tempting to let Katie's touch pave over the shame I lived with for so long, I know that fix needs to be mental and that it's on me. But I'm not punishing myself for it anymore. We all have to walk around with our faults, getting from one step to the next.

If you're lucky like me, you find an incredible girl to walk with you. But not for you.

When I hear the locks on the apartment's front door begin to squeal open, I set down my brush, leaning sideways to check the time on my cell phone.

"Honey, you're home," I call, in my best impression of a fifties sitcom husband. "Early."

Katie skids around the corner, pressing her back against the wall just inside our bedroom door. "You might want to lie down, Jack."

Ahh shit. I see what's going on here. Peeling off my ancient T-shirt, I saunter towards my girl, deciding this will be the time we leave on her infamous boots. "Did you cut your shopping trip short because you needed some Jack?" I mold our bodies together and groan against her ear.

"Can't wait to find out where those pointy heels dig in."

"Wait, I . . ." My teeth close around her ear and she sucks in a breath. "There's something important I have to tell you. Trust me, it cannot wait."

"In a rush, huh? Against the wall it is." I find her fantastic ass with both hands, lifting her off the ground, letting her feel my stiffening cock. "Slow or rough?"

My bedroom door creaks open.

And suddenly I'm looking at two unfamiliar faces. A man and women in their fifties stare back at me, eyebrows in the vicinity of their hairlines.

"My parents are here, Jack," Katie whispers. "Surprise."

I've never lost an erection so fast in my life.

"I'm as shocked as you are," Katie says, patting me on the shoulder. To let me know I still have her levered against the wall for a quickie, while her parents are literally five feet away. Over their shoulders, I see Danika busting her ass laughing on the way to her bedroom, which should have lightened my panic. But no. My current heart rate is equivalent to a man running from a bull in Pamplona. I'm not prepared for this. I'm still trying to assure myself I landed Katie. Parents were something for the future. Something I was looking forward to, sure. I want the McCoys to know I'm going to worship at their daughter's feet as long as I live, but there's no plan in place yet to accomplish that. I'm shirtless, unshaven. And I've got their little girl's ass cheeks in my hands. "You might want to set me down, Jack . . . ?"

"Oh God. Right." I ease Katie down to her feet and search frantically for my shirt. "I'm sorry—"

"Now. Don't go getting dressed on my account," Mrs. McCoy says from the doorway, chin up, watching me from the corner of her eye. "Sure, you should be comfortable in your own home."

I start laughing. Which seemed impossible a second ago, but this is familiar territory.

Katie's face turns red. "Honestly, Mam."

"What has he got that I don't?" Mr. McCoy holds up an arm and flexes. "Same physique as the day you married me. Better, even."

"Jack Garrett." Katie waves her hands around, as if trying to dispel the conversation. "Meet my parents, David and Sinead. They're like this all the time. Except for the spontaneous trips to America part. That's new."

I lunge—yes, lunge—forwards to shake their hands. "It's nice to meet you."

I'd pictured Katie's mom to be an older version of her—an adorably happy redhead—and she is. But her father surprises me. He's not the cold, anguished man I was expecting when Katie told me about the difficult training he put her through. I've been around him only a couple of awkward minutes and I can already understand why Katie would feel guilty letting him down. He's such a dad. Something I wouldn't understand, because I never had one. But I understand the way he looks at Katie. He loves her. Wants the best things life has to offer for her. We have that in common.

"We decided to bring your clothes and knick-knacks in person," Sinead says, walking into the room, purse clutched beneath her arm. "What's wrong with that?"

"Ringing first would have been nice." Katie stops battling her smile and it spreads across her face like wildfire. Knowing how much she's missed her parents, that smile makes my heart pound. She made the call to her father the morning after she decided to stay in New York, informing him she wouldn't be resuming training for the Olympics. There were enough tears to down a battleship, but I was so fucking proud of Katie for finally coming clean to her father about how the pressure was too much. They talked a lot about Sean, for the first time at length since his death and I could see, after they spoke, the load on Katie's shoulders was lighter. There's still some lingering guilt, though, but if I've learned one thing recently, it's that real, actual progress takes time. And we have that.

"I am happy to see you, though," Katie continues. "Very much. Even if it's going to take me a year to recover from finding you loitering outside the building."

David pats his daughter on the shoulder. "Ah sure, we'll be back for another visit before a year passes."

Katie's smile wavers. "Brilliant?"

Parents and daughter share a laugh, then silence falls in the room, three pairs of eyes turning to me expectantly. Katie's mother can't look at me without blushing, but her husband is the exact opposite. Brows furrowed, rocking back on his heels. In Katie's words, he wants to see what I'm at.

"I'm glad you brought Katie's clothes." Do better. Do so much better. Crossing to my dresser, I pull out the top three drawers, which I cleared out for Katie. "You probably brought a lot of sweaters, right? Because Ireland. And it's about to get cold here, so she'll need them." I go through a mental rundown of my Make Katie Happy checklist. "I've been looking everywhere for mint tea bags, but they don't have the same brand here. You didn't happen to bring any of those, did you?"

I watch in horror as Katie's mom gets teary eyed. "He's looking for her tea bags, David."

Mr. McCoy makes an exasperated sound. "What's the story with these pink lights?"

"It was the fastest way to make the bedroom as much hers as mine." Katie's mom starts to fan her face and Katie hugs herself, so I take that as a good sign. But I'm clearly still about ten miles from winning over David. I'm probably not going to win that battle today, but I'm lucky just getting the chance to fight it, aren't I? "I know this isn't ideal. Katie moving into a place with so many roommates and a small bedroom. Or with a guy who technically doesn't have a job yet." A snort from Mr. McCoy, earning himself an elbow nudge from his rapt wife. "I promise you both, though, it won't be forever."

"No, it won't. Especially since her visa is only ninety days."

"All due respect, sir, I'll be surprised if I make it that long without asking her to be my wife."

Mrs. McCoy bursts into tears.

Katie stares at me. Half in awe, half like she wishes we were alone. She's going to say yes if I ask her. I'm so sure of it in that moment—and humbled—I'm tempted to get down on one knee, right there in front of her parents. But I won't do it without a ring. Which is the first item on my Make Katie Happy list and I plan to cross it off. Sooner rather than later, now that I see the way she's looking at me. My wife. God, I can't wait to call her that. Marrying my girl means she never has to leave New York. After which I might stop waking up shouting her name in an outright panic that she's gone.

"What is that?" Katie asks, her gaze drifting past me. "Jack . . ."

Shit. I'd forgotten about my project. Sue me, though. I've been a little distracted. "You came home early, so I didn't have a chance to finish." I turn, trying to see my handiwork through her parents' eyes and hope they find it worthy. "Went down to that flea market on Houston and picked it out this morning, paid a couple guys to drop it off. I finished sanding it down, but I'm still putting on the lacquer. It's a workspace. For your purses." No one says anything so I keep rambling. Apparently Katie is rubbing off on me, but I'm definitely nowhere near as cute. "You can store materials in these drawers—"

Katie takes a running leap, throwing herself into my arms, which wrap around her automatically, tightening as much as I know she can stand. "I love you."

In a split second, there's no one in the room except Katie. "I love you, too."

"There goes our chances of luring her home," David says across the room, his mouth ticking up at one end.

Katie's eyes shine as she shakes her head. "My home is with Jack. I'm sorry, Da."

"Don't be sorry," he says. "Be happy."

"It appears she already is," Sinead sobs. In a familiar gesture, Katie's mother straightens her back and marches across the room, dropping her purse and picking up a paintbrush. "Now. Let's get this workspace finished. Do put on the kettle, David."

There we sat, the four of us. For hours. Drinking mint tea, finishing the table and putting Katie's clothes away in drawers while I listened to stories about the love of my life's childhood. And with her hand in mine, I couldn't wait to write our own.

Are you ready to watch stern, grumpy Lieutenant Greer Burns fall hard? He's already met his match and she's not going to make things easy for him!

DISTURBING HIS PEACE

Coming Spring 2018!
Read on for a sneak peek . . .

CHAPTER 1

—————— *Danika* ——————

The ground rumbles when he walks in.

Weird how I'm the only one that seems to notice.

Okay, not the *only* one. There's a trio of other female recruits parked up against the gymnasium wall that zero in on Lieutenant Greer Burns's shifting butt muscles, shaking their heads as if they're mad at it. The dudes stretching around me on the mat are a different story. They live and die by the lieutenant's whistle, but until he blows it, they're still lost in their world of women, baseball and ball scratching.

Ahh, the academy. Never change.

There's this sliver of time, twice a week, that I love to hate. When Greer is scheduled to whip our future police officer backsides into shape, I'm treated with—cursed with—a window of five seconds before he blows the whistle for inspection. During that handful of ticks, he slowly inserts that whistle between a pair of lips that make grandmothers wish for time machines. He tucks it *right* in there. And he looks at me. One cool sweep of those twin glaciers that begins at the tip of my sneakers and ends at my ponytail.

That's around the time I tell him with my eyes to *go fuck himself.*

It's a complicated dynamic.

Anyone else would get suspended for showing the lieutenant a hint of the fire I pack into my morning look. Why does he let me get away with it?

Even more annoying, why do I look forward to it?

Greer hasn't quite made it to the front of the gymnasium yet, but there's a jet stream of anticipation whipping through my blood in hot revolutions. My spine straightens and I firm my jaw, telling myself this time I won't meet his eyes. I'm distracted from my mental preparations when a male recruit drops down on the mat beside me, blocking my view of the approaching lieutenant. His timing is either terrible or perfect. My body is too confused these days to decide.

"Hey, Silva."

"Levi." I flash a tight smile at our resident easygoing, golden boy who's never without a smile or a compliment. "What's up?"

Over his shoulder, I catch the eye of my best friend, Jack, who lets his tongue loll out of his mouth like a lovesick idiot. His impression of Levi, I'm guessing, who has been flirting with me since we started at the academy, but has yet to pull the trigger and ask me out.

To which I would say . . . what? No freaking clue.

"What did you think about COBRA training yesterday?" Levi asks, grabbing his elbow above his head and stretching. "Heavy stuff, right?"

He's referring to the Chemical Ordinance, Biological and Radiological Awareness training we spent the last few days completing. "Yeah." I tear my attention away from Jack, who is now pretending to make out with himself. "There's no cute way to rock a hazmat suit, I guess."

"Oh, I don't know." Levi cuts me a look. "I think you did a damn good job."

Impressive. Ten points to Levi. See, I should be asking *him* out. He's the definition of my type. Growing up around my uncles and boy cousins meant I was always one of the guys. They didn't pull any punches while playing football in the park or critiquing my homecoming dresses with sarcasm. My mother was—*is*—amazing at making me feel girly when necessary, but there was no escaping the men in my family. As a result, I'm drawn to softer-spoken artistic types that treat me like a lady. Which is the number one reason I shouldn't be so . . . affected by the sight of the lieutenant sliding a whistle between his lips. There's *nothing* soft about him.

When Levi chuckles, I realize I've been staring into space. *Way to take a compliment, Danika.* "Uh. Thanks. You . . ." I give him a soft punch in the shoulder. "Did it justice, too."

I'm saved from having to bask in the aftermath of my awkward attempt at flirting when Jack pokes his head in between us and makes a buzzer noise. "Snooze you lose, Levi. Gave you a good two minutes to close the deal. More than enough time." He winks at me, letting me know I owe him one for his intervention. "Danika has plans for the night, anyway. She's cake tasting."

My stomach groans, reminding me I skipped breakfast. "I am?"

Jack nods. "Pays to know the lady who is catering our graduation."

I don't know what's flowing through drinking fountains at the academy, but in the months since we started, both of my roommates, Jack and Charlie, have been brought to heel by the almighty L word. And I'm not talking the fizzy stomach bubbles, let's share a soda pop kind of love. I'm talking all-out, devoted, want their women to have their babies kind of love. It's a little daunting when I have zero romantic prospects of my own and I can hear the proof of their affection through the thin walls of our apartment. Nightly. My suffering has all become worth it, though, with the utterance of the words *cake tasting*. "I'll be there—"

The whistle blows. *Loud*.

All two hundred recruits jump to their feet and form rows. Backs go ramrod straight, chests puff out. Inspection is always twice as intense when Greer is here, because he doesn't just take roll. He scrutinizes each of us for imperfections. Legend has it, he once made a recruit walk home from Twentieth Street to the Bronx to retrieve his forgotten uniform gym shorts. And that recruit was never seen or heard from again.

Out of the corner of my eye, I watch the lieutenant approach, my attention traveling down to perform their own inspection on the object of my reluctant obsession. The thighs that—against my will—changed my type from artistic, easygoing guys to big, rough-hewn enforcers. They demand to be taken seriously, as does their owner, by doing nothing more than existing. Through stiff, navy blue uniform pants, sinew creeps from hips to knee, muscles sculpted by a diamond cutter. In weak moments, I find myself wondering if they're hairy or smooth. Or ticklish? Could the man have such a silly weakness as being ticklish?

No. Not a chance.

Lieutenant Greer Burns doesn't have weaknesses. As he strides past the inspection line, the humming halogens overhead paint shadows on his face, darkness settling in the always-present frown lines between his eyebrows. When his eyes land on me, his jaw bunches. When is it *not* bunched? It tics and flexes like he's trying to suck the copper off a penny. That tension must be the reason my eyes are drawn to his brutal lips, harsh and full all at once.

He leaves my line of vision, his boots making the mat groan as he weaves behind me, and I'm not—*definitely* not—disappointed that I missed my five second stare-down with Greer today. I'm not annoyed at Levi and Jack for distracting me either. Nope. Uh-uh.

Greer is right behind me when he says, "I'll be demonstrating a new takedown this morning." I feel his gaze on my neck, heating the flesh above my collar. "Any volunteers?"

My hand goes up. It always does, even though he never picks me. Ever. I tell myself it's stupid to think he's afraid to touch me.

My theory is further disproven a second later.

"Silva. To the front."

Greer

W*hat the hell are you doing?*
I can't even *think* of the girl without getting wood. Now I'm going to wrestle her onto the mat in front of two hundred recruits?

Silva's head turns slowly, hitting me with the full force of her surprise. And not for the first time, I'm caught between wanting to lick her, head to toe . . . and telling her the gray academy T-shirt really brings out her eyes.

Idiot. You fucking idiot.

This wouldn't be happening if she'd just kept our arrangement. It's very simple. Before I blow the whistle for inspection and become her instructor, she gives me a few seconds of her undivided attention. Obviously we never made this agreement out loud. How would that conversation even start? But it's the one thing I look forward to lately.

Even if she does hate me.

Why wouldn't she? My default mode is insufferable asshole. This is my city and I've been tasked with whipping this group of young people into effective members of law enforcement. I take that responsibility seriously. So why do I like letting Silva get away with that open disdain *so damn much*? I can't tell her that she's . . . important. Special. Even if those words cram into my throat when she's around, twisting my stomach up like a pretzel. So I satisfy the urge by letting those heated looks slide and hope she doesn't sense this pointless infatuation of mine.

She's definitely going to catch on when I pin her to the floor and my cock salutes the tight, sexy shape of her. God, what is she going to *feel* like under me?

Silva isn't the only one shocked that I picked her for the demonstration. My brother, Charlie, is giving me jerky *bad idea, bad idea* head shakes, making me wonder if he's caught me staring like a fool at his roommate. If so, I need to be more careful. Recruits are off-limits. I've never had a problem adhering to that rule in the past. Not even close. They were all just uniforms with varying skill levels until she showed up.

Some jackass two rows back whispers about how *he* wouldn't mind pinning Silva, and the comment brings my focus roaring back. Jesus, it's that shithead who always wears aviator sunglasses again. He goes white when I turn and narrow my eyes on him. "I hope you don't mind staying an hour late today and wiping down the mats, because that's how you'll be spending your evening," I snap. "Try and locate some respect while you're down there."

"Yes, sir."

Christ, on top of being sex-starved for an off-limits girl, I'm now a hypocrite. Didn't I choose Danika for the demonstration because I *hated* watching her flirt with someone else? Because *I* wouldn't mind pinning her, to put it mildly. Yes. *Hell* yes. And that moment of weakness is going to cost me big-time because in a few minutes, her curves are going to be pressed to mine. I'm going to have her beneath me. She's the only one inside these four walls that could shake my professionalism with something as routine as a takedown—and I've damned myself with my jealousy.

"Was I somehow unclear?" Self-disgust makes my voice hard as I pivot to face Silva again. "To the *front*."

The way she jerks on a gasp stabs me in the gut. For a split second, right before I shouted at her, there was wonder, maybe even appreciation, in the way she looked at me. Because I stood up for her? The possibility makes me wish I'd suspended the recruit who made the comment. Or sent him on a walk to Montauk. How would she have looked at me then?

Doesn't matter now, because I ruined it.

Just like I'm about to ruin myself.

Following in Silva's wake to the front of the room, I can't help but suck in the fresh grapefruit scent that follows her. I don't know for sure, but I think it comes from her shampoo. Perfect, now I'm trying not to think of her in the shower, soaping all those black, wavy curls she keeps up in her ponytail. Trying not to think of steam clinging to her full, sarcastic lips and taut skin. Good thoughts to be having when I'm about to wrestle her in front of a crowd.

There is total silence, apart from the lights buzzing overhead and the occasional cough. In my head, though, there's a riot taking place. Will I ever be satisfied with five seconds of eye contact ever again once I've had her beneath me? Of course not. Hell, I'm not satisfied *now*.

"As you know, an officer never wants to end up on the ground. Your weapon becomes accessible to someone other than yourself. There's a lack of mobility and a potential to be assaulted by a perp. In other words, this is a worst-case scenario."

I'm about halfway through the beginning of my speech when it dawns on me that a guard escape is probably the most intimate move I could have chosen. It's not something I did intentionally after selecting Silva as my volunteer, it was on the morning agenda—and now it's too late to change course.

Silva is beside me, trying to look fresh out of fucks, but I can see the pulse going wild in her neck, the eagerness to learn in her brown eyes. It starts my own pulse hammering, that determination in her. That bravery. Just some of the reasons I can't seem to make it through an hour of the day without thinking about her.

"The goal of a guard escape is to gain back control of the situation and get your perp cuffed, as fast as possible, before you can be subdued or worse. Understood?" I wait for the chorus of "yes sirs" before lying on my back. They've seen me down here countless times, demonstrating moves—it's a vital part of their training—and I try and fail to focus on the familiarity of teaching. How can I when Silva is staring down at me, her mouth in a little O. "Feign an attack, Silva."

"On . . . you?" she whispers.

"Yes." She's nervous. Before I can make a conscious decision, the need to reassure her takes over. "This is it. Your chance has finally arrived."

Laughter ripples through the recruits and it seems to ground her. But I'm the furthest thing from grounded when Silva drops down on her knees between my bent legs. Her tits are still jiggling when she wets her lips, and I'm the furthest thing from fucked. My balls are suddenly five pounds each, pressing in around the base of my dick. *Christ*. This is already torture, but I have no choice but to get even closer. Any other time, I would continue my lecture from the ground, but I can't. I have to get this over with as fast as possible.

Her cheeks are fire-engine red as she leans over me, her dukes up, punching at the air. And with a final hard swallow, I lock my legs around her waist, bringing her head down safely into the crook of my neck to stop the supposed attack. Then I drop a foot to the outside of her planted knee and use the ground as leverage to flip her over.

It's the sound that comes out of her mouth that well and truly screws me.

That—and the way her eyes roll back, swollen lips popping open to let it out.

It's a moan. It's pleasure and excitement and need, all rolled into one little, choked noise that will probably haunt my every waking moment going forward.

Does she *like* being pinned down?

For a few seconds, all I can do is stare down at her flushed face, her body trapped between my thighs, and wish we were alone so I could—

So I could *what*?

I don't get involved with women. For very good reasons. It's a rule that has served me well. *All* the rules serve me well, and I'm breaking them right now by keeping my hips planted on top of Danika's stomach far longer than necessary.

"Find a partner and practice," I call to the room, still unable to stop staring down at Silva. "I'll come around and—inevitably—correct you."

The room breaks into motion, and so does Silva, sliding backwards up the mat and rolling to her feet. I stand, too, facing her. My pulse is pounding in my ears as she hesitates, words poised on her lips, fingers twisting in her T-shirt. But she doesn't say anything, turning instead and jogging away to partner up with one of the girls. It's a good thing my brother approaches, nudging me with his elbow. Otherwise, I might have gone after her and apologized. Or asked to pin her down again. Jesus, what *is* it about this girl?

Her moan goes off in my head, and I grit my teeth as I turn to Charlie. "*What?*"

Nothing can knock the humor off Charlie's face. Not even me. "Nothing. Just . . . you really decided to *make your move* in a literal sense." Before I can respond, he holds up his hands. "Forget I said that. Nothing was said. I'm just here to issue an invitation."

He might as well have handed me a bouquet of flowers. "A *what* now?"

"You're making this so easy." Charlie scratches the back of his neck. "Ever is baking sample cakes tonight and we're taste testing." I say nothing. "Ever is my girlfriend . . . she's the chef who's catering our graduation . . ."

My sigh cuts him off. "I know who she is and what she does."

"Considering this invite was her idea, she'll be thrilled."

That gives me pause. And an irritating tug in the region of my chest. "Tonight. Where is it and who is going?"

"Brooklyn. I can text you the address. It's me, Jack, Danika . . ."

I don't hear the rest of the names. I'm out. It's hard enough to be around Silva at the academy. Seeing her outside of these walls in regular clothes, without the visible, concrete reminder of my position as her instructor to keep me away? Bad idea.

But even as Charlie walks off to go join the other recruits, I'm looking for every excuse to drive over the bridge later.

SEP4 0317

At Avon Books, we know your passion for romance—once you finish one of our novels, you find yourself wanting more.

May we tempt you with . . .

- **Excerpts** from our upcoming releases.

- Entertaining **extras**, including authors' personal photo albums and book lists.

- Behind-the-scenes **scoop** on your favorite characters and series.

- **Sweepstakes** for the chance to win free books, romantic getaways, and other fun prizes.

- Writing **tips** from our authors and editors.

- **Blog** with our authors and find out why they love to write romance.

- **Exclusive content** that's not contained within the pages of our novels.

Join us at
www.avonbooks.com

AVON *An Imprint of* HarperCollins*Publishers*
www.avonromance.com